"I was just reading an
her girlfriends starting a b
Whisperers.' Ghastly name I know and doesn't exactly
roll off the tongue, but catchy.

"They evidently help widowed and divorced
men…newbies, they call them, get back into the swing
of life and train them how to do the things their wives
did for them, as well as getting them ready to start
dating…I think they even have a course called 'Women
101.' When I first saw their ad about four months ago, I
kind of thought it was a ridiculous idea and had no clue
Sally was involved. But it looks like they're doing really
well and have so many male clients that they're going to
branch out to females soon."

"That's charming, and I wish them all the luck in the
world, but it has absolutely nothing to do with us."

"Well, if you think about it, it really is a good idea.
It's hard for most people to start over. You know what it
was like after you and Gayle divorced. I remember what
it was like dating after Jake died, before I met you. It was
horrible. Men were absolute idiots, thinking they were
suave and debonaire. You'd go to dinner, and they'd be
putting down the ex, drinking too much, start trying to
hold your hand and talking about back rubs…" She
shivered and ran her hands over her arms. "It was creepy,
and I don't imagine it's gotten any better as we've aged."

Unrequited

by

Tina Fausett

The Widower Whisperers Series

Cover Art by *The Wild Rose Press, Inc.*

The Wild Rose Press, Inc.
PO Box 708
Adams Basin, NY 14410-0708
Visit us at www.thewildrosepress.com

Publishing History
First Edition, 2024
Trade Paperback ISBN 978-1-5092-5299-2
Digital ISBN 978-1-5092-5300-5

The Widower Whisperers Series
Published in the United States of America

Dedication

To the BABs (Bad Ass Bitches), it's because of you and our crazy conversations on girl's nights that I wrote this book. Cheryl Booze, Schelli Booze Boyd, and Christy Borelli, I thank you for your friendship.

To my granddaughter, Rhiannon Abernathy, thank you for believing in me all the years...

To Ally Robertson, my amazing editor, you are the most wonderful mentor...

And to all the men out there that gave me such terrific fodder, without you it wouldn't have been possible...

I love you all!!!

"Grow old along with me! The best is yet to be, the last of life, for which the first was made. Our times are in His hand who saith, 'A whole I planned, youth shows but half; Trust God: See all, nor be afraid!' " Robert Browning

Chapter 1

"Okay, old girl, it's show time." Sally's image in the bathroom mirror reflected her involuntary shudder. *What the hell am I doing?* She didn't have an answer. She just knew she dreaded what was about to happen. The alarm on her watch went off, startling her. "Hey, Siri, stop." One last glance, a flip of her hair and she headed for the kitchen, grabbing her purse on the way out. "Alexa, unlock back door."

Pulling out of the driveway, she told Siri to *lock back door and alarm stay* then tried to focus on not backing into an early morning jogger when her cell rang. The screen lit up with *Betty Cramer*. "Hey, Thelma, what's up?" Glancing in the rearview mirror, she hit the brakes barely missing a scantily clad young woman darting past her rear fender. "Shit!"

"Just checking on you. You okay?" There was a sly tone in her voice.

"Why? Wanting to make sure I was on my way to meet some stranger at this ridiculous hour on a Saturday morning? He could have at least had the decency to ask what time would be good for me."

"Jeez, Louise, it's not that bad. You know most adults are usually up and about at 7:40. Some actually have jobs and have to be at work by 8:00."

"Yes, I remember those days well, and I don't want to relive them. I can't...not since the accident. Besides, I like my coffee in bed, and we should be retired by now. And it happens to be the weekend. Plus, I almost hit a damn runner, probably training for a marathon."

"That used to be you. I'm sorry. Is your back hurting?"

"Yeah, some...and the hip. I'm just irritated is all. I miss my past life."

"I know you do, honey, but you're alive, and you don't know how much that means to the rest of us. I think maybe you're just mad at yourself because you agreed to meet this guy at all. You could easily have told him it was too early for you."

"Oh, I'm mad about a lot of things. But everyone keeps telling me I need to get out and about, test the waters...put myself out there. So, now that I've totally blocked Darrell and made the decision to move on, that's what I'm doing, like it or not."

"Speaking of...have you heard from him?"

Sally sighed. She was getting tired of people asking her that. "No, and I won't. I made it where he can't even email me, much less call or text. But he wouldn't try anyway...way too narcissistic. He probably loves the idea of seeing me as the evil one, gives him the perfect out." She was getting a knot in her chest. "I was thinking about him this morning...about being in my bed listening to him talking to another woman...how horrible it made me feel. He never treated me the same after the accident and surgeries. It's done. I don't want to talk about it."

"An accident and surgeries that were his fault! Sorry, okay, fine. So, this guy...did he find you on a dating site?"

Sally looked at the time. "I'm going to be late. Hold on, I need to send him a text."

"Not while you're driving, I hope. Seriously, Sally, he can wait. It's only coffee. Lord, Darrell did a number on you."

Sally elected to ignore that last part. "Done! No, I was at a stoplight. As for a dating site, you know how I feel about those. Besides...Facebook has become *the* dating site. I guess he saw that I was a friend of one of his friends, asked me to be a friend, saw that I was single, and decided to ask me out. Actually, I'm not sure about the order of what I just said."

"You mean he stalked you like the others."

"Yep, I suppose he stalked me like the others. I don't know though, there are some of them that just walk up to me out of the blue."

"I'm almost certain that's stalking too. I bet he's researched everything about you and when he saw that you write porn, he prob—"

"It's not porn, it's erotica. But if you want to keep the genre clear, it's women's fiction with erotic and paranormal elements...or something like that. My editor and I are still trying to figure it out. And we can't really call it romance because it has to have a *happily ever after*...I'm not even sure I believe in that. But, yes, I'm certain the erotica part probably makes me a bit more enticing."

Betty cackled.

"What's so damn funny?"

"Oh my God! Wait until he gets one of your lectures

about senior citizens and sexually transmitted diseases. Damn, I wish I could be a fly on the wall. Here he is thinking he's found some hot, promiscuous, old broad, ready to get it on…and then he comes face-to-face with you, the *real* you, not the fantasy one."

"Not all men are like that. Maybe he just wants companionship…you know, maybe he's really looking for—"

"A nurse or a purse. Isn't that what you always say?"

"Yeah, well, that too."

"And all the better if she writes about BDSM. By the way, Louise, it would be good for you to get laid. You know what Betty White always said, 'The best way to get over a man is to get under another one.' "

"Obviously, she had a better selection than we do. You know how picky I am. I mean first of all…" Sally hesitated as she turned into a parking spot in front of the diner.

"Are you still there?"

"Damn it, I'm going to have to get off. I just pulled in, and I think that's him sitting outside waiting for me. I'll call you when I'm done. Any chance of you contacting the girls to make sure we're still on for tonight?"

"I'm in. I'll text them and make sure they are."

"Great, I just don't want to have to lie if he asks me out or wants to extend coffee."

"You're a real trooper, Louise. Try to have fun," Betty suggested then quickly hung up.

****

The man sat at an outdoor table and watched as she crossed the parking lot, making Sally self-conscious about her limp. When she stepped onto the sidewalk, he stood. It was obvious he recognized her from her pictures on social media. As she approached, he said her name. She glanced up and smiled at his ruddy face.

"Mark?" She extended her hand, but he was already putting his on her back to escort her into the diner which was surprisingly full.

Before they were seated, he directed her to the counter to order. *Control issues?* She didn't like being herded and liked the closeness of his body practically pressing her into the counter even less. The girl behind the cash register had already taken his order while Sally stared up at the menu feeling rushed.

He moved to her right side and looked down at her. "Do you want to order something to eat?"

"No, I just thought they might have a cappuccino or latte. Sorry it's taking so long."

"They have coffee. You get it out of the thermoses over there." His voice was deep and flat.

She gave the cashier a smile. "Well, I guess I'll have coffee then."

The girl smiled back and handed her an empty cup. "It's free refills."

"Thanks," Sally murmured, unsure if she was supposed to be buying her own or not. Who knew these days when men seemed to have no problem letting a woman pay for everything? She was looking for the wallet app on her phone when he held a credit card out to the girl, and she took that moment to study him.

He was tall. She was used to that. Most of the men who asked her out were. He appeared to be in decent shape, but the too short shirt he wore was a clear indication he'd put on weight since he'd bought it, especially by the straining buttons. And he was balding.

She didn't mind…most of them were. His ruddiness was obviously from a lot of time spent out in the sun, but the weathered face wasn't unpleasant, and it didn't hold the bloated look of a big drinker like so many of them did. But that didn't mean anything, Darrell's hadn't either. His eyes seemed clear.

They finally settled into a booth, and he asked again if she wanted to order food. *I thought this was supposed to be coffee. He must be hungry.* Sally smiled sweetly. "Thank you, but I like to get my caffeine fix before I eat. Maybe later, but please go ahead if you want to."

He shook his head, and they spent the next few minutes absorbed in small talk before he asked how many times she'd been married. She told him twice then inquired about his wives, and he was off to the races. She listened attentively to his tales about all four of them and tried hard not to let what she was thinking show on her face while he was describing his current sex life…or lack of it.

Seriously? It's only been thirty minutes. He's brought up sex seven or eight times, and not once has he asked me anything other than how many times I've been married. She snuck a peek at her watch.

"Is something wrong?"

The fact Mark stopped talking long enough to ask startled her. She gave a serene smile. "Oh, no…no, nothing at all. I thought I felt it vibrate. All's well. Now, where were we?" she asked, shifting on the uncomfortable seat, wondering if this morning would ever be over.

Chapter 2

Two and a half hours later, Sally's mind was as numb as her butt sitting on the dilapidated cushion of the booth. He'd started in on another story involving sex and a woman he'd gone out with recently, and that was when it happened, the fatal blow, and she couldn't have stopped herself even if she'd wanted to…and no way did she want to.

"You know, Mark, I'm terribly worried about us Baby Boomers. Do you realize that the percentage of adults over fifty with sexually transmitted diseases has grown considerably each year? And of course it has in this day and age. We have men popping little blue pills like breath mints or using pumps on their flaccid penises. Do you realize they can even be shot up with stem cells now?"

She leaned in, narrowing her eyes, and waited for a response, but he didn't answer, so she went on. "Then we've got desperate people going online to find sex. Now, I'm not saying that's what you were doing messaging me on Facebook, but you have to understand. People might think they're doing it simply to find a companion to grow older with or they're lonely, but let's face the truth. I know women who get on a site, meet a man, and after a week they're going on dates with them, if you can actually call them dates. And first or second time, boom, they're doing *the deed*. They don't know the person they're shagging from Adam, but there they are hopping in and out of bed like geriatric Energizer Bunnies playing *tag, your it*."

She noticed that his eyes were as wide as saucers, and he was the one checking his watch now. She couldn't help but grin. "And so, here's what's happening. They start getting to know the person they should have gotten to know *before* acting like hormonal adolescents on steroids and *poof*...the fuck fest is over. And do any of them learn a lesson? I mean seriously, you can probably relate to this as many times as you've been married and divorced. No, they don't learn a damn thing. They get right back on a site and find another one within days, and it's the same story all over again. They're up there on that saddle not caring the least about how dangerous the ride could be.

"Here's a cruel fact, Mark. When you sleep with someone, you're sleeping with everyone they've slept with. So, can you imagine how much is being spread by these people who jump from one to the other? But here's the caveat. They end up with an STD. If they're lucky, it's herpes or the clap, not syphilis or gonorrhea, and they just can't understand how it happened. But here's what's really frightening. Statistics from the Centers for Disease Control and Prevention have shown that adults over the age of fifty represent around half of the population of those living with diagnosed HIV in the US, and that can be deadly for a senior citizen.

"Certainly, you're educated about what goes on in nursing homes and retirement villages. It's a revolving door for jumping from one room to the other. It's a sexual free for all. And believe me, I know. My son witnessed my own Aunt Sally slipping out of one of those rooms in nothing but a see-through negligee, and he's been scarred ever since."

Realizing the diner, filled mostly with elderly people, had gone deathly silent, she stopped to take a deep breath and looked around to find most of them staring at her, some with big smiles on their faces.

An attractive older woman sitting at the table next to them with her gray-haired girlfriend nodded, her eyes brimming with amusement. "I get what you're saying. I've got friends it's happened to. But go on and tell us what you'd do, how you'd handle things."

"Abstinence." Sally looked back at her coffee date as some of the patrons chuckled, and she smiled. "I'm serious about that, and I've been there, done it. There's nothing wrong with not wanting to be alone, but good Lord, can't people take time to get to know each other first? And I mean *really* know each other. This isn't a joke. I think it's a wise idea to be tested and for your potential partner to be tested too.

"If you're older and get diagnosed with an STD, there are big health concerns like weakened bodies and immune systems. Are we in that big a hurry? I mean hey, what a way to go, right? At your funeral, your grandkids could say, 'If Grandma had only waited for the results of the blood tests and wasn't in such a hurry to get laid.' Now that's a creepy thought."

A couple of people gave her a polite golf clap, and she looked across the table at a paled Mark, his mouth agape. She shot him a brilliant smile, gave a dramatic look at her watch, then dug in her purse for her car keys.

"Gosh, I had no idea how late it was getting. I've got to be going, but it's been delightful, really. Thank you so much. It was a pleasure meeting you." She stuck out her hand knowing people were still watching them, and this time he took it and gave a weak shake.

"How about inviting me over for wine?"

He did not just say that. "That would be lovely. We'll have to do it sometime." She extracted her hand from his sweaty one and resisted the urge to wipe it on her jeans as she hurried to the door.

She was reaching for the handle when an arm shot in front of her, grabbing it. Thinking it was Mark, she turned with a scowl and looked up into the most gorgeous pair of pale hazel eyes she'd ever seen. Eyes like the Louisiana swamps you could get lost in.

"Sorry, didn't mean to startle you. I was just getting the door for you."

His voice was soft, lips full, perfectly covering white teeth that bared as he smiled with cute little dimples etched into both sides of his mouth. For a brief moment she was paralyzed, staring at those eyes, now amused and crinkled at the corners beneath full salt-and-pepper brows. "I, uh, I didn't see you. It just surprised me is all."

He stepped back, pulled the door open, and nodded. "Ladies first."

Or age before beauty. Her mind was flipping from one thing to the next as she stepped into the sunlight. She turned to thank him, but he was already walking the other direction. She took in the full head of perfectly coiffed white hair, the broad shoulders, and long legs as he went around the corner of the parking lot and disappeared, never once looking back. Oddly, she was filled with a sense of something familiar, and an inexplicable sadness engulfed her.

Chapter 3

The BABs (Bad Ass Bitches)

Once in the car, Sally looked at her phone and saw Betty had called twice. She was calling her back when she glanced in her passenger side mirror and saw Mark standing on the sidewalk staring at her car. *Just when I thought it was safe…*

"Hey, that was a long coffee. You must have had a good time."

"Hold on a minute. He's watching me. I'm backing out before he decides to come over here."

"You never have been able to back and talk at the same time. So, I guess he's still stalking you. Must be your charmingly sweet personality. I thought you'd forgotten to call me when you were through, and I just wanted to let you know that the girls are on for tonight. Did you see my text? I knew you wanted to have your truthful excuse ready."

"No, I just saw that you'd called. I felt guilty for even glancing at my watch. That's great. Same place and time?"

"Everyone knows you aren't a happy-hour fan, so we thought sixish at the lake to watch the sunset."

"Aw, that's perfect and so sweet. What would I do without my fellow bitches?"

"I have no idea. You've run everyone else off. You

really have."

"I know. I can't afford to be around all the negativity anymore."

"So do tell, how did it go?"

Sally was relieved to have made it out of the parking lot without Mark jumping in front of the car, and she sighed. "Well, Thelma, I'll skip to the part where he goes into depth about his four marriages and divorces and how none of them were his fault. How do you think it went?"

"Oh my…that well, huh?"

"About like that, but I'd rather discuss it tonight over a couple of glasses of wine. If I tell you everything now, I'll just have to repeat it."

Betty cleared her throat. "I know only too well. Deal! See you this evening. Love ya, mean it."

"Love you more. See you later." Smiling, Sally thought how much she really did love her friend and all the adventures they'd been through together. There were things their children didn't know about, much less their ex-husbands. That's why they felt like Thelma and Louise…there had been more than a couple of times they'd both almost gone over that cliff. And from nowhere, her mind drifted to the man with the incredible hazel eyes…

****

"Woohoo, there she is, our little beauty queen." Peggy waved her napkin at Sally to get her attention.

She plopped down next to Peg, gave her a hug and peck on the cheek. "I am not a beauty queen. My second husband's second wife was. If you remember the story, I was in the miss Teenage America pageant but—"

"You dropped out when you realized how misogynistic and sexist it was," all three of the other

12

women said in unison.

She grinned sheepishly at Betty and Carole sitting across from them. "I guess you all do remember."

Carole nodded. "But we want to hear about your date this morning. Betty was just briefing us."

"I bet she was." She looked at her statuesque best friend and winked.

"Well, it's not like you gave me much to run with." Betty tucked a blonde tendril behind her ear and winked back. "Start from when you saw him sitting outside waiting for you."

"Oh Lord, you know how we couldn't find any good pictures of him on social media." They all nodded. "He was tall and in decent shape except for looking like he was ready to give birth. So many men are that way anymore."

"Well…come on now, we've all gotten a bit thicker through the middle as the years have gone by." Peggy, who was always playing the devil's advocate, pointed to her own stomach.

Sally shook her head. "I agree, but it's not the same. For women after menopause that's just where the weight seems to land, and in defense, all of us have had at least two children…some of us miscarriages, hysterectomies, endometriosis, multiple surgeries…I could keep going. To me it's a sign of closet drinking and sitting on one's ass too much."

"How old is he?" Carole asked.

"Ten years older than we are…well, not you, Carole, you're a baby."

Carole was petite with a pretty face, deep blue eyes and a full head of curly, dark auburn hair. She and Sally could have been related. "Yep, that's me…a fifty-two-year-old baby."

Betty put a hand on her shoulder. "When you get to be as old as we are, you'll look back at this and see yourself as an infant. Now, go on, Louise."

Sally savored a sip of Chardonnay. "Okay…he didn't seem to think the age difference was any big deal. You know, typical for a man. But I'm quite sure that wouldn't have been the case if I was the one that much older. When I got there, he didn't take the hand I offered. Instead, he put his big old sweaty palm on my back and practically pushed me into the diner." They all gasped. "I know, right? I'm sorry, I just don't like being touched…unless I want to be touched." She paused again and shrugged. "You know…"

"We get your drift," Carole piped in.

"I've been married to two older men and just don't want to go there again."

Betty shifted in her seat. "I warned you…*both* times."

Carole sighed and leaned back in the booth. "We all know this. Could we just hear the rest of the story, *please*?"

Peggy giggled, and Betty looked solemnly at Sally. "Proceed."

Chapter 4

"Thank you." Sally nodded. "Hell, I don't know where I was…oh yeah, he talked nonstop about himself. I really didn't want to hear about his last wife and how they had sex several times a day."

"They did? That means he can still do it." Betty offered brightly.

Peggy choked on her margarita and tossed her napkin at her. "Stop it! We all know how Sally is." Giggles and snorts rippled through the women like a pack of teenage girls.

"That's just it. She needs to get laid." Betty grinned back at Peggy.

"After the trauma from Darrell, no wonder she doesn't want to have sex with just any—" Betty kicked her under the table. Peggy's dark hair was sprinkled with silver, and she twisted a strand of it. "Oops, I'm sorry, Sally."

"Oh, good grief, I'm perfectly aware of what he did to me, and it's my own damn fault for allowing it."

Carole looked at the other women with a shake of her head. "Can we just get back to the damned story?"

Sally nodded. "All right, so my point is that this was supposed to be coffee, not a three-and-a-half-hour ordeal. He talked about himself endlessly, and none of his multitude of divorces were his fault, because of course he's such a great catch. He picked the place, the time, and in the first thirty minutes, he brought up sex at least seven times. But about two and a half hours later, when he used the words *prophylactic* and *herpes* in the same sentence, I just couldn't take it anymore and I—"

"Gave him the speech...I knew it." Betty looked at Peggy then Carole. "One time we were on a trip together and had gone to the hotel bar. It wasn't very full yet, and this man sidled up to Sally and said something like, 'I've always loved redheads.' "

Carole raised her hand. "Yep, I get that one a lot, too. Usually before I can respond, they've reached out and touched my hair. It's kind of freaky."

Betty nodded. "Oh yeah, he did the same thing, and you would have thought he'd grabbed her boob or something the way her hand flew up to brush his away. He was good-looking, dressed in a nice suit. So, she looked him up and down then turned her back to him, and he made the mistake of touching her shoulder to turn her to face him."

"Did he live?" Peggy was staring at Sally who was trying so hard not to laugh she had tears in her eyes.

Betty emptied her glass and motioned for the waitress. "Have you ever seen a bull castrated?"

"It was that bad?"

"Oh, Peg, worse! She even got a standing ovation from the women in the bar. And the funniest part was that he still asked for her phone number."

Sally wiped her eyes with her napkin and sniffed. "They always do. A narcissist never gets it. They listen to you go into a tirade, and they're thinking how spunky you are and what a challenge...and they always believe they're just the man who can tame you...you know, with that *third leg* they all think they have." She held her hands about a foot apart then brought them in a couple of inches from each other.

Peggy chuckled so hard she hiccupped, and the others burst into gales of laughter just as their waitress approached. Still chortling, Sally looked up. "I apologize. I hope you're not here to kick us out. We were talking about men…you'll understand when you're older."

The young girl rolled her eyes and grinned. "I heard. Trust me, I saw what my mom went through with my dad and then her second husband. I've witnessed pretty much every kind of abuse you can think of. I saw how it destroyed her. I'm not dealing with it. I just broke up with my boyfriend for talking to other women while I'm working all night and going to college all day…nothing would surprise me anymore."

This sobered them up, and the laughter came to an abrupt halt. "Oh, poor baby, I'm so sorry. But good for you. Don't settle. You deserve to be respected. We all do. Another round please." Sally stared at Betty unabashedly then broke into a big smile.

"Yes, guilty as accused. I gave *the* STD lecture, and you know how passionate I get and how my voice tends to get a wee bit louder."

"And what did Mr. Coffee think about that?" Carole asked.

"He wanted me to invite him to my house for wine."

"What is wrong with men today? At our ages they rarely ask us out on a regular date. God forbid one would get all cleaned up and actually be a gentleman, pick you up and take you home, *without* expecting you to split the check and your legs." Peggy handed her empty glass to the waitress and squinted at the name tag. "Thanks,

Jewel."

"No problem. You know it's not *just* your all's generation. Most men are still little boys wanting someone to take care of them. But it's not such a horrible thing when you think about it. Isn't that what we all want…to love and be loved back, to be taken care of and to take care of someone else? I want to grow old with someone and them be there to hold my hand when I take my last breath. I think men are just very confused nowadays."

She finished passing out their drinks, and all four women sat silently watching as she walked away.

Sally stared at her wineglass. "Who is that girl?"

"Our waitress, Jewel," Peggy offered with a hiccup.

"No. I mean did you hear her? She's an old soul."

"She is right you know." Carole took a drink from her glass. "Isn't that what we all wanted before life kicked us in the teeth and made us jaded old bitches?" The women smiled wanly and nodded. "Where have all the real men gone? Why are they so confused?"

"It's because of what they're used to. Take widowers for example. They've spent a lifetime having their mothers then their wives clean and cook for them. It didn't matter how hard or how many hours I worked, I'd get home and hear, 'What's for dinner?' Then after cooking, cleaning, taking care of the kids, and being exhausted, we're expected to let them roll on top, use us as receptacles, then be heavenly blessed to get to listen to them snore.

"We did it, and basically we only have ourselves to blame. But now we know that's not what we want. Women have evolved and found their voices, and they're using them. And these poor men who have lost their wives don't know what to do…they woke up from a blissful dream and landed smack dab in an unknown world called *reality.*"

"Exactly, Peg, but there's more when it comes to widowers. For the most part their wives were sick for a long time, and they weren't getting any sex. The good ones hung in there and were faithful, but now they're hornier than hell. And it's been so long they don't know what to do, much less how to go about getting a decent woman. Same goes for all newbies…even the divorced ones. The assholes more than likely had someone on the side, so they don't count.

"Back in my mom's day, women would be standing in line at a widower's door with casseroles and offers to come over for dinner. Today we're still working women with lives of our own, and we're tired of being the caregivers. No wonder men are confused, and I would think somewhat emasculated. Wouldn't it be great if there was someone out there who could teach them how to fend for themselves, step from the past into the present, and learn how to actually *court* a woman?" Sally's mind flashed to Darrell. He'd been so damn good at it during the love-bombing stage.

Betty put a hand on hers. "I for one don't have any problems with Jim. He's wonderful and understanding. We have great sex; he's always doing things for me…not that I'd ever get married again, but it's nice the way it is. I still have my freedom to be me.

"I've been where you all are. Look how long it took me to find someone and all the frogs I had to kiss. I get it. That being said, Sally, why don't you start a business? There're tons of single women out there who would love helping you. Offer different services to the newbies like teaching them to do laundry, fold clothes, or fix meals, how to dress, when it's time to get a new shirt. Or how about them learning proper ways to act around a woman…what to say and definitely what not to say?"

Sally stared at her friend, awestruck. "Training…that's what you're talking about…like being widower whisperers? Oh, my Lord, you are absolutely brilliant! We could train them how to go on a date, how to dance, open doors, ask a woman proper questions, and let her answer them. They could learn how to stand when a lady walks into the room, how to touch a woman and not touch her unless she wants to be touched…let's do it!"

She stared at the other three women expectantly, but there was dead silence around the table. *They're looking at me like I've lost my mind.* "What? Why do you all have those horrified expressions?"

Peggy took a long swig of her margarita, cleared her throat, then twisted on the seat to look at Sally. "You know how I feel about dating. I made mistakes in the past. Who am I to train anyone?"

"Well, to begin with, we've all made horrible mistakes. But you're an amazing woman who has survived so much. Look at you. You're beautiful and kind and authentic. Who better to teach others what you've learned?"

"But the rest of you have been through a lot too," Peggy reminded her.

"Yes, and each of us has our share of mistakes. But let's not forget that we all need money."

"I need extra money," Carole interrupted. "It's been hard trying to help my daughter with the two kids. After my heart surgery, I couldn't work for a long time."

Sally nodded then looked at Betty who put her hand out in front of her. "No! Nope! Nada! No way, Jose! No, you've been getting me into things since we were teenagers, and most of it was trouble. Besides, I don't need money. I have a good job."

"Humph, one you can't retire from. And for your information, *Thelma*, you always went more than willingly into whatever *trouble* I came up with. And you would be on this like white on rice if you weren't dating Jim. Like you're all innocent and stuff." Sally shook her head.

All eyes turned to Betty who smiled. "Okay, it's true, I always loved all the mischief you got us into…it was fun and exciting. But I'm afraid this could turn out to be a problem. What if they see us like surrogates or escorts?"

"Like old lady hookers?" Carole shrugged. "Well, we all still like sex."

Sally's brows drew together. "Do I have to give you the STD lecture?"

Peggy and Betty were chuckling, but Carole leaned in closer to Sally. "You have this thing about older people and sex and STDs. That's why you're so judgmental about men. Have you seen a therapist?"

"Okay, agreed, I'm a judgmental troublemaker." Sally shrugged and took a sip of wine. "Let's just get back to the training thing. You're right! People probably *would* get the wrong idea…especially men. But we could work around all that. We'd have to do research on them and have contracts detailing the services we offer and stating the services we *don't* provide. One of them hitting on one of us is bound to happen. Like we were talking about earlier, most of them probably haven't had sex in a long time."

She looked around the table at the stunned look on all three faces and shrugged. "Okay, these are pitfalls we can make them aware of. We would definitely have to have rules. I say no fraternizing with them…that we keep it professional and strictly business."

"Yeah, right! You know they're going to be lonely and want us to be their sounding boards and friends and—"

"And you know as well as I do, Carole, that no man really wants to be your new best friend unless he's gay. Look, all I'm asking is for you all to think about it when we're completely sober. Go home, do your daily routine, but think about some ways we could make it work. I'd love to hear your ideas." Sally looked up and saw Jewel.

"Does anyone want another round of drinks or anything else to eat?"

They shook their heads. "We each have to drive home. Better not…just our checks, please." Sally replied.

"I'll do it. The whisperer thing…I'll do it. I bet half the single women in here would…hell, even the married ones." Jewel shot them a big smile then turned to get their checks ready.

"See there, *she* wants to do it. Please, ladies, at least think about it. I want each of your inputs. I know we could make this work."

"Oh, all right. I'll talk it over with Jim," Betty conceded.

Peggy raised her hand. "I'll think about it and talk to Mom. At ninety-four years old, I bet she'll have a lot to say on the subject."

Carole held her hand out to Sally, and they shook. "I

think I'm in…not for sure, but I like the idea. And I'm getting really tired of living with my daughter and that abusive baby daddy. God only knows I'm not discussing this with them. However, there are a couple of guys at work I'd like to run it past. One of them actually lost his mother several months ago. He's been having a hard time helping his father adjust. First thing the old guy did after a couple of months was hook up with a much younger chick who thought he had a ton of money. It was a disaster. The other one is older and recently divorced. His wife left him after thirty-five years. He's been devastated. I want to get their takes on this."

"Sounds perfect." Sally held her glass out to the middle of the table. "Here's to the possibility of The Widower Whisperers!"

Chapter 5

Peggy

The first thing she heard when she entered their apartment was the sound of the television coming from Mona's room. She set her purse on a breakfast room chair then went into the kitchen to heat up the dinner she'd brought home from the restaurant.

"Peggy, is that you?"

"Who else would it be, Momma?"

The TV went silent, and it wasn't long before her mother was sitting in the chair next to her daughter's purse, waiting for her food, her walker propped against the table. "It could have been anyone. I have a big family, you know."

"I know. It's my family, too." Peggy took the plate from the microwave, put it in front of Mona, along with a glass of milk, and sat in the chair across from her. "I'm glad you're up. I want to talk to you."

"Is there some problem?"

"Not really a problem. Eat, it'll get cold again." She waited for her to take a bite then went on. "Tonight was fun. Sally had another crazy story about a man she had a coffee date with this morning. We all cried we were laughing so hard."

"I don't know why she does that to herself. You'd think she would have learned by now." Mona shrugged, and her tone softened. "But then again she's been burned so many times, from what you've told me, I'm not sure if she can really give anyone a fair chance."

"You are a very wise woman, Momma."

"Well, I wasn't always, and I've made my fair share of mistakes, but somehow it's easier now to just sit back and watch what's going on around me. Sally's one of those women that's been used to getting attention from men…the *wrong* kind…of both men and attention. And she uses her looks. Do you think she's a narcissist?"

Peggy watched her mother take another bite of food and smiled, glad she was enjoying it. A couple of months ago, she was in the hospital, and the family had been afraid they were going to lose her. "No, but she does admit to being vain. She was brought up that way by her mother. You're not going to believe this, but Mrs. Estes actually got mad because Sally wouldn't try out to be a Playboy Bunny. You would have boxed my ears for even thinking about such a thing."

Mona set her fork down calmly, took a sip of milk, and stared at her daughter. "Damned right I would have. And your father, God rest him, would have had you locked up for being insane."

"I know! It's the truth though. Betty confirmed it. She said Sally refused to do it because she wanted people to care about her for her mind, not just her body."

"Poor girl, seems like she attracted all the users and losers anyway."

"Yep, and this last man was no exception. I'm so relieved that one is over."

"Me too! From what you've told me he was pretty worthless. I guess it's good she's at least trying to get out there and test the waters. You should too, you know.

You've been alone way too long."

Peggy got up and grabbed a bottled water from the fridge. "I'm not alone, Momma. I've got you...my children and grandchildren."

"It's not the same thing, and you know it. You also know what it's like to have the love of your life. When Gordon died, I thought you would, too. You lost your soulmate and your mind, but you pulled yourself back together for the children and me. It's time for you to start living for yourself again. I don't plan on being around forever. I've had a good life and made my peace. Your father's been waiting for me, and when I'm gone, what happens then? Do you sit here alone in this apartment until you die?"

"I don't have a problem with being alone."

"How do you know? You've never been completely alone in your life. You had your father and me. You've always had the kids or me living with you. And there were the lost years when you went through those two horrible marriages. I worried about you so much."

"I know you did, but I don't want to discuss it. And you are too going to live forever."

Mona shrugged. "So, what did you want to talk about?" She picked up her fork and started eating again.

"We got on the subject of dating and men, especially widowers and newly divorced ones. It's like they're lost. They don't know what to do or how to go about daily living, much less how to start dating again, and they say the most incredibly stupid things."

"Like what?"

"Well, Carole told us that she's gone out with several who have told her how much all these other women want them. One even claimed that not just his ex-wives still wanted him, but their *daughters* did too! He told her they wanted some of what their momma was getting." Peggy was trying not to laugh.

Mona coughed then snorted. "Oh, please stop! Don't make me choke on my food. Nice women he must have been married to with daughters like that. And so, if these men are so sought after by all these females, young and old, what are they doing trying to get in Carole's pants? It seems like they'd be too busy elsewhere."

"Bingo! I suppose they think that by saying this stuff, women are going to find them desirable and virile when all it really does is make them look ridiculous, insecure, and desperate."

"Not much of a turn-on, is it? So, where are you going with all this?"

Peggy went back to her seat across from her mother. "Sally was talking about what it must be like being a newbie and mentioned there should be someone to help them get through it. Then Betty tells her she ought to start a business. Sally thinks it's a brilliant idea and said it would be like training…remember how you always loved watching *The Dog Whisperer*? She says it could be called 'The Widower Whisperers,' and next thing we know, she wants us to go into business with her."

Mona pushed her plate to the side, rested her arms on the table, and stared at her hands for what seemed like minutes. When she finally looked up, her eyes were twinkling. "Other than the name being a tongue twister, it sounds perfect to me."

"What? I thought you'd think it was idiotic."

"It might be, but God only knows how much help men need. We take care of them their entire lives, and they take it for granted. Some bastards even take

27

advantage of it. But there are some good men still out there that don't know shit from Shinola about how to start over again. I bet most of the older ones are playing golf or cards occasionally, having a few drinks with the boys, coming home to an empty house, turning the TV on, drinking some more *alone*, and eating pre-cooked or frozen meals in their underwear on a recliner."

"Oh, you mean like most of us?"

"With one big exception. They've got no one to talk to, no one to tell them good night, no one to give them a hug or dry their tears. Your daddy was a good man, and so was your Gordon, but both would have been completely lost without us. There's a reason men usually die first.

"So what if it's idiotic? It might work, and it'll get you out of this apartment. You work from here; you do everything from here. You need to forget your past mistakes and start enjoying life again while you're still mobile and can get around. It won't take much money to start up…do it! I'm tired, and I'm going to bed."

Seeing Mona reach for her walker, Peggy got up, handed it to her, and watched as she lumbered painfully toward her room. "I love you, Momma."

She stopped and turned. "Your daddy and I grew old together, and he wasn't alone when he died. There's something to be said for that. I love you, too!"

Tears brimmed in her eyes as she stared at her mother's closed door. She'd missed Gordon terribly after he'd died from a massive stroke. They should have grown old together too. She'd married two other times, trying to fill the void left by his absence. They had been awful mistakes, the kind you make when you're desperate, heartbroken, and alone, trying to raise four kids without a father.

She sighed and looked at the clock. It was still early. Memories swirled round in her head and hit her with the truth. She didn't really like the idea of being completely alone, and sometime in the not-too-distant future she would be. She swiped at the wetness trickling down her cheeks then picked up the dishes and carried them to the sink.

Chapter 6

Betty

As she drove home, her mind went through all the twists and turns of what they'd talked about. Part of her was excited over the idea of The Widower Whisperers' business. She hadn't wanted to say very much to the girls because they worried about her so much. But the truth was that she was tired…of everything.

She'd raised her daughters pretty much by herself, sometimes working two or three jobs at a time…and here she was still getting up at four thirty or five every morning to get ready to go to work at a male dominated office where she was the oldest one there and should have been retired by now. And when each of her parents had been ill and/or dying, she had been their only caregiver.

There was Jim…she loved him, but he was self-employed and worked twenty-four seven with truly little time off. To make it worse, he lived on the eastern outskirts of Austin and her house was in Westlake, making it a long commute and even more difficult for them to spend time together.

Betty pulled into her garage, put the door down, and walked into the house through the unlocked door leading into the utility room. The two Chihuahuas were getting so old they were going deaf and no longer whined and barked when she got home. She hurried to the back room where they stayed while she was gone, opened the baby gate, and they hightailed it to the back door. While they were busy doing their business, she went to the purse she'd thrown on the couch, pulled out her cell, and tapped on Jim's name.

He answered on the third ring. "Hey, Betty, you on your way home?"

"No, I'm sorry, I forgot to call when I left. I'm here okay. Just let the dogs out, and I'm exhausted. What are you up to?"

"Just got home, too, and letting the dogs out. I wish Roy would get settled somewhere and come get his two. Had to work late again. The new guy I hired didn't show up."

"Again? That's great!"

He sighed. "It's the life of having your own business. You know, I worry about you when you go out like that, especially driving home by yourself. I wish we were closer so I could be your chauffer."

I do too. "It's okay, we have a rule that no one has more than two drinks, and if one of us does, we call them an Uber. You know how it is, the life of old ladies going out on the town. Besides, we always share something to eat and drink plenty of water." The dogs were scratching and yipping at the back door. "Hold on a sec, I've got to let Bebe and Bobo in."

She quickly fed them and flopped on the couch. "Hey, I'm back, sorry."

"It's fine. Gave me a chance to finish taking care of this herd of wild beasts."

He was always so sweet and understanding. She was hoping he'd remain that way when she told him about what she and the girls had talked about tonight. "Jim, you trust me, don't you?"

"Of course, I do! Why would you ask a thing like that?"

"I just want you to listen and hear me out. No interruptions till I'm through. Can you do that for me?"

"Sure."

She detected doubt in his voice. "Promise?"

"I promise! Would you just get on with it? Now I'm not only curious but worried."

Betty started with Sally's coffee date and went on about some of Carole's experiences. By the time she got through with the night's conversation, ending with The Widower Whisperers, she wasn't sure if Jim was actually breathing or not. "Are you still there?"

There were a few more seconds of silence. "I'm here."

"And what do you think?"

"What do I think? Betty, how would you like me asking you if you thought it was okay for me to go out on dates with other women and get paid to teach them how to handle themselves around men again…and learn how to do what their husbands had always done for them?"

Now she was the one who was quiet.

"Betty?"

"I'm thinking, okay? All right, it probably wouldn't make me happy. But if it could be handled in a professional way with contracts and things…Shit, I don't know. Maybe there's some way I could be involved in the business and not have to deal with the men directly. I just know that if it works, we could start hiring other women to be the ones to go out and actually train the men, and it might lead to a way I could quit that job I despise."

Jim cleared his throat. "You realize you're talking about training human beings like they're animals?"

Well, he sure sounds offended. "Yeah, I do, so what? Athletes have to be trained, and that doesn't seem to bother you when you're sitting there watching them play sports all weekend. They have private *trainers* at the gym you never have time to go to." She was getting worked up now. "Our military train our people in uniform. For thirty-seven years, I've been going to the same job every day and training young punks, with wannabe macho attitudes, how to do their jobs and had to sit back and watch them make four times as much as I do while they constantly got promotions and raises because of what *I* taught them. And *men* have been training women since the beginning of time to sit down, shut up, and not be heard."

Jim let out a whistle. "Are you done?"

"Yes!"

"Good, because I'm hanging up now. I suggest you think about things, and I'll give you a call tomorrow when I have time."

Betty started to respond, but he'd clicked off. "Damn it to hell and back!" She tossed her cell on the coffee table and called for the Chihuahuas to keep her company.

Chapter 7

Carole

Her daughter had borrowed her car to pick the kids up from a friend who'd been watching them. Getting out of the same Uber she'd taken to meet the girls, Carole heard yelling the second she stepped onto the curb. *Another night in paradise.* Yet another night baby daddy, David, had forgotten, or was too drunk, to get his own kids.

She hesitated going up to the house, remembering how this fiasco had happened. She'd been recovering from open-heart surgery, wasn't able to work, and had agreed to give up the condo she'd been renting to move in with her daughter and help with the grandchildren. It had been a perfect solution for both since Dave had deserted them, and Carissa really needed the help. With her savings dwindling quickly, so did Carole.

Unfortunately, it wasn't a win-win situation for long. With Carole there to babysit, her daughter was able to get a better job and work longer hours. Soon enough, Dave caught the scent of money and came crawling back begging to be taken in *again. Poor Carissa doesn't have the strength to resist him.* Now, Carole had no home of her own to go back to.

She took her time walking to the front door, her stomach doing flip-flops as she stepped onto the porch.

She stood there a long time listening, wishing she could make the abusing bastard inside disappear. She could hear him clear enough, his slurring insults, his ludicrous excuses for forgetting about his own children, something crashing across the room…the *blood curdling screams…*

"What in the fuck is going on here?" The door slammed behind her, and she took it all in. The bowl of fruit from the dining room table shattered against the wall going into the kitchen, the baby screaming in her daughter's arms, a red mark on Carissa's cheek, Dave towering over them with his fist drawn, sweat pouring down his greasy forehead, the three-year-old, Able, clinging to his dad's leg, screeching for him not to hit his mommy again.

Carole's trained instincts took over. In one giant leap she was on Dave's back grabbing for his arm. He twisted and tried to throw her off, but she took her fist and pounded it against the side of his face. He reached behind him, clasping a chunk of her hair, and Carole let out a yelp. Carissa came to her senses and in one swift kick to his groin brought him to his knees.

"Run," Carole screamed getting to her feet. Pulling her gun from the purse still hanging from her shoulder, she swung in front of David and pointed it at his head. "You know what, you piece of slug slime? I *will* use this. You touch my family again, and I'll have no qualms about blowing your fucking brains out, what little you have."

"Fuck you, bitch, they're *my* family," he spat.

"Not if I have anything to do with it. You know where I worked before I gave that life up, got married, and had kids?"

"A whorehouse?"

"Yeah, something like that. I worked with a segment of the police force that took down pissant shits like you."

He looked her in the eyes and started to get up. That's when she took the Glock 19X and slammed it into the side of his head, knocking him out.

****

All the lights came on as Sally pulled into the drive, got out, and walked to the house. As usual, it was quiet, almost eerily so. She climbed up the steps to the back porch where more lights came on, told Siri to turn the alarm off and unlock the door, then went through the utility room into the kitchen and told Alexa she was home. Immediately, the alarm was armed stay, and more lights lit her way as she walked into the dining room, turned down the hall, and entered her bedroom.

Sally told Google Hub to turn on Pandora on speakers, and easy listening music filled the house as she started changing into sweats and taking her jewelry off. A song came on, one of hers and Darrell's. At once melancholy swept over her, and she slumped on the edge of the bed letting her mind drift to that last morning in this same room almost a year ago.

Her eyes barely opened to the golden glow of sunshine behind the blinds. She stretched, her hand coming to rest on something deliciously warm, and she rolled over to find Darrell staring at her.

"Mmm, I don't want to get up," she purred.

Fingertips ran languidly across her bare shoulder. "Let's just lay here a bit longer and—"

The ringing of his cell interrupted him, and he moved his arm to grab it from the nightstand. Peering at the screen, he smiled. "Here we go."

"What?"

He put a fingertip to his lips and answered, fluffing a pillow under his head.

Sally could hear the woman on the other end. "Hey, you, happy birthday. You have any special plans?"

He chuckled. "No, no one's doing anything special for me. But you're the first one to tell me happy birthday."

Sitting up straight, Sally pulled the blanket around her nude body and stared at him in disbelief. *No one's doing anything special for him? She's the first one to tell him happy birthday? What the hell have I been doing for the last five days?* Then the coup de grâce, she could hear the woman asking him out, and his response was like a flaming arrow to her heart.

"That'd be great, but I think I have the flu. I'm just going to stay in today and take care of myself. Maybe in a couple of days."

Quickly, Sally reached for her clothes at the foot of the bed and started putting them on as he told his *friend* goodbye.

He reached out and grabbed her fingertips. "What are you doing? I thought we were going to hang out in bed awhile…maybe you could give me a little present." He gave what he probably thought was a seductive grin.

Sally jerked her hand away. "What in the hell are you talking about? Evidently, I'm not even here. And give you a little present? No one's doing anything special for you if I heard correctly. For five days, I've been waiting on you hand and foot because you've been sick. I let you come here because your condo flooded and was being repaired. I loaned you the money to get the work started because you were depressed and having money problems and that last *big deal* of yours fell through. I have given you gifts; I've fixed your favorite foods, and yes, I've given you my body. And you laid here in *my bed*, next to me, and rudely answered the phone, knowing it was another woman, and talked to her as if you were at home a thousand miles away and I didn't even exist."

"Whoa!"

"Don't you 'whoa' me. Yesterday, you took a call, and I heard you sneak off into another room and start whispering. I'm done, Darrell. Each and every time I give you another chance, you promise me the stars and the moon that this time it's going to be different. I've known you and been there for you for fifteen years, and you treat me with absolutely no respect whatsoever. I can't—"

Her cell pinged, pulling her from the debasing memory. It was a text from Carole. *I need some help. I've got my daughter and grandchildren. Can we come over?*

Concern quickly replaced the degradation she'd felt moments before, and she sent back, *Absolutely! I have a spare room for the children and the couch in my office folds into a bed.*

"Hey, Google, stop the damn music, turn off the alarm, and unlock the front door."

"I'm sorry, Sally, could you say those one at a time?"

Irritably, she went through each command while she finished changing then threw on some sneakers, went to the kitchen, poured a glass of wine, and carried it to the front porch. She put the glass on the coffee table, lit its fire pit, then settled on the couch behind it and waited with apprehension churning her stomach. About twenty minutes later Carole's car pulled up, and she wrapped her sweater tighter around her as she walked down the long sidewalk to greet them.

"What's happened?" The streetlamps glowed behind them. She glanced at Carissa who was holding the sleeping baby, Cindy, and could clearly see the mark on her cheek even in the simi-darkness. "It's David again, isn't it? I wondered why you had to take an Uber tonight."

In Carole's arms was Able, his exhausted blond head resting on her shoulder. "Yeah, I walked in on an assault and battery. Cold-cocked the bastard with my Glock. Police were there to take him in. I had the babies stay in the car while I waited. I didn't want them exposed to that…they've seen enough already."

Sally opened the front door and ushered them upstairs to her granddaughter's room. "Aren't you going to get in trouble for knocking him out?" she whispered.

"I doubt it. They know me, and it sure isn't the bastard's first rodeo."

They tiptoed downstairs while Carissa was getting the kids to sleep, and Sally fixed them both a drink then they went back outside to sit on the porch. "But aren't you worried he might come after you all again? I know some people who might be able to help…attorneys, judges."

Carole turned to look at her. "Everyone forgets I was with the department once. It might have been a long time ago, but I still have friends in high places that will cover my back. This go around, I'll make sure he does time, enough time I can get Carissa and the kids out of here and started over somewhere he won't find them."

"But that's going to take a lot of money."

She smiled at Sally. "You're absolutely correct, and

that is exactly why we need to talk about The Widower Whisperers."

Chapter 8

Six Months Later
Elaine Fitzsimmons

Elaine was propped up in bed reading a local paper when her husband came in to check on her.

"What are you perusing so intensely? I expected you to be binging on *Outlander* or one of your other lusty series." She laid the paper open on her lap and looked up with a smile as Thomas Duncan Fitzsimmons sat on the edge of her bed and curled the paper up to see its name. "Aw, so it's the *Austin Chronicle*, now is it? And what has you so enthralled this fine Thursday afternoon?"

"Quit teasing me. You know I love to read the horoscopes and see what's going on around town. Since I can't really leave the house now, it still kinda makes me feel like I'm part of things." She shrugged. "That way, if a friend calls to check on me or see if there's anything they can do, I can always change the subject and say something like 'Oh, I hear Sixth Street is doing such and such.' I know that sounds awful, because everyone feels bad for me and wants to help, but they make me feel worse. I'm not a total invalid…well, not yet…"

Thomas leaned over the paper and planted a kiss on her forehead. "Not awful at all, Ellie. And your mind is still as good as ever. So, what's going on in town that's of interest?"

She knew he was lying...knew he'd noticed her lapses in memory, but neither of them was ready to face it yet. She forced the spark back into her chocolate eyes, gazed into his hazel ones, and brushed at a kinky strand of salt-and-pepper hair that was always falling across her face while grinning mischievously.

"Your unrequited."

For a few seconds he looked puzzled before it dawned on him. "Sally?"

"Your Sally."

"Not my Sally. I don't have a Sally. The Sally Estes we based the book off of?"

She took one of his hands lovingly and stroked it. "Yes, the same one you had a thing for in high school, but she was always dating someone else, and you all stayed *friends*. The same one you wanted me to meet when we were living in Colorado and came back here for your fortieth reunion, but she didn't remember you. The same Sally Estes we based 'The Reunion' on.

"Last year after the MS was getting worse and we had to move back to Austin full time, I started stalking her."

"Oh, love, why would you do that? It was just a high school crush. There was nothing to it. I haven't thought of her since we published the book. Well, actually that's not completely true. I bumped into her at our café several months ago. Interesting character...I stepped in as she was giving a speech on venereal diseases and Baby Boomers to an extremely perplexed-looking fellow. She got up and left, I grabbed our to-go lunches, opened the door for her, and we went our separate ways. Still didn't recognize me."

"Why didn't you tell me?"

"Don't go looking all butthurt! I completely forgot about it. It was nothing… You're the love of my life…always have been and always will be." She shifted in the bed, and he rose to fluff the pillow behind her then returned to her side.

Holding his hand again, she looked thoughtful before meeting his eyes. "It's not that. I know you've loved me. But you loved your first wife, too, and she gave you two fine children, something I couldn't do." He started to speak, but she leaned forward and put a finger to his lips. "Hush. Let me go on because I've been thinking about this for a long time."

He took her hand between his two, kissed the finger, and nodded.

"Because of Sally, we created a beautiful story together of young, unrequited love, and I don't think it was a coincidence that it was her aura that inspired our book. In the beginning of my stalking, I was simply curious. It wasn't a jealousy thing. Then as this damned illness progressed and I became more confined to bed, I really became interested in what had become of her and what her life is like now. I know you don't want to hear this, but I just have a feeling I'm not going to be here a whole lot longer—"

"Stop it. We're still doing research, and people rarely die of—"

"Multiple Sclerosis, I know the spiel, but the pain is worse with less remissions. My ticker isn't good, and you know as well as I do the doctors said I could have another heart attack. Maybe it's not imminent, but the odds are high. Jean has to stay overnight now in case I have to get up or she has to change me… Today she had

43

to help me on the computer because my vision blurred for no reason. And I've felt it, the lapses in memory. Once my mind starts to go…I don't want to live that way. Just don't make it all worse by trying to deny it. We've never lied to each other."

His head was bent, but Elaine could see the trace of a tear escape from the corner of his eye. She stretched forward and ruffled his hair. "Could we get back to Sally?"

"Yes, let's," he mumbled without looking up.

"I was just reading an article about her and some of her girlfriends starting a business called 'The Widower Whisperers.' Ghastly name I know and doesn't exactly roll off the tongue, but catchy.

"They evidently help widowed and divorced men…newbies, they call them, get back into the swing of life and train them how to do the things their wives did for them, as well as getting them ready to start dating…I think they even have a course called 'Women 101.' When I first saw their ad about four months ago, I kind of thought it was a ridiculous idea and had no clue Sally was involved. But it looks like they're doing really well and have so many male clients that they're going to branch out to females soon."

"That's charming, and I wish them all the luck in the world, but it has absolutely nothing to do with us."

"Well, if you think about it, it really is a good idea. It's hard for most people to start over. You know what it was like after you and Gayle divorced. I remember what it was like dating after Jake died, before I met you. It was horrible. Men were absolute idiots, thinking they were suave and debonaire. You'd go to dinner, and they'd be putting down the ex, drinking too much, start trying to hold your hand and talking about back rubs…" She shivered and ran her hands over her arms. "It was creepy, and I don't imagine it's gotten any better as we've aged."

"Was I that bad?" He flashed his most brilliant smile deepening the wrinkles around his murky green eyes.

She squinched her nose. "Well, actually you were *different*."

His brows drew together, and the smile dimmed. "As in?"

"As in you were a breath of fresh air, and you know it, damn it!" She tossed a throw pillow at him, and he caught it deftly. "You were such a gentleman and so bloody handsome I couldn't keep my hands from shaking and had trouble getting two words put together. You asked about *me*, and I felt like you were really interested. You talked about the things you were working on, hoping to make a difference in the world, and I was fascinated. You didn't make a pass at me but instead showed you were interested in subtle ways that involved getting to know me and not just wanting to jump into bed. You didn't talk about your ex like she was demonic…you showed respect. And you were such a graceful dancer. I thought you were too good to be true, and I still do."

"You flatter me because I was thinking there was no way on earth I deserved someone like you. So, why all this talk about Sally?"

"She's been single a long time, and I could relate to some of her experiences going out with newbies she's talked about in interviews and this article. Then it made me think about you and what you'd do when…*if* I go. I imagine you throwing yourself into the work we started together, research and more research, trying to find a way to save the world, a way you could have saved me. We've been so close and done everything together, and I imagined you…*alone*."

"I wouldn't be alone. I have the kids and grandkids. And besides, you're not going to *go* anywhere."

"It's not the same, and you know it. I had Jean bring me the laptop, and we looked up the website for The Widower Whisperers. She helped fill out a form for you." Elaine held out a hand halting what he was about to say. "I knew you wouldn't do it yourself. If something happens to me, she's to go into the system and submit it a year from the date of my passing. That should give you enough time to grieve and get your bearings about you. I'd like you to stay here in Austin for a few years so you can be close to your family."

"And to Sally Estes. Say it! Because that's what you're thinking, isn't it? That somehow this long-lost unrequited love and I are going to reunite, and fifty years will have slipped away, and she'll suddenly remember who I am."

"Stranger things have happened. Because of her, we wrote a best seller that's being made into a movie."

"Which was *based* loosely on her…not *about* her. It was fiction."

"And they say truth is stranger than fiction."

Thomas stood, kissed her on top of the head, and went to the door. "Please, Ellie, please don't make me talk about this…I simply can't…"

His voice faded as he neared the door, and her heart-wrenching love for him enveloped her with such intensity she wanted to jump from the bed, run to him, wrap her arms around him, and never let go. Yet she couldn't…couldn't get out of bed by herself, couldn't run to him…but she had to let go just as did he. "Thomas Duncan, promise me, if something does happen, you'll honor this wish…this is all I'll ever ask of you."

He turned briefly and met her eyes before going silently out the door.

Chapter 9

Thomas Duncan Fitzsimmons

He left the bedroom he'd once shared with his wife, got in his car, and headed for his downtown office then changed his mind, deciding to drive past his old high school in West Austin. The parking lot was almost empty because of spring break, and he pulled in next to the football stadium. He had been a big deal back then; active in sports, involved in all the social activities, an officer of the student council.

He was tall even as a teenager, athletic and pretty nice looking except for the occasional outbreak of zits. A buddy of his, Billy Markham, had given him the nickname, Zitsimmons, during a particularly difficult time of acne, and it had taken him years to get over it. Even with all that, he'd been somewhat popular, the girls liked him well enough, and being a straight A student, life had been relatively easy for him…except for one little thing…Sally Estes.

She'd moved to town during ninth grade, and he'd walked into chemistry class to find the strange redhead sitting at the desk he usually sat in next to Billy. He'd stopped short, watching them talking then she'd looked up at him, grinned, and his heart melted. Suddenly, he hadn't felt like the cock of the walk but was uncustomarily self-conscious. His heart thrummed loudly in his ears, palms went sweaty, and he'd tried to take a step forward, but his feet were like sandbags on wobbly legs. His attempt at smiling back could only be described as a paralyzed grimace.

Billy called out to him, and he'd awkwardly shuffled over.

"Tommy Zitsimmons, this is Sally. She just moved here from New Orleans. I told her you usually sit there but you wouldn't mind. There's an empty desk a couple of rows behind us."

She'd stared up at him with the most incredible cornflower blue eyes and held out a freckled hand. "It's a pleasure making your acquaintance."

"Well, take her hand, dummy!"

Billy's comment roused him from his stupor, and he gave her tiny fingers a cursory shake, well aware of the dampness of his own hand. "Nice to meet you." That was the first time he'd laid eyes on her, and she'd been polite but guardedly unimpressed.

Over the next three years, she'd had plenty of guys after her. So many, she grew tired of it and found herself a much older college boy to date. Though she looked down her nose at most of the high school boys trying to get in her pants, Thomas had managed to stay friendly with her, until that fateful day they were alone, working on a science project after school, and he'd kissed her. It wasn't like he'd planned it…it just happened. One minute they were in the annex doing a chemistry experiment, the next a storm was blowing in, and she was pulling him out the door just as a blast of thunder greeted them.

"I positively love storms," she'd told him, gazing at the sky. Another rumble from above and the clouds broke loose as drops of rain spattered the dry earth. She grinned, held her palms out, raised her arms to the heavens, and spun in a ritualistic, almost pagan, dance. He was enthralled with her every move, the glow on her face, the gleefulness in her eyes. When she stopped twirling, she looked up at him in utter joy and giggled. "Glorious, isn't it?"

He couldn't stop himself…he really couldn't. In his eyes she was as beautiful as an ancient goddess tempting him, luring him as she stared up at him in unabashed ecstasy. "Yes, quite glorious," he'd whispered and leaned down to gently press his lips against hers. At first, she seemed startled, pulled away, and stared into his eyes. Grinning again, she stood on tiptoe, wrapped her arms around his neck, and pulled his face down to hers in a sweet, lingering kiss. His arms had gone around her back pressing her to him, and he could feel their passion growing when she suddenly twisted away.

They'd stood gazing at each other through the soft curtain of rain until she spoke, breaking the spell. "I'm sorry, Tom, I can't. I have a boyfriend…I…I shouldn't have. It's just…I really like you and wouldn't want anything to ever ruin our friendship."

She was being kind…she was *always* kind. He felt like an idiot and lied to save face. "Hey, I know. I was just kidding around. I really didn't want to, but the guys bet me I wouldn't kiss you. We were just joking around. I hope you're not mad at me."

She'd faced him as a flush reddened her cheeks and her eyes became masked, dull, before giving him a shy smile. "Yeah, a lot of boys think I'm free game because of how I look and that I moved here from the *Big Easy*. You know, we're all drunks, hedonists and *easy*…like the name implies. I just thought you were different was all. That we were really friends."

Her comment had cut to the quick, and he was so damned full of guilt his stomach knotted. "I'm sorry. I really, really am. I shouldn't...I mean, you *are* my friend...I didn't mean it like that."

She glanced at her watch. "Yeah, sure. I've got to get going." And that was that. The rest of high school she withdrew, got deeper into her college relationship, didn't go to any of the school functions. When he'd see her in class or in the halls, she'd always smiled and nodded...sometimes she'd actually give a little wave. And in his eyes that was proof of their everlasting friendship...until their fortieth reunion.

He and Elaine had been married several years and were happily living in Colorado, working on wind power research and it's footprint. At first, he hadn't thought about going to the reunion until several of his old friends had called, one of them casually mentioning that Sally Estes was helping with it and would be there. In his mind's blind adolescent eyes, they'd had a mutual crush on each other, and the older boyfriend had kept them apart. In his delusion, he'd thought they'd remained friends. And he wanted Elaine to meet her.

When they walked in, he saw her immediately. She sat behind a table demurely checking people in along with two of her old girlfriends. The ladies smiled and gave hugs, making everyone feel welcome and wanted. He and Ellie stood in line and waited their turn, but it was someone else who ended up getting their names and handing them the badge with his senior picture on it. Oddly, Sally hadn't even looked over. But she was really busy, and so many classmates were vying for attention from all three greeters.

Later, she was at the bar by herself trying to tab out. He'd sauntered up, told her he remembered her, and showed her his badge. "Do you remember me? Tommy Fitzsimmons?"

She'd changed, but not that much…she was still as pretty as he remembered. She looked up with those crazy blue eyes now surrounded by fine laugh lines and squinched her nose. "I'm sorry. I don't think so."

By then he was aware of Elaine to the side of him, and he tried again. "Tom…you always called me Tom."

She looked thoughtful then shook her head. "I'm sorry, really. It was a big class, and there were so many boys. I guess I just have a block or something. One of the girls just pointed out some guy I went out with a few times, and I didn't remember him. Did we…"

This time he shook his head in bewilderment. He was embarrassed and hurt. How could she not remember? How could their friendship have meant so little to her? How could she have forgotten their kiss in the rain?

He brought his mind back to the present, got out of the car, stretched, and stared at the row of annexes still behind the school. One of them was where they'd been working on the science project. When he and Elaine were writing the book, it all became clear and she had explained to him that when he kissed Sally, he'd become just like all the others. Just another dumb, hormonal boy trying to take advantage of her. He hadn't been a real friend in her eyes. He'd simply faded into just another jerk wanting to have sex with her and bragging rights. *What had I been thinking all those years? I was such a damn idiot…*

He perched his sunglasses on top of his head and rubbed his eyes. He couldn't stand the thought of losing Elaine. She'd been his whole world. But he couldn't deny she wasn't getting better, and she had a weak heart. He didn't want her suffering…he couldn't take that. But he wasn't ready to let her go…not yet.

Out of curiosity, he pulled his phone from his pocket and googled Sally Estes. Maybe some of the things Ellie had said earlier made sense…hopefully, he'd never have to find out.

Chapter 10

Sally

Sally was working in her home office, which was also Widower Whisperers' headquarters, when the video doorbell announced someone was at the back door. She grabbed her cell, saw an upset-looking Carole, told Alexa to unlock the door, and met her friend in the kitchen.

"Alexa, lock the back door. What are you doing here? I thought you were supposed to be at Edgar something or other's." She started walking back to the office.

"Edgar Pervert, does that work for you? Edgar disgusting old geezer maybe?"

Sally stopped in the living room. "Hey, Google, turn the music down."

"You need a frigging dog."

"What?"

"You heard me. You need something besides Google, Alexa, and Siri to boss around. You've been alone way too long."

"Excuse me?" The front door opened, and Betty came waltzing up to them. "Alexa, lock the front door. How did you just get in?"

Betty shrugged. "I walked."

"No, I mean was the door unlocked?"

Betty plopped on the couch. "No, I have a key, remember? I can't believe you never changed the locks and codes after you blocked Darrell."

"Well, he's out in Los Angeles making his fortune with another woman. I doubt he'd show up here…not his narcissistic style."

"I just worry about you being here all alone with nothing but those *things* you talk to all the time."

"See?" Carole put her hands on her hips and glared at Sally accusingly.

"See what? What's going on?"

Carole joined Betty on the couch. "First things first. I thought you vetted old Edgar."

Sally crossed her arms. "Would you all like to join me in the *office*?" They both shook their heads. Suddenly her nerves were on edge, and she was getting irritable. She rubbed her forehead. "Damn it! Hey, Google, turn the music off. Girls, we've got to move to a regular office. And miss priss, I did vet Edgar. I very carefully and thoroughly vet everyone before Betty or I interview them. What the hell happened?"

"Oh, not much. I was teaching him how to do laundry and fold cloths. We'd gotten to the sock part…you know how men just throw them all mixed up into a drawer. I was showing him how to match them up, and one fell on the ground under the dining room table where we were standing. I figured he was probably too stiff to crawl under the table to get it, so I did. And boy, I wasn't wrong when I said stiff. As I was getting back up, he put a hand on my shoulder, stopping me midway, and asked me to give him a blow job. I jerked away, saw the tent in his pants, and flew to the other side of the room."

Betty laughed so hard she was coughing, and Sally was trying not to, but her eyes teared up. She had to sniff a couple of times before responding. "My, still waters run deep...I didn't see that one coming. No pun intended." Then the explosion of giggles happened. "So, what did you tell him?"

Carole stood and crossed her arms. "You all think this is funny...eww, gross."

"Finish telling your story, and I'll tell you mine," Betty chortled.

"Okay, well, I scolded him. I told him that he had read and signed the contracts, and he knew that every service we provided was strictly professional and there was no fraternizing with the clients. And he looks at me calmly with these big rheumy eyes and says he knows all that, but he figured we were pretty much like prostitutes and just put that crap in the contracts to protect ourselves and appear legitimate."

Sally gasped. "Oh dear. Did you explain in detail that that is *not* the nature of our business, and his behavior was unacceptable?"

"Good God, yes! And then Edgar saunters over with his John Wayne impression and throws two one-hundred-dollar bills down on the credenza next to me and says he'd make it worth my while. I told him he was fired and ran as fast as I could out of there and to my car. What else was I supposed to do?"

Sally took Carole's place on the couch. "Nothing. No, you did the right thing. You spent a couple of days working with him, but we'll just give him an entire refund. We don't want him getting angry and spreading lies about any of us, our girls, or the business in general. We can't afford rumors suggesting we solicit, especially after the article in the *Chronicle*."

"That's fine! I don't want anything he's touched. It was good, by the way."

"What?"

"The article." Carole sat in a chair across from them. "So, what happened to you, blondie?"

"I'd rather be dead than red on the head," Betty said smugly.

"Yeah, says you! Come on spit it out. What happened?"

She gave a sly grin. "You know how I've got that really cute younger client in his forties?"

They both nodded. "So, I was teaching him to do household stuff for a few evenings, and things had been going so well we decided to move on to the dating thing and work on his conversational skills with women. Things went great! He actually picked me up…don't worry, it was from work, not home. He opened doors for me, got us a beautiful table at Truluck's, held the chair out for me. He asked if he could order dinner for us, and I agreed. After asking if I preferred red or white, he picked a lovely wine that complimented our food perfectly. I was wondering why he thought he needed to work on his dating skills when out of the blue, he reached over, put his hand on mine, looked into my eyes, and asked if I wanted to be his sub."

She paused to let it sink in, but when neither woman spoke and just stared at her with their mouths open, she went on. "You know, sexual sub…as in *Fifty Shades of Gray*? I thought he was kidding, right? I seriously did, and it cracked me up. He waited for me to quit laughing and held my eyes with his gorgeous young ones. He never even smiled, just squeezed my hand. That sobered me up. I asked him if he'd been joking, and he shook his head. Next thing I knew, we were having this deep conversation about how his ex-wife had been his sex slave. How he got involved in the whole culture and BDSM stuff and that he missed it. He said he was attracted to me, and he'd always had a thing for older women."

"And you didn't get up and walk out?" Carole asked.

"Actually no, I didn't. I was flattered, and I must admit intrigued. And it was kind of sexy. It's not really what you think…most keep their relationships monogamous, but his ex had wanted to venture out and bring others into it. That's what ruined the marriage. It came out that being his sub, she did everything around the house, and he didn't have to lift a finger, so when she wasn't there anymore, he was lost. But his biggest problem with dating is he has trouble talking to women normally and brings up the sex slave stuff, or BDSM, or something that makes them run."

"You didn't," Sally pointed out.

"Well, no, because I'm not dating him, and I found it all remarkably interesting. I mean if I were younger, I might even have said, 'Hell, yes, let's try this.' But I'm not, and I really want to help him get over this urge where he thinks he has to blurt stuff out *before* he gives a woman a chance to know him."

Carole snorted her disapproval. "It sure doesn't hurt that he's a hunk. I bet the story would have been different if you'd been sitting across from old-as-dirt Edgar with his pants tented up."

They were all giggling when Sally's cell rang. She shushed them and answered. Clicking off, she looked solemnly at the other two. "It was Peggy. She wants to come over. She can't stand being in that apartment alone since Mona died. I'm worried about her. I've been trying to get her to work with us on the weekends. She keeps saying she will but…" She shrugged.

"And really, we're all worried about you. You're here all the time alone, and you talk to those damn voice-assistant things like they're people," Carole rebuked.

Betty nodded. "You really do. You should at least get a dog."

"That's exactly what I told her." Carole high-fived the air.

"Okay, ladies, seriously, we've got bigger problems than my being alone. We've been working at this business a little over six months, and I'm thrilled with the way it's been going. But we need more full-time help. I was thinking about Jewel. She was awesome helping us get it all together, and I felt bad that we couldn't give her enough time to make it worth her while to quit waitressing. What do you all think?"

Betty was giving a high five back in the air then looked at Sally, and her face got serious. "Personally, I think it would be smart. There needs to be more than just the two of you full time. And she'd be great getting the female newbie thing going. By the way, Jim said he'd love to help with it when the time comes."

Sally gave her a dubious look. "That's great as long as you won't get jealous. By the way, did you tell Jim about the sub proposal?"

Betty flashed a smug grin. "Not yet, but I'm going to. Maybe it will inspire him to be a little more adventurous."

Carole rolled her eyes, and Sally cleared her throat.

"Alrighty then, let's move on. We have got to get the business out of my house. It's going to reach a point it's not safe or feasible. We've got enough money to get a location with a good address. We need a place where clients can come in for interviews, etc. Betty, I don't like you letting this Max fellow pick you up from work no matter how hot he is. I think if we got something with a little space to it, we could host meet and greets for our male and female clients…maybe venture into a bit of dating services."

Both women nodded. "I think that would be awesome. A lot of times when I'm training a guy, I picture some woman I'd like to introduce him to," Carole said.

Sally nodded. "I do the same thing. Incidentally, we might have gotten our first female. There was a request on the website for an application to be sent to an email address that started Elaine something. Maybe she read the *Austin Chronicle* article."

"I can follow up on it," Betty volunteered.

"Thanks, I appreciate it. Last but not least, we have got to decide about protecting us and the business. I'm afraid being a corporation isn't enough under the circumstances. We've talked about body cameras or nanny cameras, but I think that would make our clients too nervous and uncomfortable. I've given it a lot of thought, and I say we go with mini voice recorders."

"But don't you have to let them know you're recording them?" Betty asked.

"I'm not sure, but we're not going to use them in a court of law or for blackmail. I intend for them to be erased…except the ones that document things like what happened with Carole and Edgar today. It's protection for us in case they make claims that we came on to them or they were led to believe we were prostitutes." She gave a deep sigh. "I'll talk with an attorney friend tomorrow and meet with Edgar. Carole, can you get with Jewel and offer her the job? Once Peggy gets here, we can figure out her salary and get busy looking for a new space. If things keep going well, someday maybe we can have a staged training area."

"And a dog," she heard in harmony behind her back as she turned toward the office.

Chapter 11

One and a Half Years Later
Thomas

Everyone had left the meeting except for Thomas who was still standing in the conference room studying charts, when he turned to see Jean nervously watching him. "Oh, hello! Did we have an appointment?"

"Well, yes, actually Elaine made it. It's been a year."

"I'm sorry, what?"

"A year since she died." Jean had stayed on as his housekeeper and to help with the dogs and occasional visits from his grandchildren.

"I'm aware." He lifted his shoulders, indicating he didn't understand.

"She said you'd forget."

"Aw, she would. Forget what?"

"The promise you made her."

"I made her many promises."

"You know the one I'm talking about."

"Do I?"

Jean pulled a heavy chair out from the table and sat. "In the event you've forgotten, I am to send your application to Widower Whisperers, LLC...today, a year from the day she died. Within, it specifies that you will deal with Sally Estes only."

Thomas's gut did a somersault. Hell no, he hadn't

forgotten, no matter how hard he'd tried. Elaine had held his hand and made him swear to her that he'd follow her wishes. And it still stung…losing her, not holding *her* hand when she died or being there when she took her last breath. It had been at the beginning of the pandemic when proper measures weren't in place yet to prevent its spread. They'd been warned by fellow scientists and put themselves in lockdown, but Ellie suffered a small stroke and had to be hospitalized for a few days that turned into months. She never came home.

Even a year later it was hauntingly vivid. Their large home overlooking Lake Austin felt so cavernous and desolate without her that he'd leased an apartment near Sixth Street, hoping the activity there would distract him. And yes, he'd been lonely and had to admit to a bit of mild stalking of Ms. Estes. But he wasn't ready to put himself out there. And in retrospect, he didn't blame Sally for blocking him from her memory all those years ago.

He took a deep breath then let it out. "You came all the way across town to tell me this?"

She shifted in her seat, withdrew an envelope from her purse with *Thomas Duncan* scrawled across the top, and put it on the conference table. At the sight of Elaine's handwriting, a tremor went through him, his heart raced out of control, and his throat constricted.

"Would you like me to leave, Thomas?" He glanced at her with tears in his eyes, but no words would come. "I'll be in your office then."

He nodded, watched as she went through the door then softly closed it and took her place in the chair. He brought the envelope up to his nose, but there was no scent of Elaine. He ran trembling fingertips over his middle name…Ellie had always called him Thomas Duncan when she was cajoling him…and she always, always got her way. The thought made him smile, and he was sure she'd known it would.

He sighed deeply a couple of times, broke the seal with her initials on it, and pulled out a single piece of stationery, his heart now stuck in his throat.

My Thomas Duncan,

If you're reading this… Just kidding! I know you're aware of what day this is. You've probably thrown yourself into a research project trying to forget. But it's here and you promised. I know you'll always love me, as I love you. At all times, we agreed that love is all there is or ever will be. That's why I want you to find love again. I want you to find laughter and joy. I couldn't bear leaving, thinking of you alone… So, you'll do this for me…you'll give it a chance, even if you feel you're not ready…and no lies, to her or yourself. You and Sally don't have all that much time left, so don't waste it on more grief…it's time to move on…until we see each other again…

Never forget, Thomas, my love is eternal…the frequency lives on…and so must yours.

Forever,

Elaine

A tear fell onto the paper as he put it back in the envelope. He snatched a tissue from the travel pack sitting on the conference table. Jean must have discretely put it there before she left. Those two thought of everything. He smiled. Elaine had remembered how he scoffed at the movies, books, and lyrics with the overused, *if you're reading this then it's too late, or I'm gone, or already dead…* Of course, she had, and through everything she'd been through, she'd never lost her sense of humor.

****

He found Jean patiently staring out the window in his office. "When did she write this?"

She looked over her shoulder then back at the view of the street. "The day after I helped her fill out the form and she had the talk with you. She knew things, damn it, Thomas. You know she did. She knew she would be dead within the year. I didn't want to believe her. She was my sister, and I didn't want to lose her. But she was in so much pain and ready."

She swiveled his desk chair to face him. "We talked a lot, and she told me things she'd never have told you. She felt bad about what you did to Sally Estes. About you telling her someone had put you up to kissing her and you hadn't really wanted to. It must have hurt her terribly. She understood you were just a teenager trying to save face, but she still had empathy for the young girl who'd trusted you."

He spread his arms out from his sides as if asking for help. "I understand, I really do. But Ellie and I talked about all this when we were writing the book. Besides, we were children and—"

"And children are easily scarred. Perhaps that was reason enough for her to block you and the memory. Maybe you weren't important enough to remember. Or it's possible she's lying and she does remember you. The point is you had a huge crush on this girl, and your friendship with her had meant enough to you that you'd wanted to introduce Ellie to her.

"It's simple! Honor her wishes. You said you would. So what if you and Sally don't click after all these years?

You could possibly meet someone else through the process. The worst that could happen is you could learn to move on and start over, maybe even cook and clean."

"Humph, like you'd let me."

"Because Ellie wanted me to take care of you."

"I know how to do all that stuff anyway. Who do you think took care of everything when she was so sick before you moved in with us? I get along just fine in the apartment."

"I imagine seeing me at the house reminds you of her."

They definitely had the same family traits but completely different personalities. Ellie was the fun-loving playful type while Jean was more somber and steadfast. "There have been times, yes."

"Then move on so that *I* can. Do it for me, for Ellie…for yourself and possibly Ms. Estes."

He sat in one of the guest chairs opposite her and sighed. "What's the next step?"

She picked her phone up from his desk and tapped around for a minute. "There, second step done. I just sent your application in."

"Now what?"

"I wait for a call back. I'll be acting as your secretary to make sure you work directly with Sally."

He grinned at her not-so-veiled accusation. "Are you saying I might not take care of that myself?"

She gave a sly grin back, showing they understood each other. "My, wouldn't that be such bad luck?" She nodded. "I'll be talking to you when I know something." They both stood, and he was walking her out when she turned and threw her arms around him and squeezed. "I had her a lot longer than you did, Thomas. I miss her too!"

They pulled apart from the hug and stared into each other's weepy eyes then without another word she was down the hall and disappeared into the elevator. All he could do was stare at the closed doors, letting the tears fall as he whispered brokenly, "Ellie, Ellie, what have we done?"

Chapter 12

Betty Cramer thought she'd finished the emails with requests for Widower Whisperers' services and was shutting down her desktop when she got a notification on her watch. She squinted at it and saw it was another email, picked up her cell, and opened it. She recognized elaineduncan@gmail.com from a couple of years ago. She'd asked for a form, they'd sent it to her, but she'd never returned the application.

Curious, Betty booted her computer back up. She hated trying to work from her phone. Her eyes were getting worse, and arthritis made it hard for her to type on the tiny keyboard. There it was…the filled-out application. She flashed back to them thinking it was their first woman client, but that clearly wasn't the case. This was for a Thomas Duncan *Fitzsimmons*. She quickly read through it, hit print, stood, and grabbed the copy. "Holy shit, Sally," she screamed, running from the room. The dog was sitting in a chair next to her friend and growled as she burst into the office.

"It's okay, Bruce, it's just your crazy Aunt Betty." Sally Estes ran a hand over the Chipin's head and stroked his neck before looking up. "Are you okay? I haven't heard you scream like that since you and Jim broke up."

Betty gave an exaggerated shiver, sat in a chair, and tossed the papers on Sally's desk. "Don't remind me about him. I can't believe he turned out to be such a creep. Read this application." She waited expectantly for something to click in Sally's eyes as she studied the form, but when she looked back up, they were void of any recognition. "Well?"

"Well, what?" Sally asked.

"Fitzsimmons?"

"So?"

"We went to high school with him. *Tommy Fitzsimmons?* Just one of the cutest, hottest, sweetest boys in the whole school. Don't you remember?"

Sally shrugged. "You know I don't remember that much about high school. Once I started dating Patrick, I didn't really hang out with any of those people."

"Including me."

"Well, you were little miss popularity now, weren't you? On that dance show on TV in your cute skirts and boots, while I on the other hand was going to college games and frat parties. Our worlds weren't exactly colliding."

"You really don't remember, do you?"

She shook her head.

"Well, did you notice under special requests that he asks to work directly with you and no one else?"

Sally stuck her readers back on, glanced at the bottom of the second page then stuck them back on top of her head. "Impossible!"

"No, it's not! Why?" Bruce had wandered over for some loving, and Betty picked him up. "It's not like I can't take care of the emails and vetting since I quit that dead-end job and started working here full time."

"When we moved into this headquarters, we had an agreement that as long as I was keeping this end running, doing the promotions, interviews, and marketing, it would be a bad idea for me to actually work with a client. When you were able to come on and help with all that, we agreed again that we could not afford either of us getting caught up in some sort of uncomfortable situation with someone we were working with.

"If you haven't forgotten, we are the face of this company. People recognize us when we're out in public. We both have gotten letters and emails directly from men wanting to get to know us better...in your case women, too. You know all this. Why would you even suggest breaking our own rules?"

"He was so cute—"

"Then you take him on as a client."

"He wants you."

"Well, he wouldn't be the first, would he?"

"Did you know him?"

"I don't know. You know I didn't pay much attention to the boys in school. All with their raging hormones...all trying to have sex with the redheaded girl with the big boobs. I don't know how many times I heard I'd screwed someone I didn't even know. It was awful back then."

"You didn't even remember dating that guy from the Episcopal school."

"So, I've blocked things. Which guy was that?"

"It doesn't matter. He died. But he was cute, too. Tommy must remember you from back then. What are you going to do about it?"

"Nothing!"

"But you have to respond."

"No, I don't."

"That means you expect me to do it."

Sally nodded. "You opened the email. See if you can

set him up with Jewel. She's younger, and men seem to like her. She really has a way of dealing with them. As pretty as she is, they all manage to treat her like they would a daughter."

"You won't even make the call and explain?"

"Nope!"

Betty picked Bruce up and carried him back to his chair. "Sorry, little man, your mommy's a bitch. I've got to go handle something unpleasant."

She was almost out the door when Sally stopped her. "I don't want to start making exceptions. You'd be better anyway. You remember all those people from high school. Did you know him very well?"

Betty turned and shrugged. "Not really. He was really brainy...hung with a different group. He probably won't remember who I am."

"Are you kidding? There isn't anyone from school that doesn't know who you are. At that reunion ten years ago, this one guy was carrying on about how every boy wanted you and every girl wanted to be you."

"Not you. You were the girl that looked like a movie star and didn't give a flip about any of us, plus you were smart."

"Well, I'm flattered you saw me that way. And I'm sorry I'm making you do this. It wouldn't be any different if someone from high school asked especially for you, probably because he had a crush on you then and saw this as a good way to get to be around you. That's not what we're about."

"What if that's the case with Mr. Fitzsimmons?"

She looked down at the application then back at Betty. "It's not...I don't even know him. Go on and get it over with. I see the contact is a Jean Reynolds. A female...possibly a family member or secretary. Let me know what she says."

Back in her office, Betty called the number and asked to speak to Jean.

Chapter 13

Sally

"Remind me one more time why I'm here." Sally stood outside the hundred-year-old brick warehouse and looked at the address on her phone.

Betty sighed before responding. "Because I talked to Jean who explained this was her dying sister's last wish. I met with and vetted Tommy. He's still so cute. I wish I'd been at that reunion ten years ago. He and his wife were. She was something of a fan of yours. From what he told me, she followed your interviews about Widower Whisperers and thought it was a wonderful concept. Her MS was getting worse, and she had a feeling she wasn't going to make it another year and asked Tommy to agree to it. But you were the only one she trusted him to work with."

"Right, so I'm breaking my own rules because of a dead woman I never met…God rest her soul."

"Wrong! You met her at that reunion."

Sally racked her brain but couldn't place it. "I still don't remember that. But so many people were coming up to me, and I didn't really remember any of them, and you weren't there to tell me who they were." She sighed. "Oh well, let's get this over with."

"He said just to go in the doors on the south side and straight ahead you'd see the elevator. He indicated it was rather old fashioned."

Sally followed her instructions, put on her mask, and once inside the building, lifted her sunglasses to the top of her head. It was shadowy and cool as she squinted, searching for the elevator when a voice startled her in the stillness. "Ms. Estes, so nice of you to come all this way."

She turned abruptly, and the first thing she saw were the most alarmingly pale hazel eyes staring into hers, and her breath caught. They looked like they'd seen a lifetime of laughter, and her eyes drifted to the brilliant smile, feeling her own lips lift at the corners. Intrigued, it took her a couple of moments to acknowledge the hand held out to her.

"Oh, I'm sorry. I saw your car parked out front and thought I'd come down to welcome you so you wouldn't have to take that ancient ride to the top on your own. I forgot to throw my mask on. Do you mind? I've been vaccinated, but I can run up and get it." He withdrew his hand. "We could always bump elbows, if you'd prefer."

Suddenly, she came back from wherever her head had been, pulled off her mask, and held her own hand out. "No, you're fine, actually. I've had both of my vaccinations, too." Her mind kept tugging at her, registering something vaguely familiar about him, but she couldn't pull it out of her thick skull.

He reached out again, and they shook. "The Covid was what actually got her. With the MS she was already immune compromised but also had a weak heart."

Sally took her hand back, and the smile left her face. "Betty told me. I'm so sorry. But a year…do you think it's been enough time?"

"Please if you'll allow me." He extended his arm to

indicate the freight elevator. "Ladies first."

There it was again, some memory jolting about her head, ready to explode out of her brain, yet stuck. Why did she feel such déjà vu? She had a chance to really look at him as he went about the business of manually closing the brass gate. He was tall, but not overly so. She'd guess about six foot two. He'd probably been taller but had done a little shrinking as they all had by their age. He had a full head of nicely styled white hair and a bit of salt-and-pepper scruff on his not overly weathered face.

She was thinking about what a damn good-looking man he was when the elevator lurched, announcing its start of the journey up. Startled, her hand flew to his shoulder in an effort to brace herself.

He turned quickly and took her arm to steady her. "I should have warned you. She has a way of getting off to a bumpy start."

She looked in his eyes and saw both humor and sincerity. Most men who'd grabbed her arm like that would have used it as an excuse to flirt with her, or she'd feel them giving a slight rub by now. But there was none of that. "I'm fine. Just wasn't prepared. Thanks for the support." As soon as he was sure she had her sea legs under her, he removed his hand.

"So, I know you're probably wondering why I wanted our first meeting to be here."

"Well, yes, I was. It's a bit outside Austin. I supposed it had to do with work."

"I'm sure you read in the application that I'm a scientist."

She nodded as the elevator came to an abrupt stop, and she again reached for him, mentally cursing herself for wearing high heels. "Betty told me a little. That you're into research, but not exactly what."

He opened the gate and waited for her to step out then indicated she turn to her left. "We typically have any number of projects going at once. I have a facility in Colorado as well as here. I was going to give you a tour, but I don't want you twisting your ankle in those shoes." He glanced at her feet then opened a door and lead her to an old-fashioned worktable. "Sit, please. Would you like tea or water? Possibly coffee?"

She shook her head. "I'm fine really. I could do the tour."

He sat next to her. "No, we'll do it another time when you're not so dressed up."

Her face flushed. She didn't know why it had been important for her to wear a stylish suit and squeeze her feet into shoes that only accented her limp, which he'd obviously noticed.

"You look lovely by the way."

She might as well fess up. "Thank you. I usually don't do this, as I'm sure Betty explained to you. I only dress this way if I'm giving an interview or doing pictures for an ad. I have to admit my feet *are* killing me. I was in an accident a few years ago which required emergency surgery. Unfortunately, it left me with a lot of pain and a limp. So, again, thank you for giving me an out. I usually have a bag with sneakers in it, but I forgot to throw it in the car this morning."

His expression changed, and he looked solemn. "No, I'm sorry. Would another surgery help? Is there anything else they can do?"

She leaned back in the chair and shook her head. "Probably not. It was a long time before they got me into surgery, and my body went through severe trauma.

Going under again could be too dangerous."

"What do you do for the pain? Are you on opioids?"

She smiled and thought how understanding he was. "No, except for an emergency. I was fortunate to have gotten caught up in the cannabinoid movement and took some courses. My daughter introduced me to it, and I got involved with quite a few knowledgeable people. I'm not a big believer in meds. The upshot…I wish I could teach every older person how to use cannabinoids and get rid of the pills. Oops, sorry, didn't mean to preach."

He leaned forward and grinned. "That's one of the things we've researched. We're typically hired by the government or big corporations, but Elaine and I did that project on our own. We were looking for something to help with the MS."

"And did it?" Sally was surprised at how easy he was to talk to.

"Well, as you know, it didn't cure her, but it did ease some of the pain. CBD allowed her to go on lower doses of medications. She was weaning off some of them when she had the stroke and was hospitalized. I'd warned her that she was rushing it, but she told me she didn't have much time left." He shrugged. "We didn't have the chance to find out if it would continue working or not."

His candor and vulnerability had put Sally at ease, and she reached over to put a hand on one of his resting on the table. "I'm so sorry for your loss. But, Tom, I don't want this to sound like another lecture, but I truly don't feel that you're ready to move on just yet. And, honestly, it appears you're handling work, grief, and yourself better than most. I really don't know what I'd be doing for you or even why—"

Chapter 14

Thomas

"You called me Tom."

She withdrew her hand and looked taken aback. "Oh, should I have called you Mr. Fitzsimmons? I apologize if I was too informal."

The contagious grin was back on his face. "Not at all. It's just that it's been an exceptionally long time since anyone's called me that. People I grew up and went to school with called me Tommy or TD. As an adult, I've been Thomas. Elaine liked to call me Thomas Duncan when she was trying to wheedle me into letting her have her way."

"Huh?" Sally leaned back in her chair and gave a small shake of her head. "Sorry, don't know where it came from."

Because that's what you called me in school. You said Tommy was too babyish and Thomas sounded like an old man. "Nothing to worry about. Speaking of lectures, I happened to have been privileged enough to have heard one of yours."

Her brows drew together, and she gave him a puzzled look. "Like in an interview or something?"

"No." He was mildly enjoying her discomfiture. It made her seem far less formidable. He got up, went to the refrigerator, brought back a pitcher of lemon/cucumber water and two glasses. "It was in person, a couple of years ago." *Let her think on that a minute or two.* He was aware of her scrutinizing him as he poured her a glass.

"Had we started the business yet?"

"Not sure." He looked at her askance, and she was giving him a sly grin. "What?"

She waited for him to sit and held her glass up in a toast. "Here's to strange men in diners."

They clinked glasses. "Did you just figure it out?"

She shook her head. "It was eating at me the moment I saw you, but I couldn't put it together. Then when you extended your arm and said, 'Ladies first,' I felt this déjà vu sweep over me and thought I must be crazy. You opened the door for me at that…"

"Joe's Café."

"Yes, Joe's Café. I'd never been there before."

"If I may be so blunt as to ask, why were you there then?"

Sally took a gulp of her water. "Hmm, that's good." She set the glass down and grinned at him like a Cheshire cat, accentuating dimples that he remembered weren't as deep fifty years ago. "Well, the truth is I was on the unending coffee date with a man I'd never met before who picked me up on Facebook. You know…a friend of a friend. It was a weird time for me. I'd gone through a breakup a few months before, and everyone kept telling me to get back out there, test the murky waters…" She squinched her nose. "How much did you hear?"

She's candid, has a sense of humor about herself…none of that's changed. It dawned on him that he was actually having a good time and matched her grin with one of his own. "I'm fairly sure most of it. I'd ordered lunch to take back home and was waiting at the counter. I didn't mean to eavesdrop, but I'd turned to lean against it and saw you. You were so animated, just like in school. Your booth was right there, and I couldn't help but hear. I think it started with something like, *men popping little blue pills like breath mints*."

"No!" She laughed and put her hands over her face then peeked out between spread fingers. "I did…I did say that, didn't I? Oh gosh and so much more." Her heels did a little pattering on the wood planks of the floor. She put her hands in her lap and brought her laughter down to barely controlled giggles and sniffs. "I was so tired of listening to him drone on about sex. And to be indelicate, my ass was killing me from sitting there for three and a half hours."

He was chuckling with her now. "Not indelicate at all and I can't say as I blame you. I have to admit I actually enjoyed your speech. It took guts to stand up to him like that."

"Oh, I don't know. Maybe I was being mean. I was writing women's books with erotic elements back then, and men seemed to have this obtuse idea it meant I was hot to trot. I mean really, it's just fantasy. And why they'd picture I'd want them in my fantasy, I have no idea. Oh my, I've said too much." She giggled again and wiped at the tears threatening to roll down her cheeks.

Sally was charming and funny, and for the first time since he'd lost Elaine, he felt himself relaxing. "No, you haven't said too much. My wife was a follower of yours and liked your writing. I don't think she would have wanted your coffee date in her fantasies either. When she told me about stalking you and The Widower Whisperers, I told her about your speech, and she couldn't quit laughing and saying *Bravo*. She was a big fan."

"So, you recognized me?"

"Absolutely!"

"From high school?"

"Yes, and the fortieth reunion."

"But I didn't recognize you?"

He shook his head and turned his chair to face her so he wouldn't have to keep twisting back and forth. "No, but it's okay. There's no reason you should have." *That's not really a lie*, he told himself and Ellie if she was listening.

Sally followed his lead, scooted her chair around, and looked earnestly into his eyes. "Did we know each other?"

He shrugged. "We had a few classes together over the years. Science, chemistry…I think one or two psychology classes."

"I just don't remember much from back then. I always tell Betty I must have blocked it, or I have high school amnesia. Maybe I've hit my head too many times, or it's the onset of dementia. I just know I wasn't like everyone else. I enjoyed staying home reading a classic or spending my nights painting. People went to concerts; I went to lectures. When Woodstock was the big thing, I was listening to *Dream with Dean*.

"I met Patrick, and he was older, kind of a nerd in this completely geeky fraternity, and he understood me." She stopped to giggle again. "To this day, Betty thinks those frat parties I was at were wild and crazy *Animal House* kind of events, but they were really more beatnik. I'd tell her the truth, but I wouldn't want to ruin her image of me."

She glanced at her watch. "Gosh, I really should be leaving. Since we're not doing the tour, I want to beat the traffic back into Austin."

Thomas had been listening, enthralled with her story, but stood, held out his hand, and gently helped Sally to her feet. "So, are we good here? Should we set up our second appointment? I'll make a point of being at the office downtown. My apartment's off of 6th Street and an easy walk from there…if you wear comfortable shoes."

"I'm not much of a walker since the accident."

He noticed that she didn't volunteer to tell him what happened but figured it might be hard for her to talk about. "It's really around the corner. I'll give you an arm to lean on if you need it."

She smiled sweetly, and he felt it coming…the rejection. "I just don't feel like you need my services, and I still don't understand why *me.*"

Thomas thought about his answer as he walked her to her car and opened the door for her. When she turned with her hand out to make her goodbyes, he took it, but not to shake.

"Sally Estes, I told my wife about you soon after I met her. You and I had been sort of friends in school, and I had the biggest crush on you from the first time I saw you. I always thought of you as the one that got away, but I never even had the nerve to ask you out. Elaine loved that story, and when she met you at the reunion, she was intrigued…all the more so when you didn't remember me.

"All these other women were coming up telling her stories about me, and admittedly it was giving me a big head…then you, the one I told her about so often, the one

I thought I'd stayed friends with, had no idea of my existence. I was totally shot down. Ellie started referring to you as my *unrequited.* When she thought she was dying and you'd started the business, in her mind it was perfect. She and Jean, her sister, filled out the application. I only saw it right before Jean emailed it, along with a letter Ellie had written to remind me she didn't want me to be alone and that a year was enough time for me to grieve."

"But Tom…is that what I used to call you?"

He nodded and let go of her hand. *There, I've blurted it all out, Ellie. Are you happy?* He glanced at the sky briefly then looked back into her eyes expectantly. "But what?"

Chapter 15

Sally

She stood on one foot then the other. *Damn it, why did I wear these shoes?* Sally was uncomfortable in more ways than just physically. With the bright Texas sun shining behind him, she had to squint to look at him. "But what did your wife think was going to happen?"

Thomas ran a hand through his hair then reached up and pulled her sunglasses from her head, handed them to her then stepped to the side to block the glare. "For God's sake, I don't know. She told me the worst that could happen was I learned how to get on with life. She asked Jean to stay on at the house to take care of me after she was gone." He raised his arms in exasperation.

"I saw Elaine everywhere, and Jean reminded me too much of her, so I got the apartment. I'm not that bad of a cook, but I have my pick of restaurants in the area. I do a fair job of…well, really nothing. I just throw myself into work, wine, and research. I wouldn't know how to date or ask a woman out. The idea scares the hell out of me. And quite frankly, Jean is definitely ready to get on with her life. She's still there at the house, waiting for me to return in the event she still needs to help me. And the only fucking person my wife trusted with getting me to move on, is the one fucking woman who doesn't fucking remember me and… and it's a fucking mess…sorry."

Sally was confused but thought she was beginning to see the big picture. "So, Elaine wanted me, though I have no recollection of you, to be your trainer, so to speak, and get you back on track because she trusted me *why*?"

She could tell the question frustrated him. "Look, Elaine *knew* things. She had a sixth sense, always listened to her gut, and it was rarely wrong. I'm not the type of man that flits about and flirts with women. I rarely notice them…don't get me wrong. I love females and have tremendous respect for them, but I've always been a one-woman man. I think the medications were messing with her mind that last year. The way she reasoned it was since I'd had a crush on you all those years ago, and she'd researched you thoroughly, she could trust you to…" He raised his arms again as if helpless to explain.

"I'm going to be truthful. I didn't want to do this. I really didn't. But I promised her, and I never lied to her. And then, just now, I found myself talking so openly to you…laughing with you. I was enjoying myself and realized I really do want to live again. I know this is a lot to digest, but please think about it."

Sally was nonplussed, staring at him blankly before turning and getting in the car. Once inside, she tilted the glasses up and stared into his troubled eyes. "I'll think about things, but you should too. It really would be best if one of the others took you on as a client. I'll be in touch." She closed the door, not giving him a chance to reply, started the car, and headed for home, her mind boggled by what he'd told her, but more so by how much fun she'd had visiting with him.

****

Betty brought Bruce home from the office where she'd been watching him while Sally was gone. "So, how did it go?" she asked unhooking the leash.

Sally bent, picked him up, and flopped on the couch. "Hey, baby, did you have a good day with crazy Aunt Thelma?" She smiled up at her friend. "So, when you talked to Mr. Fitzsimmons, how much did he tell you?"

Betty shrugged and plopped down next to her, both women kicking off their heels. "You go first. He's cute, isn't he? And that hair! Why can't all men have hair like that? Why can't I have hair like that? And his lashes. Women would kill to have his lashes." She glanced at Sally who was playing with Bruce. "Okay, spit it out. What did he say to you?"

Sally pulled a dog toy out from under her and threw it for Bruce to fetch then told Betty most of what had happened and was said. "There, that's it. Did you know all this after your meeting with him?"

"Oh, jeez, Louise, I knew some of it. And don't start in with any negative bull crap. It all kind of made sense to me. I could understand his wife trusting his taste in women and his instincts."

Sally sat up straight. "Thelma, look at me. I mean it. Look at me." Betty sighed, threw the toy again, and turned toward her. "We are not a dating service. I repeat, *we are not a dating service.*"

Betty stood and put her hands on her hips, assuming her Superwoman pose. "Now, you look here, you mean, lonely old bitch! You do not talk down to me! I am not one who's ever going to put up with your shit." Sally started to respond, but Betty's index finger was wagging back and forth in her face. "Don't! Just sit down, shut up, and listen. You just told me he said he wanted to live again. Well, it's about time you realize that you're dying a slow miserable death alone. No one can undo what Darrell did to you, not even Bruce. But it's time to *move on*.

"I am sick of your rules and regulations. You're worse than the IRS. Nobody gave the rest of us a vote. There is absolutely nothing wrong with any one of us falling in love with a client. If it makes both people happy, who gives a damn? I think that's why you decided to keep us in the office and not work with the men. You didn't want to take a chance of getting too close to anyone. After Jim and I broke up, I would have dated that Max guy in a New York minute if it hadn't been for your damn rules. Plus, *you're* the one always talking about delving into some dating services."

Sally tried to jump to her feet, but her spine popped, and she fell unceremoniously back on her butt. "Ooowww!"

Betty lunged forward and helped her sit up straight. "Are you okay?

"No, I'm not okay." Sally tossed a throw pillow across the room. "I wore those damn shoes today. I don't know what I was thinking. I guess I was trying not to look ancient. I mean, you'd told me about how good looking Tom was, and I just didn't want him to see me like this, all gimped up, and be a disappointment."

Betty sat next to her. "Aw, you could never be a disappointment. You're as beautiful as ever. I know women in their forties that have back or knee problems and don't get around as well as you do. You worry way too much about how people see you. Most don't even notice the limp."

"Oh, I know, it's just that I have this anger because

of the way it happened. I'm grateful, especially to you, I really am and to be alive and able to get around at all. But sometimes the anger seeps in, and I get so frustrated. You're right, I am just a mean old bitch…but I'm not lonely!" She reached over and ran a finger between Bruce's ears, who'd brought the toy back to be thrown.

"Darrell did a number on you. The accident was all his doing, and you're the one suffering. I don't blame you for getting angry. Sometimes I wish the son of a bitch didn't exist. But move on…not everyone is going to hurt you. There are some good men out there, and I think Tommy's one of them. Didn't you tell me he was concerned about your comfort and put off the tour because of your shoes?"

Sally was giving Betty her full attention now and nodded.

"Okay, and when he noticed the sun was in your eyes, he handed you your glasses to put on and stepped over to block the glare. That was sweet. It sounds like he does things like that automatically because he truly is a considerate guy. You've been with men who would use you as a shield in the face of bullets flying at them."

"Yeah, kind of the same way yours have. You've got a crush on one of the clients, don't you? Who is it?"

"Nunya."

"What?"

"None of your business because I don't…but I wish I did."

"Who is it, Jewel?" Betty was shaking her head when the bell rang, and Sally glanced at the Echo Show. "What's Carole doing here with a man?"

Her friend shrugged and gave a sheepish grin. "I was trying to tell you." She glanced at her watch. "Sorry, they're early."

Sally scrunched her face in consternation. "Carole? I'll never date again or sleep with another man, *Carole*? Is this one of your jokes?"

Chapter 16

"No! Seriously, listen to me…she was the one here working herself to death with you to get this business started when the rest of us still had full-time jobs. You need to keep your pretty little mouth shut and hear her out." Betty got up, opened the door, and ushered the couple to the living room. "Don't try to stand, Sally. You remember Calam Bennet…you vetted him and his son, Michael, a few months ago."

Sally held out a hand and stared at the handsome face as he took it and brought the back of her hand to his lips. She remembered him. How could she forget the kind gray eyes, the flawless golden-brown skin, the slight east Indian accent, and perfect manners? His wife died of breast cancer well over two years ago, and he'd still been struggling raising a son and working as an ER doctor, especially with Covid raging. She had vetted him several months ago over Zoom. "It's good to see you in person. How's that adorable son of yours?"

He glanced at Carole then gave a killer smile. "Adorable and ornery and growing like a weed."

She nodded and gave Carole a skeptical look. "Sit! Something you want to talk about?"

They settled in the armchairs across from the sofa, and Bruce ran over and jumped in Calam's lap. He appeared to have a way with dogs *and* people. "Look, Sally, I'm here as support for both of you. Carole explained the rules set up when the business was started, and I understand why you made them that way. But sometimes the unexpected happens, and there really are miracles. Trust me, I see them all the time."

"I'm really sorry. I never meant to break your trust in me. I didn't believe it was possible to have these kinds of feelings. In the beginning we were having lessons over Zoom. Michael had a nanny staying with him, and Calam was having to be tested all the time because of his ER work. Once I'd had Covid and had been through quarantine, we thought it was okay for me to go to the house and meet Michael. Calam was so sweet and kind, and we would include Michael in some of the training. He's such a little man."

Carole stopped and looked adoringly over at Calam then back at Sally. "I was teaching them to do chores together. It was so endearing and beautiful to watch them working side by side, laughing and kidding around with each other. We included Michael in learning how to act around women and in the dating lessons. I don't know what happened. The three of us were getting so close and just bonded.

"Then one day, I went by to drop something off. Michael was there with his grandmother. He'd just fallen against the coffee table and had a gash on his forehead. She doesn't drive, so I called Calam, scooped him up, and drove them to the ER. Calam was waiting for us, and after getting his son checked out and stitched up, he brought him back out and said he'd be okay. I was so relieved I was crying and hugged both of them then kissed Calam on the lips. When I realized what I'd done, I felt horrible, apologized, and asked them when they wanted their next dating lesson. Michael looked up at his dad and said, 'Why do we have to date? Why can't we just marry Carole?' "

Sally smiled. "And that's just the push you needed to acknowledge your feelings for each other. I have to admit, I didn't think you had it in you, Carole. And the age difference?"

"I'm older than I look. Because of med school and internship, I wasn't interested in children. Once I'd built my practice up, Simone had her own career. We were late bloomers familywise. The difference isn't that great. I'm not that much younger, and I wouldn't care if I was." Calam reached over and squeezed Carole's hand.

"It's a second start for both of us, all three of us. If you'd told me this was possible two years ago or I could be this happy, I wouldn't have believed you. But it's possible, Sally. If you want me to quit, I will."

"Calam, what would you like Carole to do?"

"Working makes her happy. She likes helping people. I trust her with my son and with my life…I don't think she'd ever give me a reason to be jealous. I want her to do what she wants to do."

Those were the right answers. How can I not be elated for them? Sally took her time getting up as the group watched her expectantly. When she reached Carole, she bent and hugged her. "I'm not an ogre. The only way I'd let you quit was if *you* wanted to. I'm so happy for you. Maybe we need to work on changing the bylaws."

Carole nodded, held out her hand, and wiggled her fingers, the overhead light causing flashes to spark off the beautiful ring. "He proposed last night, and I accepted."

Betty was on her feet now, examining the yellow

diamond. "Then let's celebrate! I'll call Eddie V's or Truluck's."

Calam stood and put his arm around his fiancée. "Sorry, we have a date with a little boy. We want to tell him together."

When they'd left, Sally and Betty hugged each other, and Betty cried. "That's so beautiful. Do you think he's got a father or older brother?"

Sally pulled away. "You're incorrigible!"

"Well, we deserve to be happy too!" Betty wiped at a tear. "How about we go out and celebrate for them?"

"How about we put it off till the weekend? I can barely walk, and I'm exhausted. We can just drink here, and you can sleep over or call an uber."

****

About halfway into their second bottle of wine, Betty asked, "So what did you really think of Tommy?"

Sally put down the piece of cheese she was getting ready to chomp on and took a sip from her porch glass. "He really is good looking. I got so nervous when I saw him. I couldn't place it at first. But remember the guy I told you about when I had that insanely long coffee date?"

"Yeah, Diner Man?"

"What?"

"You brought him up so much we started calling him Diner Man."

"Nice." She nodded. "Anyway, I finally put it together when he told me he'd heard one of my speeches before."

Betty started laughing and got choked on a cracker. "Noo! Diner Man is really Tommy Fitzsimmons? Well, imagine that! What a crazy small world. I'm pretty sure that's an omen or something. When you told us about him opening the door for you, I thought you were going to swoon describing how handsome he was and what gorgeous eyes and hair he had. Truthfully, we were wondering if you'd hallucinated. I mean some guy that good looking…"

"Really sweet. I'm glad you all have so much fun at my expense. Don't laugh with your mouth full. I don't want to have to give you CPR. There's something else I left out."

Betty looked at her accusingly. "You held something back from me?"

"Well, I felt funny, like I was betraying Tom's confidence in me. He said he had a big crush on me in high school. I don't even remember him, but I'm sure I would have been crushing back."

"You're old. You don't remember anything."

Sally shrugged. "About high school, no."

"You like him, don't you? I can tell. You've brought him up several times. Why not just go out with him?"

"Because he hasn't asked me out, because he promised his wife he'd be our client and learn how to start over again. I'm not sure if she meant for him to date me or really just trusted that I would do my best to get him on the right track. I guess neither of us wants to break her trust."

"Well, all the more reason to take him on as your client and not pawn him off on one of us. However, if things don't click between you two, I'd be delighted to take him off your hands." Betty held her glass up in a toast and grinned.

They were enjoying their time on the porch couch, but Sally leaned over and pinched her.

"Ouch! That hurt!"

"Don't you dare try to take him before I even have him."

"Did you just say *before you even have him?* My, that sounded a bit territorial. The lady doth protest too much, methinks."

"That's just the lady's drunk ass talking. But he is good looking and kind, and he still has a cute little butt…you know it wasn't all spread out and flat like Sponge Bob—"

Betty was racked with chuckles and had to set her glass down to keep from spilling it. "My, oh my, little miss STD lecture queen noticing a man's butt. That was about the last thing I ever expected to come out of your mouth."

Sally gave a sly grin. "Well, I don't tell you everything." *Most, but not everything…if you only knew…* No, some things she just couldn't share, like telling her that even though he was blocked, Darrell had used a different number and left a message on her phone that morning. Or that even though her gut told her to ignore it and move on, she still wasn't sure what she intended to do about it.

Chapter 17

Thomas

Jean cleared her throat, and Thomas looked up from the reports he was studying. "They're wanting to have an intervention, you know."

He took off his glasses and rubbed the bridge of his nose. "Who?"

"Your girls, their husbands, the three older grandchildren...the babies don't really care. I'm sure given a vote, Domino and Ace would concur."

He stood and pointed to the chair across the desk. "Sit, please." He waited for her to get settled. "What's this all about?"

"Elaine made sure to talk to the children to explain her wishes. They loved her; you know they did..."

"But?" He sat, waiting for the other shoe to drop.

"But she was sick for an exceptionally long time, and you were kind and loving, and she couldn't have asked for anyone to be better to her. *But* she felt guilty...even the girls realized it. You rearranged your lives for her and around her, and Victoria and Annabelle watched you give up so much of your own life...for them then for Elaine. They want to see you happy like you were when you and Ellie were first together. How long has it been since you've seen them or your grandchildren?"

He set his pen on the desk and leaned back in the chair. "Okay, it's been a while, I admit it, but—"

"It's been since you got the apartment in town. They used to come to the lake house. There was plenty of room for them to play and the dogs to run. They still come to see me occasionally. You've been too busy or out of town."

"Okay, it's been two or three months. I took everyone to dinner that time."

"Six months ago! It's been six months, Thomas. They're worried about you. I'm worried about you. I know you're obsessed with why you couldn't save Ellie, and every spare second goes into more research. But she's gone and we're here."

They had a stare down, and Thomas was the first to look away guiltily. "You're right. Sometimes I forget. When we lived in Colorado, we'd go months without seeing the family. But Ellie was so good about staying in touch, planning things."

"How did the meeting go with Sally?"

He shrugged. "It's been a week, and I haven't heard anything."

Jean grinned. "You do know your private number was not on the application. Mine was, remember?" He scrunched his eyebrows in confusion, and she continued. "You neglected to give her your cell number. Betty called and told me Sally agreed to take you on as a client."

A smile spread across his face. "Really? I was fairly certain she'd turn me down. Is that why you're here?"

"Well, I'm here for several reasons. I do get lonely at that house by myself with nothing but the dogs to talk to. I like to come to town. I'm actually looking at houses.

It's time I leave, and I want to be in the city closer to everything. I've even considered moving to Dallas to be near my children."

"But I thought you'd stay on…thought you and Ellie had an agreement."

"When I sold the big house and moved in with the two of you, it was always meant to be temporary. She wanted me to have a life too…maybe find a man and not be alone. It's time. I want *my* life back. Oh, and I wanted to warn you that the entire family will be showing up here in about an hour to take us to dinner, probably Chuck E. Cheese or someplace like that."

Thomas stared at his hands then looked back up with haunted eyes. "God, I'm such a selfish bastard. I didn't think of you. I—"

"Oh, stop it! You're just a man. I needed that time with Elaine before she left us, and I needed time to grieve, too. I wasn't ready to decide where I wanted to go or what I wanted to do. The last year has been good for both of us." She reached in her purse and pulled out a slip of paper with a phone number on it and slid it across the desk. "I suggest you call Ms. Estes and set up a schedule before she changes her mind. I know it'll feel awkward but do it and get it over with. I'll just step out."

"Wait!"

She was at the door but turned back to face him. "What?"

"Now?"

She gave a small chuckle. "There's no time like the present. By the way, when I mentioned Sally willing to take you on, your eyes lit up, and it was good to see you smile again."

Once Jean closed the office door behind her, he

made the call, got her voicemail, and left a message. "Sally, it's Thomas…Tom from our meeting last week, Fitzsimmons. I'm sorry I forgot to give you my number, but this is it, so if you could…I mean Jean just told me I'm to be your client, so I'm not sure how this works. She said something about scheduling. Anyway, if you could give me a call or whatever back when you get this…or when it's convenient for you, I'd appreciate it. Thanks…bye."

He quickly hung up and ran a hand over his forehead, wiping away anxious beads of sweat. *Holy Mother of God, I sounded like a complete lunatic.* Just then his cell pinged, and he glanced down at the message. *Vetting an extremely nervous young man. It might be a while. How about I come to your office around 11ish tomorrow? I'll be wearing sneakers. You can show me around, I'll buy you lunch, and maybe we can see if I can make it to your apartment. If you have time…*

Thomas grinned, checked his calendar, called his secretary, emailed a client then picked up his cell and texted back. *I just made time.*

****

"Excuse us, Carl, we need to take a little break." Betty stood and ushered Sally out of the conference room. "Bathrooms are down the hall on the right, if you need them," she called over her shoulder.

Once in her office, Sally turned. "What is wrong with you? I didn't need a break. He was just starting to get comfortable."

"Who was that?"

"Who was what?"

"The voicemail, the texts? Was it Tommy? I talked to Jean this morning and told her it was a go."

She bit her lip trying not to grin and played Tom's voicemail on speaker. "I'm sorry, but it was so cute…the way he wasn't sure what to say. You know, you don't find that very often."

Betty sat and gave her an *I told you so* face. "See, I knew he wasn't like all those other guys. You could tell he felt awkward. So, what did you text back?"

Sally went to texts, handed her phone to Betty, and leaned against the closed door. "I was trying to make him feel more comfortable."

"Aw, good girl. You did a great job."

"Thelma?"

"Huh?"

"I have a confession."

Betty waved a hand at her. "Oh, I know…you like Tommy."

She had trouble looking her friend in the eyes. "Well, I think I do, yes. But I don't really know him, and I'm trying not to think of this whole thing like a courtship, though it kind of feels that way. But that's not it. I…I, uh, heard from Darrell."

"That's not funny."

"I'm not joking."

"You blocked him."

"I did, but he called from a number I didn't recognize and left a long message about how he's in therapy and he's been sober for a year and a half and—"

"And it's been almost three years since you've seen him, six years since the accident. When was this?"

Sally gave a sheepish shrug. "A week ago."

"You knew this when you met with Tommy. That's why you didn't originally agree to him being your client. You knew when Carole and Calam were there, when I stayed the night at your house, and we drank?"

She chewed on her lip and nodded. "I was confused."

Betty stood. "*Confused?* About what? I knew this would eventually happen. What did you do?"

"I thought long and hard about things. I know I could never trust him. I know I've always been his last resort when things haven't gone his way. And I've always been there to pick up the pieces. I know liars don't change…at least not permanently. I know I don't ever want to be treated the way he treated me again. I thought about a man like Tom and how caring he is… I didn't respond, deleted the message, blocked the number, and here we are."

There was a knock on the door, and Sally turned to open it. "Sorry, Ms. Estes, this is where they said you might be. Could we finish up? I have to pick my daughter up from school in an hour."

"Of course, Carl. We just had some business to go over." Both women put on smiles, straightened their cloths, and walked back to the conference room in silence…both wondering what the other was thinking.

Chapter 18

Thomas

Thomas stared out the window at people bustling up and down Sixth Street, then turned his chair back to peruse the documents on his desk. In seconds he was up, walked to the door, and looked down the hallway. He paced to his desk and back wondering if he should have offered to pick Sally up but decided that would have been too much like a date. *This is business after all.* But he wasn't the least bit certain he believed what he was telling himself.

He was just about to sit again when his secretary, Barb, buzzed to let him know Ms. Estes was here. "I'll be right out." He did a full circle for the hundredth time to make sure the office looked perfect, wiped his damp palms on his jeans then headed down the hallway and stopped short when he saw her.

Sally Estes looked even younger and more beautiful than when he'd last seen her. She was wearing a faded pair of jeggings, a loose-fitting blue blouse, and her coppery hair was windblown and tousled around her sun-kissed face. She was carrying on an animated conversation with Barb, her smile reminding him of the teenage girl he'd once known and was immediately put at ease when she turned her glistening eyes on him, as though they had some special joke between them.

"Oh, there he is, the man himself. It was so nice meeting you, Barb. I hope to see you again. And hang in there. You'll find a good man when the time is right. Tom." Sally stepped in front of him and held out her hand, but for some unknown reason, Thomas ignored it and gave her a quick hug instead then glanced at her feet.

She did a little twirl for him. "As promised, sneakers."

"And you look just like you did in high school." He pointed to his handsome running shoes. "So, we seniors are all sneakered up. Are you ready for a small tour?"

"As long as you don't call us seniors again. Just for today, let's pretend fifty years hasn't gone by." She winked, and he felt even more at ease.

"Scout's honor!" He held up two fingers then offered his elbow.

She laced her hands in the crook of his arm and looked at him askance. "Were you really a scout?"

Walking her down the hall, he realized he had a smile spread across his face and tried to look serious. "Oh, yes indeed! I was an Eagle Scout. Never fear, you're safe with me."

"Hmmm, that's nice to know in case we ever go camping, which by the way is never going to happen." She awarded him with a cute little smirk.

He patted her fingers around his arm and led her into his office. "Do you need to sit for a few minutes?" She nodded, and he pointed to the chair across from his desk with the best view. "I hope you didn't have to walk too far."

She sat and looked up at him. "I used to be an expert on this part of town. When I was quite young, I had a small house not far from here. That being said, Betty drove me. The parking can be hellacious, and I didn't trust myself having to walk any great distance."

Damn, I knew I should have offered to pick her up. He took the chair next to her. "I'm sorry, I would have come to get you."

She waved a hand. "No, no, I wouldn't have let you. Betty had a client to vet, and she was meeting him at the InterContinental, so it was on her way. He's from Dallas, and we're opening a branch there, but he couldn't wait and wanted to come in person to get things rolling." Self-consciously she ran a hand through her hair. "I must look a mess. She insisted on putting the top down on her car."

He leaned back admiring her. "Actually, I was thinking how absolutely beautiful you look all casual and disheveled like that...like you..."

He'd had to stop himself. He almost said something she'd probably consider too forward.

"Like I what?" She grinned at him mischievously.

"Nothing. Hey, about the view?"

She glanced out the window. "It's lovely. So is your office." She turned back to him smugly. "Like I'd just gotten out of bed. Is that what you were going to say?" She bit her bottom lip like she was trying to keep from laughing.

He sighed. "Yep, that's what I was going to say. But I didn't want you to take it like I'd been thinking about you in bed, or anything like that...it's just—"

She held a hand up and shook her head. "I get it, really!" She chuckled. "No offence taken. I'm really not that touchy...except when I'm expected to sit for several hours and listen to a man, I don't even know, tell me about his sex life. No lectures, I promise."

Or lack of one. He felt a mild sense of relief and

quickly changed the subject. "So, how would you like to handle today? You mentioned lunch."

"Yes, lunch! I'm starving. I saw that The Hoffbrau Steakhouse is open for lunch on Fridays. Does that sound good to you? I used to save up my pennies when I lived down here so I could afford to go there at least once a week. I've only been a handful of times since moving when I got married. Don't judge, but I've been craving their chicken fried steak and the fried catfish. Decisions, decisions…"

"Both good choices. I always enjoy going there. I think it's an excellent idea. Since you're famished, how 'bout we take a quick tour of the offices? My car's close. I can pull up front, pick you up, and then we can talk about the training over lunch."

Sally stood. "That sounds perfect. Let's do it."

Thomas grinned. "My, you are hungry, aren't you?"

"Oh, you have absolutely no idea." She grabbed his arm. "Lead the way, Mr. Fitzsimmons, and I'll follow you anywhere as long as it leads to food."

Her openness and honesty were so charming Thomas actually felt joy…something he hadn't felt in a very, very long time, and it scared the hell out of him.

Chapter 19

Sally

"You didn't have to do that, but I'm sure glad you did." Sally grinned like a little kid, took a sip of tea, and leaned back in her chair.

Thomas put his fork down and cocked his head to the side. "Didn't have to do what?"

"Split the catfish and chicken fried steak with me so I could have some of both."

"They sounded good to me, too. It was a win-win."

"Are you always so accommodating and easy to get along with?"

"Probably not. I'm sure some people think I'm a complete asshole." He picked his fork back up and started eating again.

I seriously doubt that. There was something intriguing about him. He was smart, kind, funny, humble, and incredibly good looking. She had to remind herself that most people put on a good front early in a relationship, and her mind drifted to how positively perfect Darrell had been when he was in hot pursuit. She gave an involuntary shudder.

"Are you okay?"

"Sorry, just a flashback I'd rather forget. It's nothing." She glanced at him surreptitiously, almost positive Tom would find it hard to be fake just to get what he wanted. "I talked to Jean. I don't know if she mentioned it or not."

"She did not."

"I hope you don't mind, but I was trying to get a little insight since she was the one who made initial contact. It helped. I understand things a bit better now. She told me about your home overlooking the lake and that she'd moved in there to help with Elaine."

"She did, and I'll never be able to thank her enough. She promised Ellie she'd stay on and look after me, but I couldn't do it. I couldn't stay. Everything reminded me of her, and it seemed so quiet and empty, even with Jean there. I moved into the apartment a month or so after she died. I was staying late at the office trying to drown my sorrow in work, and it was close to there. I thought the activity downtown would be good for me."

Sally nodded. "Do I still get to see the apartment today?"

"Your wish is my command."

"Be careful with that. You have no idea what I might be capable of wishing for."

"It wouldn't matter." He placed his napkin on the table and stood. "If you'll excuse me a moment."

She watched him walk away and, once he was around the corner, signaled for their waitress. "Could you bring me the check, please?"

"Oh, no, that's not possible. Mr. Fitzsimmons already took care of it."

Sally was confused. "When?"

"When he called to make sure his favorite table was available, and I could be your server."

There was a tiny pang in Sally's chest that felt vaguely familiar as she looked up at the pretty young face of the blonde girl. She shook her head trying to convince herself that she hadn't just felt a twinge of jealousy.

"Is there anything else I can get you?"

A double dirty martini. "No, no thank you. Does Tom…Mr. Fitzsimmons come here often?"

"Oh, sure." She leaned in confidentially and lowered her voice. "He's always alone and kind of sad looking. I try to cheer him up. I was so relieved to see him with you today and smiling." They saw him walking back, and she started cleaning the table.

"Hey, Ginny, thanks. You did a great job."

She blushed, said thanks under her breath, and scurried toward the kitchen.

"What a delightful young woman. I tried to pick up the tab since I'd told you I was going to take you to lunch, but she said you'd already taken care of it." She could have kept quiet, but she wanted to see how he'd respond.

He sat, took a drink from his water glass, and looked her in the eyes. "Guilty as charged. Does it bother you? Do you feel like I went behind your back?"

Well, he just put it all right out there. "I was just surprised. You didn't mention you were a regular here or this was your favorite table…and I was the one who offered to take you to lunch." Sally hoped she wasn't looking at him accusingly. Her mother always told her anything she thought was written across her face.

He sat back and stared as if appraising her. "I don't know what kind of men and/or clients you're used to. But as both, I'm old fashioned and not into letting women pay for me *or* themselves. I was going to mention it before you expected the check to come, but you were

108

quicker than I anticipated. Would it be possible for you to try to relax and let a man be a man?"

She was fidgeting with her napkin. "I'm not sure I know how to do that. Much less know any *real* men. The last one I went out with told me he wanted to find a wealthy old woman on her death bed with no family."

"Charming. I'm sure that was a delightful experience."

"You wouldn't believe some of the things we hear our clients say."

"Well, I'd like to consider myself a *real* man. That being said, maybe there are some things I can teach *you*. As for not telling you I was a regular as you call it, was it important? I'm probably considered a regular at most of the restaurants around the area. Have you forgotten I don't cook for myself?"

She shook her head.

"Sally, you might not be used to this, but I'm not the type you have to be suspicious of. I try to be completely transparent. If you ask something, I'll give you an honest answer, even if it's one you don't want to hear."

She'd been staring at her hand playing with the napkin but looked up and met his eyes. "It's the things unsaid...I have a fear of what's not said. I'm sorry, I can't explain it."

"Are you talking about lying by omission?"

She shrugged. "It's just I've been duped so many times by liars, and yes, a lot of the time it's the things they left out." She smiled and tossed her hair over her shoulder. "I didn't mean to get into all of this. I'm supposed to be here for *you*, helping you. Not pouring my heart out over past injuries."

"Maybe, just maybe, you *are* helping me by being

so candid. I haven't quite gotten used to this being alone thing. I used to tell Ellie absolutely everything. But sometimes I'd just simply forget because it wasn't important. As Jean would say, I'm just a man. You were so enthusiastic about Hoffbrau being open for lunch it didn't enter my mind to start going off about myself and how often I come here. All I was thinking about was making you happy because it gave me joy to do so. Am I making sense to you?"

She nodded. "I really am a fucktard. I'm just not used to men worried about my happiness...it's usually been about what I can do to make and keep them happy. And I do appreciate you not going on about yourself all the time. It's one of my pet peeves."

"I know."

"You do?"

"I've got to confess to a fair amount of stalking you. You've said in almost every interview and blog how tedious it is to sit and listen to men go on endlessly about themselves."

Sally felt her ego get just a little plumped up, and she grinned. "So, Mr. Fitzsimmons, has your research of me been more or less since I met you at your warehouse?"

He looked thoughtful for a moment. "Let's just say it's been more *in depth*."

"Meaning?"

"Meaning you're all over the place. From your books and your blog to the business. You're not shy about doing interviews, and from outward appearances, it would appear you're as open as I am, except..."

He paused, stared into her eyes, and she felt like the wind had been knocked out of her. *Except what, damn it?* Her mind was whirling with all sorts of things he could have found out about her that really weren't public knowledge. She had ghosts in some of her closets as did everyone. "Except?" she asked urging him to go on.

"What happened to you, Sally? Your accident…how did it happen? I can't find anywhere that you've talked about it."

She took a deep breath and exhaled. "Huh, well, that's because I don't like talking about it. But since you're curious…I was in a pair of high wedges, tripped, my right foot went sideways off the wedge, and damaged the soft tissue. The swelling was so bad that I only made it as far as the couch when I got home that night. I propped it on throw pillows I'd put on the coffee table and fell asleep like that.

"I woke up in the middle of the night in excruciating pain. My foot was the size of a football and turning black in areas. I couldn't find my phone; it wasn't in my purse. I tried to stand to go look for it, but the pain was so excruciating my legs went out from under me. I collapsed, hitting the edge of the table on the way down. I damaged my spine and broke a bone in my hip. I tried crawling and ended up passing out from the pain. Betty found me hours later, and an ambulance came. The doctors did the best they could to repair me, but so much time had passed, and several surgeries later, here I am today. A little worse for the wear." She raised her shoulders indicating that was it.

Chapter 20

Thomas

She looked uncomfortable relaying her story. There was something more to it, something she didn't want to relive, but Thomas wasn't going to press her about it. She was nervously playing with her napkin again, and he reached across the table and put his hand over hers. "I'm sorry. The memory has to be painful." He looked around the restaurant and smiled. "I think we should probably leave so they can finish getting ready for the evening crowd."

Sally looked relieved to have the subject changed and scanned the empty room then glanced at her watch. "Oh my, I had no idea we'd sat here so long. We're the only customers left."

Thomas stood, pulled her chair out, and helped her stand. "I enjoy visiting with you. This has been nice."

"Well, it was supposed to be business, and I'd hoped we'd get to talk about things you need help with…but, yes, it was nice…very nice." She held gratefully onto his arm as he escorted her to the front where the valet had his car waiting.

Once they arrived at his apartment, he quickly showed her around then got her settled in a comfortable chair and sat across from her on the couch. "So, what do you think?"

She smiled, her eyes sparkling with mischief. "Well, all I can say is, what do you need me for? Everything's perfect. Did it come like this, or did you hire a decorator?"

"No, it was empty. I did it myself."

"The decorating? With no help?"

"Hmmm, yeah, is it that bad?"

"No! It's perfect. And everything's so immaculate."

"Aw, well, I can't exactly take credit for that. Cherry came in this morning and tidied up."

"Cherry?"

"Yep, Cherry. She's the daughter of one of my daughter's best friends and needs to make extra money while going to college, so she comes in a few mornings a week before classes."

"Is that all she does for you?"

For a second, he thought she was suggesting sexual favors. He stiffened before it hit him then he relaxed. "Okay…so you mean like taking my clothes to the cleaners and picking them up, washing the linens and towels, grocery shopping, etc." She nodded. "Yes, to all the above."

Sally chuckled and shook her head.

"What?"

"You are so spoiled."

His eyes widened as he feigned shock and pointed at his chest. "Moi?"

"Oui! Very, very spoiled. You hire someone to do everything for you. You eat out or have food brought to you. I don't see one possible thing I could help you with."

Thomas leaned forward. "Can I be honest with you?"

"By all means, please do."

His arms rested on his knees, and he rubbed his hands together. "When Ellie first got bad, I took care of her and the house. Someone would come in once a week and do the heavy cleaning, but that was it. I tried to work from home as much as possible and include my wife in everything I was researching and working on. That's the way we were. Her diet was important, and I'd prepare special meals, take care of all her needs…she didn't want strangers looking after her. I even washed the clothes to make sure there were no chemicals that could trigger some kind of allergic response in her."

He felt a lump in his throat and cleared it before going on. "Occasionally, we'd have a treat, and I'd pick up her favorite chicken salad from Joe's Café, like the day I saw you there. I ran the errands, did the grocery shopping, and always tried not to leave her alone for long. Her being sequestered like that was hard on both of us, and quite frankly, I was exhausted. And I was angry. Nothing I did was enough; nothing was helping her get better."

"Tom, you don't have to—"

"No, please just let me finish. I tried to hide it, but she knew. Jean had been divorced for a few years and was selling her home, so Ellie asked her to move in and help. At first, I was hurt…like she didn't trust me to take care of her anymore. Then I realized she knew she was getting worse, even though I refused to let myself admit it. And somewhere in there, I just gave up, quit functioning around the house…I was in denial."

"I understand, but—"

"But the point is, if I need to, I can do everything around the house and take care of myself. I just haven't wanted to. I needed a break to concentrate on work and research without worrying about anything else. So, no, Sally, there really isn't much you can do to help me in that area. What I need is the part about learning to live again. And as for women, I wouldn't have the slightest idea how to go about dating…I'd be lost."

She sat quietly for a moment before commenting. "You seemed to do a pretty good job of it today."

"What?"

"Going on a date."

"But it was business, not really a date."

"Was it?"

Heat rose in his face. "Yeah, it felt kind of like a date."

"Well, either way, you were charming, funny, interesting…a complete gentleman. I enjoyed it. And I think Ginny our waitress might have a tiny crush on you."

He started to protest, but she put her hand out in a warning gesture. "It's a girl thing. Men are oblivious." She shrugged. "Anyway, back to business. I'd like to see the house at the lake. I feel like you need to face it, Tom. It's been almost a year of running away. Though this is all wonderful, it's temporary. I'm sure there are things you miss about home."

He stood and paced in a small circle. When he stopped, he was smiling. "I miss the golden retrievers, Domino and Ace, magnificent animals."

"Then that's our next assignment. We go to your real home." She looked at her watch. "I'm sorry. I'm supposed to be meeting Peggy at headquarters. She's part of all this but hasn't been working much since her mother passed away. I think she's ready to get back to it now." Sally dug in her purse and retrieved her buried cell. "Excuse me, I need to call an Uber."

Thomas reached down and gently took the phone from her hands. "No, you don't. I'll drop you off. Please, it would be my pleasure."

He gave her cell to her, and she returned it to her purse. "Well, put like that, how could I possibly say no?"

"I have a feeling you say no a lot more than you say yes."

She took the hand he held out and let him help her to her feet. "Maybe that will have to change," she said cryptically with a sly grin, leaving Thomas wondering just what in the hell she meant by that.

Chapter 21

Peggy had her briefcase hanging from one shoulder, her purse from the other, her Hydro Flask of green tea in the left hand, her cell in the right prepared to get her assignments and get back to work. She was standing in front of the new headquarters, trying to figure out how to free a hand when the door flew open almost hitting her, and she dropped her phone. She knelt to pick it up and bumped heads with the owner of the café au lait hand that beat her to it. She stood and rubbed her head.

"I'm sorry, I didn't mean to run you over," he said and held her cell out to her.

"No, it's okay, really." She stuffed it into an outside pocket of the briefcase.

"Can I help you carry some of that? It looks like you've got your hands full."

For the first time, she looked up, *way up*, into golden eyes fringed in thick black lashes, and her stomach lurched. She ran her free hand self-consciously through her hair. "I, um, no, it's fine really. Just a little bump." She swallowed hard. "Okay, I won't blame you if you think I'm a nut case…but I've got to say this."

His brows drew together, and she saw the red mark above the wrinkles between his eyes where their heads had collided. He gave a slight nod. "Okay."

She took a deep breath then let it spill out. "You are drop-dead gorgeous. I know you've probably heard that all your life, but I just had to tell you. I don't know. Maybe it's the bump on my head or—"

He held out a hand to stop her and stared down at her a moment before breaking into an intoxicating smile that spread to his eyes. "I think you're probably the first and only but thank you. I might have to get a neck brace just to help carry my head around, it's getting so big. I have a feeling I'm really going to enjoy working here." He stuck his hand out. "Frank, Frank Wellston. Are you a client?"

She shook his hand and shifted the weight of the items she was carrying. "No, oh, definitely not. No, I helped get the business started…my mother passed away a while back. I was staying at home…you know, working from there…but I'm ready to get back in the saddle…swing of things. Eager to get going again…" She was rambling.

People were behind him wanting to leave the building, and he stepped out of the doorway, let them pass, then held the door as Peggy stepped inside. "You're in one of those pictures in Sally's office. I remember hearing about you. I didn't recognize you 'cause you're even prettier in person. Nice to finally meet you. Hope to see you around…"

"Peggy, or Peg. Peg's fine…you can call me Peg."

More people came through the doorway pushing him along, and he gave her a small wave then headed down the sidewalk. She watched till he was out of sight and finally took a deep breath she didn't realize she'd been holding.

Within minutes, Peggy burst into Sally's office and shut the door. "Okay, who the hell was that?"

Sally looked up from her computer and stuck her

reading glasses on top of her head. "Well, hello, nice seeing you, too. Who are we talking about?"

"The man. Damn it, I was so out of it I forgot his name." She held her hand over her head indicating his height. "Caramel skin, older with gray in his hair, and golden eyes that just melt you when you look into them. My God, I almost peed myself."

Sally chuckled. "You ran into Frank?"

Peggy sat and dumped all her baggage onto the floor except for her drink which she took a big gulp of. "Yes, Frank...that's what he said. We literally ran into each other. He was coming out the door and almost hit me with it. I dropped my phone, we both bent down for it..." She reached up and touched the small knot that had formed above her right eye. "I said something I might regret but it just tumbled out."

"You didn't cuss him out, did you?"

She wrapped a long, dark tendril around one finger and whispered, "I told him he was drop-dead gorgeous."

Sally burst out laughing. "You? You said that to a man?"

The color rose in her face. "I know, it's totally out of character for me. But something's changed. Since Mom's been gone, I've had this overwhelming urge to just say whatever I'm thinking. She sincerely wanted me to learn to live and love again, and I don't know...it's like this wave of pent-up emotions has just been flooding out. Is he really working here?"

"Yes, he is. Frank's a retired psychiatrist, so I doubt you shocked him. He's probably heard everything."

"He said I was the first to tell him that."

"Oh, well, congratulations. It's always nice to be a first."

Peggy grinned. "He thinks I'm pretty. Is he single?"

"Well, you know damned good and well you're pretty! Don't be such a coquette. He is single. But I have no idea if he's dating anyone. We got to know him through Calam. You've met Carole's fiancé?"

"Oh, sure! They've been over to help me with some things after Mona passed away. I'm so happy for them. I never thought Carole would date again, much less be engaged. After we started making some decent money and she was able to get her daughter and grandkids started over in another state, I suppose she was able to relax and enjoy life more."

"Yeah, she's been like a whole new person. We couldn't be happier for her. Anyway, Frank's wife died a few years ago after battling Alzheimer's for a long time. He'd been doing volunteer work at the hospital when Calam's wife passed away. They became close friends, and Frank was a big help during the grieving process. We all went out to dinner to celebrate the engagement, and Frank joined us. He was fascinating to talk to about grief. We found out he'd done some seminars on diverse and multicultural relationships, too."

"Okay, but what does that have to do with us?"

"Diversity has become a big issue. So has grief counseling. Betty and I were intrigued with his knowledge and experience. He was interested in what we're doing. We met a couple more times. I seriously thought he was going to ask Thelma out, but that hasn't happened. Anyway, we were all having drinks one night, and he mentioned being a little bored with retirement. I suggested he come work with us part time. He has family in Dallas and doesn't mind going between here and there, so it's perfect. He doesn't want or need a lot of money. He likes helping people and is someone easy to relate to."

"What do you mean you thought he'd ask Betty out?"

"The two of them were flirting a lot, but that doesn't mean anything. She flirts with everyone. Just because he's single doesn't mean he's not dating anyone though, and I haven't asked."

"So do you."

"So do I what?"

"Flirt with everyone."

The smile left her face. "I do not."

"Oh, come on, Sally. I'm sorry, but I just don't have a filter anymore. You flirt with men, women, children...even pets. At least Betty admits it. If I'm a coquette, I had the two best teachers in Texas. So, do you think she's interested in him?"

Sally wasn't sure how to take this new babbling brook of honesty. "I think Betty is still in contact with that younger Max guy. I have no idea if Frank's even interested in her. And no, he hasn't hit on me either."

"Then he's fair game."

"What?"

"I want to know when he's going to be working at the Dallas office, and I want to go there and help. It would be good for me to get out of Austin and that apartment."

Sally was mildly surprised by the determination in her friend's voice but thought it would be good for her to get away for a while. Plus, it was refreshing to see her show interest in a man after all these years. She pulled the glasses down on her nose and picked up the calendar next to her computer while Peg sat silently watching. When she looked up, the smile was back on her face. "He'll be at the new office two weeks from tomorrow. There's a client Jewel already vetted that's all yours, plus we'll need help interviewing and hiring more trainers. I'll come up when I can, but it'll be back and forth. Jewel has a two-bedroom apartment if you want to stay with her for a while, till you see how you like working there."

"Oh, how is she? I miss that beautiful face of hers. Is she homesick at all?"

"I'm not too sure. I think she's in love."

Peggy gasped. "Really? Bless her heart. Have you met him?"

"Her."

"Her?"

Sally nodded. "She's lovely. Debra…tall, blond, pale…the complete opposite of our little Hispanic firecracker. They're gorgeous together. Betty and I drove up there to spend a couple of days going over last-minute details that needed to be done to the office space."

"I didn't see that one coming."

"I don't think any of us did. The men are all so crazy about Jewel…maybe too crazy about her."

Peggy took off her glasses, thoughtfully cleaned them on the hem of her shirt, then stuck them back on. "Are they living together?"

"They are."

"Then if it's all the same to you, maybe I could just stay in a hotel for a few days. I'd feel like an intruder."

"I know they'd love to have you, but I can book you at The Mansion or the Crescent if you'd like…at the company's expense."

"Really? You'd do that?"

"Of course, I'd do that! You're part owner of this business. It would be good for you to luxuriate for a few days. Maybe invite Frank to join you for drinks and dinner after work one night. He'd probably enjoy that after staying with family. And he's such a gentleman. I'm sure he'd want to see you safely to your room."

"Girl, you are bad…"

"Oh, I used to be."

"Trust me, you still have it. It's just been buried by all the shit you've been through." Peggy looked around. "Speaking of, where is that little shit? Has something happened to him?"

"Ah, you must be referring to Bruce. He's at the doggy daycare and spa. I had a very long and pleasant meeting. I'll pick him up in the morning after he's groomed. He has a big day tomorrow…a playdate with two golden retrievers."

"Are you going to be okay without him at the house?"

"Oh, sure! I've got Alexa, Siri, Google."

There was something Peg understood now after spending so much time alone since Mona's death, and she had to get if off her chest and apologize. "Sally, I know we used to make fun of you about all those, but I get it now, and I'm sorry. After everything you went through with Darrell and the accident, not being able to get to your phone for help…I understand why you filled your house with all those assistants, why you refuse to take your watch off except to bathe. You don't ever want to be in that kind of situation again. I get it…and something else. I've had plenty of time to think about what happened and how terrified and what kind of pain you had to have been in, and I don't blame Betty for wanting Darrell to rot in hell...I don't blame her at all."

With that she stood and looked deep into Sally's misty eyes. "I'm going to go unpack this stuff and get my office set up again before it gets any later. If you need anything or want me to come over and stay with you, please let me know. I've missed you, my friend." She walked around the desk and gave her an awkward hug then retrieved her bags from the floor and headed out the door, fully aware of the tears in Sally's eyes that would stream down her face the second the door was closed.

Chapter 22

Sally

"So, who's this little guy?" Thomas asked, opening the glass door for Sally and her companion.

"This is Bruce, for Bruce Wayne. He's kind of my bat dog with these ears. I hope you don't mind. I thought he'd enjoy getting out and making some new friends." She'd been carrying him but set him down and let him sniff Thomas's shoes and pant legs. "He hasn't barked. I think he likes you. I can leave him in the car if you prefer."

"No, on the contrary, I think it's a great idea. Actually, Jean used to have a little dog, and the big guys were crazy about it...protective even."

"Where are they?"

He led them through the foyer and into the great room overlooking the gated yard and lake beyond, pointing at the floor-to-ceiling windows. "They were so excited when I got here I had to let them out for a bit to burn off steam."

Sally stared out at the view and the magnificent golden retrievers taking turns chasing each other. "They're beautiful...the view, the house, all beautiful."

"I played fetch with them for a while but have to admit they wore me out. Plus, it's starting to get hot. Let's let them wear each other out a bit more before introducing them to Bruce. I don't want them scaring him."

She glanced at the dog sitting quietly next to her feet. "He has little-man syndrome…has absolutely no idea how small he is. He'd take on a bear trying to protect me." She made a circle taking everything in. "Is Jean here? I was hoping to meet her in person."

"She thought it best to give me some time here to myself and the two of us time alone. You feel up to a tour or would you rather sit for a bit?"

"No, I'm good. Did plenty of sitting in the car. Is it okay to take Bruce's leash off?"

"Absolutely." He bent, picked Bruce up, gave him some loving, and unclipped the leash.

Sally was moved by the show of affection, and her mind flashed to Darrell and how he hated animals, remembering that when his own mother's beloved dog had a broken leg, he had it put to sleep.

"Sally, are you okay?"

She felt startled and brought her attention back to the two guys in front of her. "Yeah, I'm good. Why?" *He's looking at me oddly…*

Thomas put Bruce down, rolled up the leash, and set it on an end table. "Because out of nowhere you got this look of disgust on your face and did that shiver thing like you're chilled or something."

She plopped down in the closest chair and gazed up at him apologetically. "Oh gosh, I'm sorry. I don't even realize I'm doing it. Betty swears it's like PTSD. These flashbacks out of nowhere. I dated this man a few years ago, and he did awful things. But I didn't see them at the time. He covered them up with lies and excuses…tried to make me think I was crazy." She shrugged. "Typical narcissistic behavior. But I didn't get it then or the damage he was doing to me."

Thomas sat on an ottoman across from her. "I'm sorry. I know a little about it because Jean's husband was like that. It's abusive and devastating conduct. Are you still in touch with him?"

She shook her head. Darrell had texted her again last night from yet another number she didn't recognize, asking her to please talk to him, and she'd blocked that one too. "I went no contact."

"Good for you!"

"It's that just now I was thinking about how nice it was seeing you showing Bruce attention, and without warning the thought of how much he'd hated animals popped into my head...I guess it made me shudder. I really am sorry." She stood. "So, how about that tour? Then I want to meet the retrievers." He looked concerned as he stood and lead her to the kitchen. *He doesn't believe me. He's wondering if I still have a thing for Darrell...if I'm still talking to him. Damn it to hell and back, Darrell Normand, get out of my fucking mind and quit trying to contact me.* He glanced back at her, and she smiled.

"Oh, Tom, this is amazing! I bet you adored cooking in here. I love the way it opens into the great room and has the big farm table in the area by the fireplace. This table...is it French or Italian? It reminds me of one at a friend's house in Provence."

"Good eye. It's actually French. It really *was* fun cooking when Ellie was still able to get in here with me. We could spend hours sipping wine, talking, chopping, tasting...experimenting and coming up with our own recipes. Baking was therapeutic. My favorite was bread.

All that flour everywhere, getting my hands into the dough and kneading, waiting for it to rise then punching it down and kneading some more. There were a lot of good times."

His hazel eyes were glowing with the memories, and Sally found herself strangely envious of Elaine and the relationship she and Tom had shared. She'd never had one like that and had to force herself to put the thought aside. "You're a fortunate man, Tom Fitzsimmons, to have had that with someone. Just curious, what about your first wife, the mother of your children? What happened between the two of you?"

He smiled. "Ah, we're still great friends. Gayle and I got married really young. Had a child almost immediately. We were always more friends than anything...the years went by, we grew apart. I think we both wanted to know what true love was like once we got a little older. The divorce was mutual, and there were no hard feelings. She met someone about three years later and has been happily married for about thirty-five years now to a man she's insanely crazy about. It took me almost five years to meet Elaine but was well worth the wait."

Sally couldn't help but wonder what it was like to be loved that much, and her stomach knotted as she glanced around the area. "You must miss this. I know you miss Elaine, but you must miss the house...the dogs...family meals in front of the fireplace..." Seeing the light go out of his eyes, she paused and took a gulp of air, trying to calm her gut. "Oh, God, I'm sorry. That was stupid of me."

Tom had been leaning with his back against the countertop but pushed himself upright and ran a hand through his hair. "No, Sally, you're fine. I have to face it sometime. The truth is I do miss it. Playing with the dogs before you got here, I caught myself staring at the view of the lake, remembering the girls and their families here for holidays and birthdays…the sound of the grandkids laughing and splashing around in the pool. And for a brief second there, I was imagining what it would be like to open the fridge and have you help me make lunch."

Her breath caught, and she didn't respond as he started pulling things out of the refrigerator. "Aw, we're in luck. Jean got the recipe for Joe's chicken salad." He turned and looked at her. "You game?" She nodded, and he put a covered bowl on the island. "Lettuce, tomatoes? I'm a pickle fan…she's got kosher spears."

He handed her the items as he pulled them out, and she in turn lined them up next to the chicken salad. "The pantry's through there. Do you mind checking to see what kind of bread and chips she has?"

Sally shook her head, looked for the light in the huge walk-in pantry, and felt lost.

"Sorry," he said flipping the all but hidden switch. "We always kept it really well stocked because the kids were here a lot with friends. Since Jean's been here by herself for almost a year, I'm not sure what's in there." He stuck his head in and pointed to a lone bag of kettle chips on an otherwise empty shelf. "What a sweetheart. She probably went to the store yesterday after I told her we were coming this morning."

Sally grabbed the chips and just below them saw a fresh loaf of whole wheat bread. As soon as she set them down, Tom was handing her a cutting board and knife. "I'll do the lettuce if you do the tomato slicing. According to Ellie, I was awful at it and made them way too thick for her liking."

"And here I was thinking you were absolutely perfect."

He looked at her askance, gave a crooked grin, and she felt a little piece of her heart thaw.

Chapter 23

Thomas

"That was delicious, and I'm stuffed." Sally sat forward in her chair and smiled as Tom grabbed another pickle spear from the jar. "Do you mind if I ask you something?"

He knew there would be a lot of questions. That was part of what this was all about. It was also part of how people got to know each other better, but he felt leery by the way she asked it. "Can I finish my pickle?"

"You weren't kidding, were you?"

"What? Is that the question?"

"No. Just an observation. I was referring to the pickles."

"Oh, well, no, I wouldn't kid you about pickles." He took another bite and checked the jar to see if he'd finished them off. "Fire away! Ask me anything you want."

"Would you mind talking to a psychiatrist?" She held her hand up before he had a chance to protest. "Hear me out. Carole is one of our partners, and she ended up in a relationship with a client, a widower, which originally agreed we wouldn't do. You know, the fraternizing with a client thing. That being said, he's a charming doctor with a young son. They both worship the ground she walks on, and we've all become friends.

He introduced us to a gentleman who happens to be a retired psychiatrist. He's been doing a lot of volunteer work trying to fill his days, and I suggested he come to work for us. He doesn't really care about the money but thought the offer was intriguing."

Thomas wasn't crazy about the idea of seeing anyone and wondered what this had to do with him, but silently listened to her explanation. He folded his arms across his chest and leaned back. "Go on."

"I thought he might come in useful when we vetted people. You know, get a better idea if they're actually ready for our services, if he feels they might benefit from grief counseling…if there are too many anger issues…particularly with some of the divorced ones. Betty and I aren't trained like he is. Anyway, I thought you could kind of be a guinea pig for us, so to speak."

"Because you still don't believe I'm ready."

"It's not that, Tom. It's just I want to be sure. Damn it, I like you. I really do, and I didn't plan on it. I get the feeling you like me too, but I don't want us jumping into anything if the timing isn't right. I'd just feel better if you talked to Frank."

She said she likes me… He was quiet as he processed everything she'd said.

"Are you upset that I asked you?"

"Let me ask *you* something, Sally. This thing with your flashbacks, are you sure *you're* ready to move on?" He didn't like the idea of memories of another man coming between them before they'd even gotten together.

She looked away then back into his eyes. "I can understand what you're getting at. But mine are painful memories, not good ones. Betty had me talk to Frank. At first I refused." She shrugged. "When I finally convinced myself to do it, it turned out to be a good thing. He explained so much to me about the mental trauma that can happen from narcissistic abuse. It helped me understand *me* better."

The idea that someone had treated her so badly made him feel uncharacteristically angry and also terribly sorry for her. "And what if this Frank doesn't feel like I'm ready?"

She shrugged again. "Well, maybe he can suggest someone to go to for counseling."

"I have an idea. Why don't we talk about this later? You're here to see the house, meet the dogs. Where's Bruce by the way?"

"Oh, damn!" She jumped up and started looking around until she found him on the back of a cushioned chair, gazing at the other two dogs who were staring back through the glass door. "Looks like he's introduced himself."

The golden retrievers were animated and wagging their tails. "Then it's time they get up close and personal. You might want to hold Bruce initially until the beasts calm down." He pushed the door open, and a hurricane of energy and love came rushing in. Bruce was so excited he jumped from her arms, and before they knew it the three dogs were playing and chasing each other through the house, easing the tension between their owners as they both laughed.

****

The dogs had finally worn themselves out and were lying on the kitchen floor while Tom and Sally finished cleaning up from lunch. She was drying her hands and glanced at her watch. "Oops, I've got to get going. I promised Peggy a formal introduction to Frank this afternoon."

"Oh right, you told me about her mother passing away. How's she doing? Is she wanting grief counseling?" He took the towel from her hand and gazed at her with a cute smirk.

"What's that look for?"

"Hmm, I don't know. I was just thinking about when you said you liked me...*really* liked me." She turned away from him. "It's kind of endearing when you blush."

She picked the dishtowel up again and made a show of wiping down the island. "You're embarrassing me. And no, Peg bumped into him yesterday, literally, and I guess has a huge crush. She intends to stalk him. It's the new Peggy Russo."

"Good for her! I like her style." She turned back to him and looked so much like she had in high school he leaned down and planted a gentle kiss on her lips before she could say anything else. When he pulled away, her eyes were closed and stayed that way. "Are you okay?"

She gave a slight nod. "Just trying to remember you."

He took her by the shoulders, kissed her again, and enjoyed the feel of her lips parting and her breath getting deeper. He stepped back again and released her. "Did that help you remember anything?"

She shook her head, opened her eyes, and grinned as her arms went around his neck. She stood on tiptoes, pressing her mouth against his, her tongue tracing along his lips and teeth, snatching his own breath away. His arms went around her waist, pulling her into him, and he resisted the urge to pick her up and carry her to the bedroom, not sure he could still pick a woman up and carry her anywhere. His heart was beating faster and thought became impossible.

Somehow they ended up on the couch, and he had no idea how long they'd been making out when barking penetrated his senses. He rose up, released his hold on Sally, and realized Bruce was on the couch with them, snapping and scratching his pants' legs, while Domino was attempting to wedge herself between them almost knocking Sally off. "Bad timing," he muttered.

"Hmmm, perfect timing." Sally giggled and sat up. "I almost forgot where I was supposed to be." She looked at the three dogs. "A little jealousy, you think?"

"Maybe a little." He smiled. "They're going to have to get over it."

"Will they?" she taunted with a flirty grin, and standing, she straightened her clothes. "I was thinking about seeing if Peg and Frank wanted to go have some hors d'oeuvres and drinks after the formal work introduction. If that turns into a thing, would you like to join us? That way you could get to know Frank and maybe feel more comfortable about talking to him. Plus, you'd get to see more of me. It's a Saturday. We should be able to find someplace with live music."

"Actually, leaving here, going back to the apartment, and spending the evening alone isn't something I'm looking forward to. Your plan sounds much better. How about this…if your attempt at matchmaking doesn't work out, I pick you up from your house and we go it alone? I'd like to see where you and Bruce live."

She'd put the leash on Bruce and was picking up her purse when she stopped and smiled at him mischievously. "Now why didn't I think of that?" And not waiting for an answer, headed for the door.

Tom stared after her completely intrigued. *I think you probably did think of it and managed to segue it into me extending the invitation. Well done, Sally...well done.*

Chapter 24

Sally

"Sorry I'm running so late." Sally moved a stack of files off one of the chairs in Peggy's office and sat. "What are you doing?"

"Honestly, I had no idea how many meetings and things there were on Saturdays. Betty asked me to help with some interviews, vetting, and other stuff since you weren't here. When I had a break, I decided to go through some of the active files, so I'd be more knowledgeable about what's going on. How was Bruce's playdate?" She looked up from the papers on her desk for the first time. "And what in the name of everything holy happened to you?"

Sally sat up straight. "What do you mean what happened?"

"This." Peggy took her hand and moved it in circles around her mouth. "Why are you so red and splotchy? And why is Bruce sitting across the room not even looking at you?"

"Really, it's red?" She gave a whimsical smile and sighed. "Our little man's mad. He thinks I cheated on him."

"Well, did you? Betty got me up to speed on the Thomas Fitzsimmons issue." Peg pushed the intercom. "Can you come to my office please? We have a

137

situation." She looked at Sally. "Well?"

Before she could answer, Betty flew into the room, took one look at her, said, "Holy Mother of God, is that whisker burn?" crossed herself then broke out laughing. "Uh, Louise, I hope you didn't run into anyone else. You might want to freshen your makeup." She did the same thing Peggy did with her hand around her own mouth. "You know, and maybe run a brush through your hair…"

Sally's eyes got huge. "He let me leave like that and didn't tell me?"

Peggy giggled. "I'm pretty sure that's not what was on his mind at that moment."

"Oh my God, I passed two clients on the way up."

Betty sat on the edge of the desk. "I hope you had your sunglasses still on."

"Why?"

Peggy took a mirror out of the desk drawer and handed it to her. Sally's breath sucked in sharply, and she started wiping under her eyes.

"A word of advice from someone who's had sex in the last decade. Always wear waterproof mascara or get lash extensions so you don't have to worry about it. How was he?" Betty gave a salacious smirk.

"We did not have sex!"

"Why?"

"Well, contrary to what everyone thinks, I'm really not that easy. It took Darrell twelve years before I slept with him."

"Yeah, and we all know how that turned out."

"Betty's right. You need to get back in the saddle again. You're too old to wait twelve years this time. You'll more than likely die waiting."

"Well, that's a romantic thought." Sally set the

mirror on the desk.

"You're not getting any younger, and neither is he. You must have liked kissing him though to let it get as far as whisker burn."

"Ya think?" She gave an impish grin at the memory and stood. "You all go ahead and laugh, but it made me feel seventeen again." She glanced at her watch. "I better get to my office and freshen up before the introduction to Frank."

Betty waved a hand. "Not to worry. We thought you might not make it in today *at all*...at least we were hoping you wouldn't, so I took care of it."

Sally felt a little left out. "How did it go?"

"Great! I asked him to go out tonight. But I didn't make it sound like a date. I said we were all going out to celebrate my coming to work full time and helping with the Dallas office."

"Oh, you did?"

Peggy tilted her head. "You can go, can't you? I should have talked to you about it first, but when Betty and I decided to go ahead with the intro without you, I just ran with it. I figured since we used to always get together on Saturday evenings, it'd be okay."

"No, actually, it's perfect. I was going to suggest something similar...kind of play matchmaker and asked Tom if he wanted to go."

"And?" Betty and Peg asked at the same time.

Sally grinned again and ran a hand through her tangled hair. "He said yes and if you all couldn't, he'd come pick me up and we'd go it alone."

"Good work, Louise! So, like a date...alone at night. Maybe you should just go with that...drink a little, dance a little, go back to your place." Betty stood and walked toward Sally just as Bruce jumped from his chair and stood looking up at them, his pointy bat ears straight back against his head. "Oops, you think he knows what we're talking about?"

Sally looked worried as she stared down at him. "He got kind of upset when we were kissing. I think maybe he's just trying to guilt trip me. Maybe I shouldn't go at all tonight."

Peg pushed away from her desk so hard her chair hit the credenza behind it. Startled, they turned to look at her as she hit the desk with the palms of her hands and stood. "For Pete's sake! What is wrong with you two? Of course, Bruce isn't happy. He's spoiled...we've all spoiled him. He's been the only male in any of our lives. He thinks it's his job to protect us. But come on! He's got to get used to you having a man around...at the very least going on dates. So, don't even start this shit! And do not ruin it for me with Frank. Sally, go home and freshen up. Betty, did you reach Adonis?"

Sally still wasn't used to the new Peggy and gave them both a puzzled look. "Adonis? I'm confused. Is it a client I haven't met?"

Betty crossed her arms. "Remember Max the BDSM client?" Sally nodded. "Well, you know we stayed in touch." She picked up Bruce and plopped down in the chair. "I was tempted a couple of times to go out with him, but it was the age thing. My daughter's older than he is, and I didn't want to interfere with him finding someone else. Anyway, he moved to Houston, but we stayed friends, and a couple of months ago, he told me he's engaged to a lovely woman of Greek descent, Angelina."

"Still confused. Is Adonis a nickname for him

because you've always found him so hot?"

Betty waved her arm in front of her. "Would you just let me tell my story?"

Sally sighed and sat on the arm of the chair. "Fine! But it's late, and I'm getting older by the minute, so could you kind of condense it a bit?"

Betty looked over at Peg, mouthed *Bitch,* and they both shrugged. "Alrighty then. Short version. They're going to move back to Austin because her father's living here. Max wanted me to meet her, so we set up a lunch. Her father, Adonis, unbeknownst to me, was included. Max swears he knew we'd hit it off. I've been out with him four times now and feel like we know each other well enough to introduce him to my BABs. And yes, Peg, he said he'd be delighted. Any luck getting in touch with Carole and Calam?"

Sally felt shell-shocked. "So, I knew nothing about any of this...*why?*"

"We've been busy...really, really busy. And it took so much just to get you to agree to take Tommy on...I wanted to keep you focused. Besides, I could have sworn you were wanting me to hook up with Frank, who is nice...but...I don't know. After all the stuff with Jim and then you being so against me keeping any kind of relationship with Max...I just kept it to myself."

Sally took Bruce from Betty. "Right...so, he must be awfully good looking for you to call him Adonis."

"That's his name, Adonis Drakos. His family calls him Adi. He'll be there tonight; you can see for yourself."

"Where?"

"Terrace59 at Speakeasy at eight."

"Eight? Most of us are getting ready for bed around

141

then."

Betty gave Bruce a pat on the head. "Be brave! There's a whole big world out there, and I want us to start experiencing it before we die."

Or it kills us, Sally thought, now in a hurry to get home to take a nap.

Chapter 25

Sally

They were chuckling as the Uber pulled into the drive at the back of Sally's house. "Oh, my gosh, I haven't laughed that hard in a long time. Carole's dance was hilarious. And the way Calam just calmly went along with it. I wasn't expecting that at all. He seems so reserved. Did you see the way those young people were looking at us?"

"First off, pretty much everyone's young compared to us. And secondly, I believe, my little dancing queen, that they were awestruck by your performance. What amazes me is that you can still dirty dance like that. That's what I found unexpected."

"Only when blitzed, Tom. And I'm pretty sure I'm blitzed and will be mortified in the morning. Just because I can't move my feet very well doesn't mean I can't move my body." She felt herself grinning from the inside out, put a hand on his shoulder, and met his eyes. He leaned in to kiss her, but she stopped him. "Okay, maybe that didn't come out quite like I meant it. But not tonight. I had a great time…the best time I've had since…" She shrugged. "Since I can't remember when. I don't want anything to ruin it, and I don't want something to happen that one of us might regret in the morning because of our adolescent behavior tonight."

He took her hand and kissed it. "It's already morning, and you're absolutely correct. May I at least walk you to the porch? It's so dark."

"Of course, you may." She put her fingers on the door handle.

"Oh no, you don't. Sit there like a lady and let me help you out."

He stepped from the backseat and walked around to the other side of the vehicle as lights popped on all around them. "I should have known," he said, opening the door and giving her his hand.

She accepted it gratefully and leaned on him as they climbed the three steps to the porch where more lights magically beamed at their approach. "Well, thank you, I had a really wonderful time." She pressed the code on her keypad then turned and kissed him softly, stopping when she heard Bruce's whines on the other side of the door. "Do you want me to pick you up tomorrow and take you to your car?"

"Aw, you're very chivalrous, but I can handle it."

She opened the door, let Bruce out, and laughed at his spider-monkey mode of excitement. "Guess he's glad to see us." She turned back to Thomas as he bent to give the little guy some loving. "Maybe I'm not chivalrous at all but looking for another excuse to see you."

He straightened and grinned. "Oh, that. Hmmm, in that case how about we both sleep in then you come pick me up late morning. Jean's leaving for Dallas for a few days to look at property and see her family. I need to be at the lake house to watch over Domino and Ace. I've had groceries delivered, and Jean's put them up. We could fix a fabulous brunch, perhaps with a couple of mimosas, sit out in this beautiful weather, and enjoy

144

watching the dogs play…the activities on the lake."

Sally stepped inside and leaned on the open door waiting for Bruce and smiled. "Why is it I'm pretty positive you didn't spontaneously come up with this just now?"

He took a step back with his hand on the gate. "Because you're a wise woman, Sally Estes, a very wise and beautiful woman. Well?"

She felt the heat flood over and through her. "Elevenish…your apartment?"

"Perfect!"

She picked Bruce up and watched Tom unlock the gate, take the steps down, and hop in next to the Uber driver. Something was surging through her…something exciting and wonderful…so wonderful it was scaring the hell out of her, but she didn't want it to stop.

****

Peggy

Frank had followed her to make sure she got home okay. She hadn't had much to drink, worried about what he might think of the tipsy Peggy, and he hadn't had anything. He'd come into the apartment complex with her, gone up the elevator, and had waited for her to unlock the door.

"You want me to come in and make sure everything's okay? I always used to do that for my sister before she got remarried. We'd go hang out together, and I'd make sure she was safe inside before I'd leave to go to my own place."

Does he think of me like a sister? "Sure, that would be nice. It's still weird not having Mamma here and the sound of the television when I get home."

They stepped in, and he gave a quick look around

while she grabbed a couple of bottles of water. She handed him one. "For the drive home. I really appreciate you doing this for me. I was worried you weren't having a good time. Do you not drink? I mean it's okay if you don't. I was just curious."

He took the bottle from her, unscrewed the cap, and took a long pull. "It depends on the situation. I'm not much for public drinking and intoxication. Tonight, I was meeting new people and possibly trying to impress you a little bit."

Peggy felt the blush rushing over her and quickly opened her water bottle, trying to act nonchalant.

"I didn't mean to embarrass you. I just say it like it is. I like you, and tonight was a blast…it really was. You know, I kept looking over at Adi, and he had this sour look on his face, and I was like whoa, dude, are you mad about something?"

Peg almost spit her water out. "I know! I kept thinking this is one grumpy old man…then out of nowhere there's this booming '*OPA*' and he was on the dancefloor doing that squat/kick thing. I almost fell out of my chair it was so unexpected."

"I noticed!"

"And did you hear what Betty said to me when I told her it was amazing the way he could still do that?" Frank shook his head. "She said *he* was amazing and had great stamina then winked. I think I got a pretty clear picture."

He chuckled. "Uh, me too, but I'm just going to try and put it out of my head. You were having such a good time you kept a smile on my face the whole night. Thank you for that. As for drinking, I prefer to do it in a more relaxing, *intimate* environment. So, would you like to have an early dinner with me tomorrow night?" He looked at his watch. "Make that tonight…nothing too late. We both have to be at work early on Monday. Someplace casual where we can sip wine and visit…get to know each other better."

She twisted the cap back on the bottle. "Oh gosh, let me think about it."

"Sure," Frank said, his expression clouding over as he turned to leave.

She reached out quickly and grabbed his arm. "I'm kidding, Frank! I'd love to."

"I knew you were." He smiled. "But don't scare me like that. Rejection's not good for the heart at my age."

"At any age."

"I'll touch base with you midafternoon. Sleep tight, Peggy."

She nodded, and he bent and planted a light kiss on her cheek. Peg held the door open watching him go down the hall to the elevators, her mind whirling with excitement and all the possibilities opening up to her. Mona had been right. She'd needed to get out of this apartment and her timing had been perfect.

****

Betty

Betty and Adi were kissing the second the door closed behind them. The dancing, the booze, it had all been an aphrodisiac. They were working their way through Betty's living room, stripping each other's clothes off as they went, when Adi suddenly swooped her up in his arms at the threshold of her bedroom. He took several steps then screamed and awkwardly dropped her onto the bed before falling to his knees.

He screamed again, rolling onto his side moaning. Betty finally came to her senses, realized something was

147

terribly wrong, found her robe in the bathroom, threw it on, and rushed back to him. Fear engulfed her as she watched him writhing on the floor, and she got down next to him, grabbed the bedspread, and tossed it over his naked body.

"My God, what is it? Are you having a heart attack?" Sweat had beaded his forehead, and he groaned, barely able to shake his head. "Okay, uh, can you stand?" Again, the slight shake as if even the smallest movement sent waves of agony.

She stood up, trying not to panic as she went through the entry hall and living room picking up their shoes and clothes, ignoring the whines and barks coming from the dogs. "Okay, we've got to do something." She finished dressing and set his clothes next to him. "Take some deep breaths and try to tell me what's happened."

He grimaced. "My back...legs...just out...like something split in two inside."

She put a pillow under his head. "Just stay calm. Keep breathing. I'm going to call Max and Angelina."

"Still in Houston."

"I don't give a damn where they are." She tapped on Max's name, and it went to voicemail. "Hey, I hate calling this early in the morning, but Adonis is at my house and can't move. Something to do with his back. I'm going to call Carole to see if Calam's available. I can't move him, so I might have to call an ambulance. Get back to me, please."

Carole answered on the second ring. "Betty, what's up?"

"Hey, you all left early."

Carole glanced at the time on her phone. "Calam's on call, and we wanted to spend the afternoon with

Michael, not be out too late. What's happened? Why are you calling so early?"

"Where's Calam now?"

"He had to go into emergency."

"Okay, okay…I'm here with Adi. We've had an accident, and he can't really move. He says it's not his heart…something to do with his back…oh, shit, hang on." Max was calling her back. She put Carole on hold and accepted the call.

"What's up, Bets?"

"Max, I don't know. Adi just kind of screamed then went down in a ball of agony. He can't get up. He—"

"Betty, this is Angelina. You're on speaker. What was he doing? It's been so damn hard to convince him he needs to stay down. Since his back surgery, he thinks he's got superhuman powers…"

"His back surgery? When was that?"

"A little over six months ago, before the two of you met. We were waiting for him to get completely healed and us moved back there for him to have knee surgery."

"Knee surgery?" Betty stared down at Adi expectantly, but he didn't look up at her, and she was starting to get pissed off. "Well, your father had a bit too much ouzo tonight and was out on the dancefloor yelling opa and doing a rendition of *Zorba the Greek* to the applause of people young enough to be his grandchildren. And when we got to my house, he picked me up like he was Rhett Butler in *Gone with the Wind* before collapsing naked on the floor at the foot of my bed."

There was a gasp from the other end, and she heard Max chuckling in the background. "He did what?"

"You heard me." Now there was total silence except

for Max's laughter.

"It's not funny, damn it! Your bedroom floor?" Angel sounded like she was trying to stifle some giggles herself. "Would you call an ambulance, please? I'll have to throw some things together but can be there in about three and a half hours."

"I've got Carole on hold on the other line. Calam's working emergency. Don't rush, he'll be in good hands," Betty assured her and went back to Carole. "Okay, I'm calling an ambulance. He's too big for me to help get him in my car. Can you text Calam and let him know? He's had back surgery in the last six or seven months and was scheduled for knee surgery once he'd healed enough. Men!" she snorted, hung up, and called nine-one-one.

Betty perched on the edge of the bed, saw his head was finally resting on the pillow and his breathing had calmed. She reached down and felt his throat to check his pulse. He was clammy, and there was a trace of a tear streaking his face. Suddenly, her heart stopped. The shock had worn off, and she cringed, imagining how much pain he was in...not just physical but emotional, and she got on her knees beside him and ran a hand over his bald head.

"I'm sorry, Adi. We were having so much fun," she whispered. "But you didn't need to prove anything. If I'd known, I'd have made you take better care of yourself. I care about you. I really do. There's no shame in us not being able to do the things we used to...we're old now."

He sniffed, blinked a couple of times, and a giant hand enclosed hers as he gave a nod. She sat next to him, waiting for the sound of sirens, and squeezed his hand, wishing she could make his pain go away. Wishing they could go back in time, and she could have met him when he'd been able to dance the night away and could still carry her, like Scarlet, up that flight of stairs. They were right, getting old isn't for sissies…and neither is falling in love.

Chapter 26

Thomas

Sally and Bruce had picked Thomas up, taken him to his car, and followed him to his home overlooking Lake Austin. They were in the kitchen sipping mimosas as they prepared a late afternoon brunch.

"That's really awful about Adi. How did you find out about it?"

She wiped her hands on the apron he'd provided her and took the plate of bacon he held out. "Carole called as I was on my way to pick you up. It's a good thing Calam was already in ER. Looks like Adi needs to have another back surgery. And he completely blew out the knee. He'll have some long months of physical therapy and healing ahead of him. From what I understand, Angelina is probably going to quit her job, come here, move in with him, and take over running the Greek food business."

"What about Max? I thought they were supposed to be getting married."

"The good news is, he can run his oil and gas business from anywhere, so I guess he'll be going back and forth until the house in Houston sells." Sally shrugged. "I have no idea what the wedding plans are now, or if they'll be getting a house or live with Adi since he'll require so much recovery time. He could be down

152

for months."

"So, how did it happen? Was it from his *opa* dance last night? He seemed fine when we were all out waiting for our rides. Maybe a little drunk but he was walking okay."

She snatched a piece of bacon off the plate, popped it in her mouth, grinned, and indicated with a hand gesture that her mouth was full.

"Oh no, you don't. I know that grin. Spit it out." She feigned shock and quit chewing. "Okay, miss priss, you know what I meant. Finish chewing then swallow." He couldn't keep the smile off his face as she made an exaggerated show of doing just that followed by gulping sounds. She started to turn to the hash browns, frying golden in the skillet, but he stopped her. "If you're trying to make me crazy with curiosity, you're doing a damn good job. However it happened, it couldn't be that bad."

She tilted her head. "Well, fine. I was going to wait to talk to Betty in person, because I hate not getting it straight from the source, and since I heard it from Carole, and she heard it from a really freaked-out Betty…"

"I get it. Since it's second hand, it would be like gossiping behind your friend's back. Okay." He held his hands up then went to the pan of sizzling potatoes and flipped them. "Eggs fried or scrambled?"

"Scrambled would be great." Sally snatched a couple of plates from the cabinet next to him, set them on the island, opened and closed drawers until she found silverware and napkins, then went about setting the farm table. "Tabasco?" He pointed to the fridge. She rummaged around until she found some, along with a jar of black raspberry jam, and put them in the center of the table next to the salt and pepper.

Thomas watched her stilted movements out of the corner of his eye. "You can't stand it, can you?"

"What?"

"That I didn't cajole you into telling me."

"Please. Why would you think that?" She leaned against the countertop and crossed her arms.

"Because you really want to." He turned the gas burner off the eggs and faced her.

"You'll think it's funny."

"Is it?"

She bit her bottom lip, but he could see the amusement in her eyes. "You'll laugh."

"Try me."

She untied the apron and pulled it from around her neck. "Evidently, Betty and Adi have been sleeping together. *Supposedly*, they were so turned on when they got back to her house last night they started making out and tearing each other's clothes off as soon as the front door was shut."

He took a sip of his mimosa. "Interesting but not funny. Go on."

"Well, they made it as far as her bedroom when he swooped her into his arms and right at the edge of the bed he felt a pop, dumped Betty on the mattress on his way down, and crumpled into a naked heap on the floor, screaming in pain."

"You have a very warped sense of humor." Thomas filled their plates, carried them to the table, and waited for Sally to sit. "Poor guy." He started to take a bite then put his fork down. "What was Adi thinking? Betty's almost as tall as he is. I mean he looks like he's in good shape, but he's not that big of a guy, and you mentioned he'd already had back surgery." *I am not going to laugh*...

"I don't know. But, Tom, the image of them buck naked and him picking her up..." She stifled a giggle. "Those long legs of hers, you know, dangling and his *thing*...hanging in the breeze." Her hand did a little wave, swinging back and forth over her plate.

He grinned. "Very genteel way of describing it. I think I get the picture. You can stop waving and spare me the visual...I'm trying to eat."

Suddenly, she exploded into uncontrollable giggles and started rocking in her chair. "Can you imagine the paramedics when they got there? Evidently, she couldn't get him dressed, and all he had was the bedspread thrown over him. Nothing like the dead weight of a seventy-two-year-old nude man."

"We can only hope he hadn't taken a little blue pill."

Sally almost choked she was laughing so hard and put her piece of toast down. "Oh, God, Tom, I hadn't even thought of that. We have to stop."

He raised an eyebrow, gave her an accusing look, and pointed his fork at her. "Uh, I think if you look around, you're the only one that's finding it so amusing."

"You *know* I think it's awful. After everything I've been through, I wouldn't wish it on anyone...it's just the way it happened. Come on, if you knew the hell Betty puts me through and the way she picks on me, you'd probably see more humor in it. And don't go acting all innocent. You're having to keep yourself from cracking up. I can see it in those amazing hazel eyes of yours. They get this sparkle and turn lighter somehow."

My amazing hazel eyes? He felt the blood rush to his face and looked down at his plate.

"Are you blushing? You are, aren't you? What are

you thinking?"

"You really want to know?"

She gave an impish grin and nodded.

"I was thinking it would be worth a broken back to be able to pick you up and carry you to the bedroom, buck naked and all." Her cornflower blue eyes looked like a deer in headlights. He watched in satisfaction as her cheeks flamed scarlet, and for once she was speechless. *Who's blushing now, Sally? That should give you something to think about.* "I really and truly thought about doing it yesterday when we were having our make out session but wasn't sure I could carry you."

She looked up from her food, and her eyes were impossibly wider.

"That was not an insult. I doubt I could carry anyone heavier than my six-year-old granddaughter. But I would have loved to try."

"Oh."

She was suddenly focused on her food again, and he stood, got the pitcher of mimosas, and refilled their glasses. "Drink up. I'll make more when we go hang out by the pool."

****

They reclined in chaise lounges and watched the sun paint the sky in hues of yellow and red, reflecting dark and purple on the lake as it slowly descended behind the hills. Sally sighed. "That was beautiful, Tom. It's been a wonderful day."

Bruce was sprawled across his stomach, and the retrievers were flanking Sally's chair, everyone at peace and happy. "It's not over yet." He gently moved Bruce and reached for the bottle of wine they'd switched to and started to pour.

"No more, I've already had too much. I might have to call an Uber."

"Stay."

"I can't."

"Why can't you?"

She shrugged. "I just need to get settled in, check on Betty. Jewel's coming to town tomorrow, and we have a lunch thing with her and the others. She's having a problem with one of the clients and thinks we should fire him. It's got to be really bad to do that, but it does happen occasionally."

He stood, climbed over Domino, and sat on the edge of her chaise. "Betty's a big girl. I'm sure she's fine. She has Max and Angel in town now. You told me Peg is on a date with Frank, and I'm pretty certain Carole and Calam are making sure everyone is taken care of. Can't you just relax…ever?" He leaned in and brushed his lips against hers.

Her breath caught when he pulled away and stared down at her. "No. I don't think so…I don't know how. And I'd feel awkward."

"You could stay in one of the guest bedrooms if that would make you more comfortable. I'm not going to push anything on you." He grinned. "I'm not even sure I'm attracted to you." His eyes twinkled as he kissed her again, just long enough and soft enough to tease her.

This time a tiny whimper escaped her throat, and she felt a flip-flop in her stomach just before he drew his head back. Standing, he called the dogs and headed for the house. "What are you doing?"

"Just going to get these monsters fed and ready for bed. I'll be back in a few minutes."

Sally was debating whether to call an Uber or stay,

stay, or call an Uber. She checked her messages and didn't have any. There really wasn't anything she had to take care of, and it was so nice here. Bruce was enjoying having other dogs to play with and had really taken to Tom, following along when he led them inside without even looking back at her. And damn, when Tom kissed her, she really and truly wanted to melt. She hadn't felt like that in years, not since…since Darrell…in the beginning.

She shivered, pushed the thought aside, and closed her eyes, breathing in the cool night air as darkness shrouded Austin with welcoming arms. After a few minutes, she looked up at the stars and moon and thought this moment would never come again, when music wafted out to her. Curious, she got up, her body stiff from sitting too long, and ambled in its direction. As she approached, the glass door opened, and Tom took her hand. When they reached the great room, it was lit by at least a dozen candles, and soft dance music filled the house. He drew her arms up around his neck, put his around her waist, and pulled her to him.

"Hang onto me." His voice was husky and low, and she felt like she had no choice but to comply…to cling to him. She rested her head against his chest, breathed in the maleness of him, and fifty-three years were gone in an instant. She didn't feel like a crippled old woman anymore. The constant pain she carried and tried so desperately to hide had magically disappeared. She felt alive for the first time in such a long, long time…in her head she was seventeen again and *safe*. Something she'd never been before.

Chapter 27

Thomas

The dogs were whining at the bedroom door, and Tom was the first to stir. He squinted at his cell charging on the bedside table, but it wasn't there. For a brief second, he was confused, until he heard her soft purr of a snore. He felt her roll over and kick one leg out from under the covers and turned to face her. She was sprawled on her belly like a kid with legs and arms flung in all directions, a sure sign of a woman who was used to sleeping alone.

He sat up and tested his legs as he tried standing, the bed and his bones creaking as he did. He moved slowly to his reading chair and retrieved his bathrobe, found his slippers, and headed for the door when he heard her giggle.

"You really wear a robe?"

He glanced over his shoulder and raised an eyebrow. "Doesn't everyone?"

Sally sat up, plumped a pillow behind her, and drew the sheet up over her breasts. Her face was ruddy from whisker burn, there were little black smudges under her eyes, and her hair resembled Medusa with a touch of rat's nest, but to Thomas she was the most gorgeous creature he'd ever seen.

"No, absolutely not. Most men seem to love

bouncing around au naturel. Are all of you exhibitionists? And what's that smug look all about?"

He ran fingers over the top of his head and wiggled them. "It's cute."

She reached up and touched the scrunchy blob of hair. "Oh that. You have to promise to ignore the little bald spot. You ignore mine and I'll ignore yours."

"Oh slam, that was brutal." He turned to the dressing table mirror and saw his normally, perfectly coiffed hair was sticking straight up in the back and tendrils coiled across his forehead, but he made no move to smooth it down. "Deal." The dogs were really crying now at the sound of their voices. "They probably thought one of us was getting murdered in here last night."

"Not a bad way to go. What time is it?"

"Don't know, haven't located my watch or cell yet."

"You need to get a Google Hub or something."

"Elaine had one in our old bedroom."

She sat up straighter. "This isn't the master?"

"No, I moved in here when she became so ill. She wasn't comfortable with me sharing a room with her. Hated me seeing her as bad as she'd gotten."

Sally grinned. "So, this is a *first* in here."

He pivoted to look at her and smiled. "Oh, trust me, there were a lot of firsts that happened in here last night, and in the living room, maybe even the kitchen…"

She tossed a pillow in his direction, falling short several feet. "Stop, you're going to embarrass me."

"Oh, I seriously doubt that," he cajoled.

"Do you have another one of those?" She pointed at his robe.

"I'll get one from one of the guest rooms."

"No time. I've got to pee, and my bladder isn't what

it used to be."

He took a few steps toward her, slipped the robe off, and tossed it to her. "Call me an exhibitionist." Lumbering back to the door, a robed streak flew behind him. He opened it just as the bathroom door slammed, and the three dogs came bounding in, sniffing, and jumping on him. Bruce had his ears down, went to the closed door, and whined.

"Come on, guys, let's go outside. You must be ready to burst." He made a stop at one of the other bathrooms, snatched a robe from its hook, put it on, then let Domino and Ace out. A few minutes went by before he realized Bruce wasn't in the backyard with the big dogs and called for him.

"He's with me." Sally entered the kitchen wrapped in Tom's robe, her face washed, and hair partially brushed, carrying Bruce. "Hope you don't mind, I borrowed some of your stuff…brushed my teeth with a washrag."

"When did you suddenly become so modest?" He kissed the top of her forehead and turned to make coffee.

"There are just some things people shouldn't have to see in the glaring light of day. Where did we leave our clothes?"

He nodded behind him. "Should be some scattered around the floor where we were dancing then more by the couch."

She set Bruce down and opened the back door for him, but he just sat on his haunches and stared up at her. "I think he might be scarred for life…totally traumatized."

"He'll get used to it," he said absently. "Espresso, cappuccino, latte?"

"I think an espresso is definitely called for. Tom?"

"Sally?"

"I've been afraid to ask, but how well did we *really* know each other in high school? Something's been tugging at the back of my mind. I have a feeling there was more to it than just having a few classes together. I've been having these little déjà vu experiences again."

A knot formed in his stomach as he put the steaming cups on the island, let the dogs in, fed them, then took his espresso to the farm table and stared out the window for a minute, waiting for her to join him. When she sat, he rubbed his eyes before looking into hers. "Are you sure you want to do this right now?" What was it in her expression, confusion, distrust?

"I haven't been completely honest with you. That was a really tough time for me back in high school…all the little boys with raging hormones pawing at me…the rumors, the girls giggling and snickering when they'd walk past me. The things said behind my back that I heard anyway. I've blocked a lot of the unpleasantness, but there's something nagging at me trying to come to the surface. Did something happen?"

He shifted uncomfortably and looked down at his untouched cup. "We were friends. I've told you I had a crush on you." He reached out and put a hand on hers. "Look, this isn't the time. You've got a lunch meeting, and I have to go out to the warehouse then back to the office to take care of some paperwork. Let's get together this evening when we have more time to talk, and I promise we'll try to figure this out."

****

Something was wrong; Sally felt it. She gave a slight nod and watched him scoot his chair back and stand.

"Finish your coffee. I'm going to take a quick shower and get dressed. Maybe you can get Bruce to go out if I'm not here."

As Tom left the room, she was suddenly filled with fear. Fear of the unknown, fear of the past…fear of her memories bursting to the surface and drowning her…fear of ruining what she and Tom had now.

She left her cold espresso, carried Bruce outside, and watched him wag his tail at the other dogs. A low rumble made her look up at the threatening sky. The wind was getting stronger as clouds billowed, and the heady scent of rain filled the air. She'd always been fascinated by storms, the electricity and energy exciting, never ceasing to overwhelm her. But this time she shivered in anticipation of it bringing with it something more ominous.

Hurrying inside, she shucked the robe, picked up her clothes, and threw them on. She was tying her sneakers when Thomas came in fully dressed, towel drying his hair.

"That was quick. Are you leaving?"

"Have you looked outside? I'd really like to try to beat the storm home. Plus, I have to get cleaned up and ready." She grabbed Bruce's leash from an end table and held the back door until all the dogs were in. "I hate to do this, little guy, but we've got to get going." Tom tossed the towel over the back of a chair and picked him up so she could clamp the leash to his collar. She snatched her purse from the commode in the entryway and turned to take Bruce.

"It's okay, I'll walk you all out."

At her car, she took the little dog and got him fastened to a seat belt, closed the door, and faced Tom just as a boom of thunder reverberated over the lake and a gust of cool air brushed against them. "Gosh, I love thunderstorms."

"I know you do." His disheveled hair blew across his forehead, his eyes lit up, and he suddenly looked so young…so young and *familiar*.

"Do you?"

He nodded as the first raindrops splattered across the driveway. She looked up at the sky, laughed, and raised her arms in the air and did a little spin as gracefully as she could. "It's glorious, isn't it?" She stopped and stared up at him smiling, and he matched it with a devilish grin of his own.

"Yes, very glorious." Leaning down, he kissed her, a lingering kiss as the rain beat against them.

For a moment, she was lost in the taste and feel of him until her mind drifted to the look in his eyes that left her breathless, to his lips just before his kiss consumed her, to the words *yes, very glorious*, the rain pounding them as their mouths searched deeper, consuming each other. A feeling…a vision so strong it was more like a memory. And, suddenly, her heart twisted in pain, and she knew. Jerking her head back, she stared at him, her chest heaving, not with passion, but barely contained rage.

"Sally?"

She shook her head and pushed against him. "It's coming back! The deja'vu…those bits and pieces. I remember now. You bastard, it's all coming back."

Was she imagining it, or did he suddenly go pale? "I know who you are, who you were. You were a jock, Mr. Everything. You and your group of popular guys, all so mighty and studly. You all made mean girls look like a cakewalk."

She started to get in the car, but he twirled her away from the door and leaned against it. "Let me explain."

Now, she was furious and tried to move him out of the way, but he wouldn't budge. "I liked you, damn it! I thought you were different. The great Tommy Fitzsimmons…or was it Zitsimmons? Wasn't that what your dear pal, Billy Markham, called you? You remember Billy, your best bud, the guy who raped me? I'm sure you all got some great laughs over that one."

Through the sheet of rain, she saw the expression on his face change and knew she'd hit a nerve. He reached out and grabbed her arms, and for a moment she was afraid of him and tried to pull away.

"Stop it! What are you talking about?"

She was crying now. "I really, really liked you. I didn't want to believe you were like the rest of them. The kiss in the rain. I…I kissed you back…you telling me the guys had dared you and you didn't mean it. You and Billy and all the other little macho pricks…I bet you all thought it was a great joke, especially after Billy forcing himself on me the week before. I was so embarrassed and ashamed, and here I'd believed you were different and really cared."

"I didn't know…I never had any idea. I still don't understand. You have to believe me."

The downpour had turned into a soft shower, but the shock of remembering was making her head swim, and she felt nauseous and weak. "I believed and trusted you once…and you…you devasted me. But not again, *Tommy.* Let me go."

She could swear there were tears in his eyes as he stepped to the side and held the car door open for her.

She climbed in, wiped the rain and tears from her face as he tried to lean in to say something. Without looking at him, she closed the door, forcing him to back away. Once she was heading down the drive, she glanced in her rearview mirror and saw him still standing there in the rain, his thumbs locked in the belt loops of his jeans, wet hair falling across his forehead…but in her mind's eye, he was still that teenage boy from all those years ago. The one who had rocked her world then destroyed it.

Chapter 28

She stood on the back porch, punched in the code to unlock the deadbolt, went inside, and was ready to tell Alexa to turn off the alarm when she noticed it wasn't beeping. *Shit, I didn't turn it on when I left yesterday.* Sally took the leash off Bruce, hung it in the utility room, stepped into the kitchen, and smelled coffee. *Great, I must have been in such a hurry to pick Tom up I left the pot on, too.*

The Chipin sniffed the terracotta floor, bristled, and took off barking toward the front of the house. "Bruce, what is it? Come back here." Sally went after him in her fastest hobble. Rounding the corner to the living room, she ran into someone. Her blood-curdling scream filled the house, as she dropped her purse and started swinging her arms, her heart pounding out of her chest.

"Hey, hey…hold on, damn it! It's me."

She knew that voice, the hands gripping her wrists…she knew the scent of him. She stopped attacking and focused on his face, laboring to calm her breath. "Jesus fucking Christ, Darrell, you scared the shit out of me!" She jerked one arm then the other free and rubbed her wrists. "What in the hell are you doing here?"

Bruce was barking and snapping at his feet and pant legs. He tried to shoo him away with his foot but failed miserably. "What is this thing?"

"It's a dog."

167

"Would you call it off?"

"It's a *he*. Bruce, it's okay, calm down, big boy. You did a really good job." She bent and rubbed his head. When she stood, her hands were on her hips. "So?"

"You won't answer or return my calls."

"And you just show up after what…three years and let yourself in?"

He gave his little boy grin that used to madden her and shrugged. "You didn't change the code. I was kind of surprised about the alarm not being on though. I did try calling to let you know I was here, but it went straight to voicemail."

"My phone's been dead."

"I tried texting. Didn't you see it on your watch?"

Without thinking, she looked down at her wrist, but it wasn't there. "It's dead too. Just like you are to me, Darrell. Dead's dead."

She threw her hands in the air and started to plop down in the closest chair when he reached out for her arm. "Hey, hey, baby, don't do that. You're soaked."

She twisted away from him and sat down anyway. "Don't tell me what to do and not do. And *do not* call me *baby*!" She bent to pick Bruce up, and when she turned back to Darrell, he had a smirk on his face. "What?"

"The top and back of your hair…I know that look."

"What look?"

"That nursing-home hairdo you get during sex where it gets all knotty like those Brillo things and your little bald spot shows. Remember, it used to take me forever to help you brush them out. It's worse than gum stuck in your hair." He stepped back and assessed her. "Baby, I wish I could say you have that freshly fucked look, but it's more like rode hard and put up wet."

Her eyes narrowed, and she clenched her teeth so hard her jaw hurt. *If only this look could kill…* For a brief moment she thought about retorting something caustic but decided not to give him the satisfaction of jerking her chain. And besides, it was none of his damned business. "When did you get here?"

"Last night. I stayed on the couch waiting for you."

"I bet you did. Do I need to count the silverware, check to see if you emptied the safe?"

"Aw, come on. That's beneath you, Sally."

"But not beneath you, Darrell." She stood. "My, so sorry you have to leave. Thanks for stopping by." She painfully walked to the door, opened it, and waited.

"Come on, bab…Sally, don't you even want to know what I'm doing here?"

"I suppose it has to do with the messages you left me. All your crap about being sober, getting counseling. You know I've heard this all before and—"

"It's real this time. I'm not lying. Being sober for over a year gave me a lot of time to think about things. But there are these lapses where I don't remember… I know I did and said terrible things."

"If this is part of your twelve steps program, great, you made amends. You can go on your way now, knowing you smoothed everything over. You're not just an alcoholic, Darrell, you're a complete asshole narcissist. What happened to your big money-making scheme you moved to LA for? Another one gone down the tubes, another unsuspecting woman bit the dust?"

He sidled closer and shook his head. "You don't think I know what I am? I want you to fill in some of the blanks. I want you to let me have it and not hold anything back. The hardest part was remembering and not being able to numb the feelings with booze. I remembered what you'd meant to me and all you did for me. And sometimes I get flashes of what I did to you, how I treated you."

She tilted her head to the side, hoping the gesture said *do I look like I care*, and planted a hand on her hip. "Darrell, I am in no mood for your shit. I'm not in the mood for anyone's shit. I'm tired, hangry, wet, and have a meeting to get to in an hour. So please, get the hell out of my house before I become hysterical, sic Bruce on you, and call the police."

He crossed his arms. "Your phone's dead, and so's your watch."

"I'll have Alexa do it."

"She can't call nine-one-one."

"She can call the neighborhood patrol."

He shook his head. "You never change…always have to be bantering with me…always have to be right, have the last word."

"Get out, Darrell, now!"

He walked up to her, and she got the nostalgic whiff of coffee on his breath when he grabbed his hat from the coatrack behind her, stuck it on his bald head, and sighed. "You're going to talk to me, Sally Estes, I promise you that." He gave her an infuriating wink and swaggered his way across the front porch, tipping his hat to the mail lady on the sidewalk. In spite of herself, Sally smiled at his effrontery and shameless charm.

Once he was safely in his car the smile faded. She closed the door, sighed, and let the tears flow freely. *Not this, not now, I can't take it.* Immediately Tom filled her mind with the vision of him standing in the rain, his wet hair in heavy ringlets over his forehead, thumbs in the loops of his jeans, watching her drive away.

****

The girls were all at the restaurant waiting for her. She'd called ahead to let them know she was running late and made her apologies all around before noticing the looks on their faces. "What's wrong? Has someone died? Oh damn, is Adi okay?"

Peggy was sitting next to her right and put a hand over hers. "Frank got a call from Thomas, and they're meeting as we speak. We don't know what's happened, but Frank said he didn't sound like himself and that he's worried about you."

"Is there anything you want to tell us, Louise? What did you do to Tommy?" Betty crossed her arms over her chest and gave her the *I know you* look.

Sally pulled her hand away, sat back in her chair, calmly took her silverware out of the linen napkin, placed it on the table and the napkin in her lap. "First of all, stop calling him *Tommy*. We are *not* still in fucking high school. Secondly, it's none of any of your all's business. I appreciate the concern, I really, really do…" Her throat constricted, and a whimper escaped. She brought the napkin to her eyes as uncontrolled tears trickled from them, and suddenly everything came spilling out, the wonderful day and night she and Tom had had, that morning remembering who he was, the story about being raped…a story she'd repressed all these years.

"Jesus, Sally, you never told me. What did your parents do? I'm surprised they didn't kill Billy."

"I never told them. It was the sixties…always the girl's fault. It caused shame to a family to admit their daughter had illicit sex. Don't you remember how my parents were always telling me not to cause a scene, and a woman who slept with more than one man her entire life was a whore? It was a man's world back then. And date rape wasn't even a thing…supposedly the girl always asked for it or led the poor guy on."

"Yeah, well, it was an archaic system back then. I'm so glad things are changing. Now I know why you've always been such a bitch to men." Betty reached across the table. "I'm really sorry."

Sally took the offered hand, and Peggy, Carole, and Jewel each put their hands on top of the last one down. Withdrawing hers, Sally looked around her, and people were staring at them, but she didn't give a damn. "I just want to say thank you. I've held this in for fifty-plus years. I blocked the whole thing, even what happened with Tom. I was crushed. I'd really thought he was one of the good guys, but he was just like all the rest of them. And the truth is, it devastated me. I remember hearing he'd gotten some girl pregnant our senior year and she'd had to leave school. What a bastard. So many things are coming back to me now."

"I was abused as a little girl." Peggy's voice was barely above a whisper. "A family member."

"Me too," Jewel volunteered with a slight raise of her hand. "One of Mom's many boyfriends."

Carole put her hands out in front of her like a cop at a crosswalk. "Everyone knows what I've been through, and most of it I brought on myself. That's why I joined the police force and went to work in the sex crimes unit. Growing up in the seventies and eighties wasn't any easier, especially with a single mom who didn't know who my father was. I'm pretty sure there's a lot I don't remember. It's okay that you blocked it, Sally. That's what a lot of victims do. It's called dissociative amnesia. Sometimes it's the only way people can deal with things like that."

"I feel like such a fool about Tom now. He completely played me, and like I always do, I jumped in feet first. God, it's like he's still laughing at me from high school."

Betty had been quiet. "I haven't had all the horrible things happen to me that the rest of you have, but I've got a gut feeling about Tommy. I don't remember him that way. Yeah, he ran with the popular crowd and was a jock, but for the most part some of his closest friends were the nerds…the smart kids like you. I remember something about a girl getting pregnant and leaving school, but he always seemed like the type that would have tried to make it right. There was so much going on back then with Vietnam and classmates dying." She shuddered.

Sally looked her friend in the eyes. "Thanks for giving him the benefit of the doubt, but I saw the look of guilt in his eyes. He should have told me everything, encouraged me to remember…at the very least he should have been transparent and honest."

"I don't think he was lying." Betty's face was stern.

"Let's see what Frank has to say. I'd love to know what they're talking about." Peggy gave them a bright smile. "I'll be glad to go with Betty to do the interviews today."

Sally shook her head. "No, thanks anyway. I need to keep busy, or I'll just sit and stew in my own juices. By the way, did I mention Darrell Normand was waiting in my house for me when I got home this morning?" Looking at the stunned expressions around the table

173

made her actually grin, and she was more than relieved the topic of conversation had changed.

Chapter 29

Thomas

Thomas had finished relaying his story. "The thing is, Frank, I know what I did was shitty, but I had no idea about Billy raping her. And no way would he have let it get back to me. He knew I had a crush on her and would have been afraid of me beating the living hell out of him."

Frank looked at him thoughtfully. "Are you prone to violence?"

"I was a teenager. I think we all were a little wild during those years. But to answer your question, no, I'm not. Vietnam was going on, and I watched two of my best friends in the world get drafted and then die in a foreign country where we didn't have any business being. I was a conscientious objector. War and killing didn't make sense to me. I think the only thing that saved me from the draft was getting married right out of high school and having a child. But all of that aside, would I be capable of taking on someone who harmed a person I care about? I think we all are."

"I understand what you're saying. A basketball accident my senior year spared me from that war I didn't believe in. But as for Sally, you didn't tell her any of this? You just let her memories come to the surface on their own?"

"Look, I know what I did all those years ago was horrible. For me to tell her that the guys had dared me to kiss her, that I didn't really mean it. I could never have been so cruel if I'd known what Billy had done to her. But I was young and stupid and trying to save face. When this first started, I was going to be straight up with her right at the beginning. I promised Elaine I wouldn't lie to her *or* myself. But when I realized how much I liked being around her, how it made me feel alive again. I...I was afraid of ruining it before it even got started."

Frank stood and stared at the landscape surrounding Thomas's warehouse. "I think I know how you feel." He turned back to the other man and nodded his head. "That feeling-alive-again thing. I kind of feel that when I'm with Peggy. We barely even know each other, but there's something so damn refreshing in the way she just pops out whatever she's thinking and feeling. Funny how we spend so much of our lives trying to impress people, say and do things to make others like us. Then you reach what's supposed to be our *golden years*, and it's not what you'd thought it would be, and suddenly, you just don't give a fuck about what anyone thinks."

He sighed and sat back down across from Thomas and looked him in the eyes. "You were a kid; you didn't know anything about your friend raping her. If you had, he would have lied and said she'd *wanted it*. I remember how guys thought and talked back then. As humans, we spend our lives saving face. If she hadn't been violated and obviously traumatized, she wouldn't have taken it so hard...she might not have turned you down either. You might have ended up together. We'll never know. But I get it, you not wanting to ruin it with Sally. However, I just have this gut feeling that if you'd been more upfront, she would have heard you out. She might have been taken aback, but what happened this morning could have been avoided."

Thomas ran his hands through his disheveled hair. "It all just moved so fast. I thought we'd have plenty of time, but it was so natural, the way we were drawn to each other…bonded. Maybe I just moved too quickly."

Frank's deep laugh boomed through the breakroom. "I think that at our ages it's okay not to have a really long courtship. Besides, fifty years waiting is a long enough time. You know, in your shoes I might have hesitated telling her, too. Like with Peg. She's adorable. I mean from the moment we literally bumped heads and she looked up at me from behind those glasses and told me I was drop-dead gorgeous; I've been smitten with that woman.

"But I don't want to rush things because I know what these ladies are doing with their business and how they're helping people. I don't want to be one of those men they think are just looking for sex. When my wife was so ill for so long and didn't even remember who I was, I'll admit, I got lonely. And I thought about what it would be like to have a female friend, someone to talk to, have dinner with, maybe have sex again. But there were rare times when I'd get brief glimpses of my Molly, moments where she'd be lucid, her eyes bright with recognition, and I knew in my heart I couldn't be unfair to her or to another woman. As long as there was a breath left in her, she was my wife and I still loved her."

"It was the same with me, only Elaine's mind stayed fairly sharp throughout. She knew who I was and worried about me. I still had her to talk to, to share things with. Hell, she wouldn't have blamed me if I'd wanted or needed someone for sex. But I didn't. It never entered my mind. And even when she came up with the crazy thing about signing me up for The Widower Whisperers and reconnecting with Sally, sex wasn't the goal. And then what did I do? I blew it right out of the starting gate."

"No, I disagree. If you'd blown it out of the starting gate, you wouldn't have scored. It's more like a horse winning the derby and then they find out it's been drugged, and they disqualify it."

"Thanks for the analogy…terribly helpful. So, you're really a retired psychiatrist?"

Frank laughed again and slapped his thigh. "You know they say we're the most fucked up." He put his elbows on his knees and leaned forward. "But it's completely okay to be fucked up. It really is. We're both good men, Thomas, but we don't have to be perfect. Give Sally some space. Maybe reach out to Betty. They've been friends since way back then. I just don't think trying to explain yourself and push her is going to work right now. She's going to have to come to terms with these suppressed memories coming to light and the emotions they evoke. It's going to be a lot for her to process."

Thomas shook his head then let it hang in defeat. "My God, the idea of her remembering being raped. It's got to be horrific. It makes me sick to think about. I can't fathom the hatred she must have had for me…thinking I knew, and it was like some kind of joke to me."

"But hey, you *didn't* know. She'll probably come around. Just give it time. Do you mind if I talk to Peg about this, or would you prefer keeping our conversations confidential?"

Thomas looked up with tears burning the backs of

his eyes. Unshed tears of rage toward Billy Markham, sadness, and shame for Sally. He splayed his hands in a gesture of resignation. "Please, talk to Peg if you think it might help. I don't have anything to hide. It's all out on the table now. And thank you for coming out here and meeting with me. Sally wanted me to talk to you anyway. She wanted to make sure I was ready to move on."

"She mentioned it to me. And I'm delighted to say that I believe you are. I can see how much you really care about her."

"It was all just so perfect. The way she and Bruce slipped into my old lifestyle at the lake house. I couldn't imagine being happy there again, but when she walked in the door carrying that little guy, all my doubts and self-pity disintegrated. And she loved the place, even joked about christening it when…you know. We have the same interests and causes that matter and are important to us. That doesn't happen very often."

"And you have *history* together. Now that she's unblocked part of that, she needs to remember the rest. How close had you all been in high school?"

Thomas sighed and wiped his eyes with the back of a hand. "We were both into science and psychology. We hung out some, did lab work together, usually partnered up. Sometimes she'd get squeamish and couldn't force herself to dissect a frog or something, and I'd do it so she wouldn't get in trouble. She helped me with chemistry."

"If I were a betting man, I'd say you probably didn't need too much help in that department. Sounds like there was plenty of chemistry going on between the two of you."

He smiled. "You're a smart man, Frank. We had something special. What's that called when you need a mental connection with someone before being attracted to them sexually?"

"Demisexual?"

"Yeah, it was like that with her. I mean, I was blown away when I first saw her. Stumbled all over myself. She was so young and beautiful, in an ornery, mischievous redheaded way. I know most of the boys thought of her as a challenge and wanted to shag her, but all I wanted was to get to know her. Is that weird?"

Frank wagged his head back and forth. "Maybe for a teenage boy with raging hormones. But, no, not really. I bet if a lot of those boys hadn't been working so hard at being macho and legends in their own minds, they would have loved to have basked in her light.

"You know, I was like that with Molly. I was kind of a prick in high school...check that...I was a giant prick. I did the jock thing, too. My specialty was basketball. I thought I was *the dude*. And girls were never in short supply. But all the while, I had this hidden desire to find out what made people tick. My mom was mixed Haitian and my dad as white as you could get. We moved up north when I was a kid because their relationship was more accepted there. Yet those two were so damned in love even though they came from such diverse backgrounds. And then there was me. I didn't fit in with the other blacks, and I wasn't part of the white cliques either. Maybe that's why I was such a prick."

Both men chuckled. "It must have been hard on you."

"That's the strange part. It really wasn't. I ended up with my own group of ragtag misfits and kind of reveled in my uniqueness. That's the way I thought of myself…unique. Anyway, when I got to college and met Molly, she opened my eyes to a whole new world. She was as blond as Betty and as fair as Sally. But she didn't seem to notice I was any different than she was. She was majoring in psychology, and before long, so was I. And the funny thing is, all those girls, I didn't even remember them after getting to know Molly. I loved her mind. I loved the way she saw the universe. Not black or white, but multicolored and she opened up a whole new world for me. Hell, she *was* my world."

Frank glanced at his watch. "This has been good. I could stay here and reminisce all day, but I promised Peg I'd meet Jewel today and discuss some of the problems she's having in Dallas with a couple of clients. If Sally asks me anything, do you want me to talk to her?"

"I'll leave that to you. I know you're right about backing off. She's got so much on her plate right now with trying to get the Dallas office open. I just worry about her trying to do too much."

They both stood. "Don't. From what I know about that woman, she does her best when she's busy. I think most of us do. Look at you, still working, hands on in your businesses. Me, volunteering because I don't like retirement."

They walked to the elevator, and Thomas silently went down with him and walked him to his vehicle. They shook hands, and Frank was about to open the door when Thomas stopped him. "Could we maybe get together again sometime? I know we only just met the other night, but when Elaine got so sick, I sort of lost touch with most of my guy friends. It was hard seeing them with their wives or listening to them talking about other women. Plus, I wasn't exactly much fun back then. I could use a new friend, especially one who's been where I have."

Frank nodded, opened the car door, got in, and put the top down. "We kind of exclude others from our lives when we're living that kind of nightmare. It's hard to watch the person that means the most to you slowly dying before your eyes. Calam has been a lifesaver for me, but he's got Carole and his son. I could use a new friend, too. I'll be in touch." He pulled out of the gravel drive with a waving hand.

Tom glanced up at the steaming Austin sun and wondered if Elaine was looking down at him, shaking her head over what a mess he'd made of things. He felt like the day's events had taken everything out of him and was suddenly so very, very tired. Slowly, he made his way back into the coolness of the warehouse and wiped at the tears and sweat trickling down his face, and his mind drifted to how happy he'd been yesterday, spending it with Sally and Bruce. "Oh, what a difference a day makes," he said aloud and headed to the elevator, remembering Sally on that first meeting, wobbling on her high heels and grabbing for his arm as it lurched upward. Despite himself, he smiled.

Chapter 30

Sally

Sally and Betty had left lunch to do a couple of interviews, promising to meet Jewel back at the office later that afternoon. When they walked in, Peg was sitting at the receptionist's desk.

"Where's Lily?" Betty looked upset.

"Oh, she wasn't feeling well. I told her she could go home."

"I'm sorry. I hope she's okay. Have you been up here since she left?" Sally was particular about everything running properly.

"Well, no, not really. I had some work to do in my office, and she told me there wasn't anyone else scheduled to come in today. Why?"

Sally had a funny feeling, and her feelings were usually right. "Have you been to *my* office?"

"No, I was just checking something on Lily's calendar. I couldn't remember if I'd scheduled that problem client for tomorrow."

"Which one?" Betty asked.

"What difference does it make? Seems like that's all we have right now. I don't know what the hell's in the air," Sally tossed over her shoulder in a hurry to get up to her office. Once there, she flung the door open and took it all in. Darrell leaning back in her chair, his feet

183

on her desk, Jewel on the couch surrounded by files.

"Oh, hi, baby, come on in." Darrell put his feet on the floor and sat up straight.

Jewel looked up. "I was checking to see if you'd gotten back and found him in here. I've been babysitting. You can thank me later. And yes, your friend's already hit on me."

"What the hell is *he* doing here?" Betty had been right behind Sally, followed by Peg.

"That's what I'd like to know. Darrell, get out of that chair, out of my office, and out of my life."

He rested his arms on the desk and looked at her innocently. "I really wasn't hitting on her. You know how I like to flirt."

"So, you *flirting* with me, and me telling you I'm a lesbian with a significant other then you asking if we could have a threesome, was not *hitting* on me?"

"Darrell!"

He shrugged.

Sally turned to Jewel. "What did you tell him?"

"That it had been my experience most men couldn't handle pleasing one woman, let alone two. Then he asked if he could at least watch."

"Jesus, Darrell, I thought you were all sobered up and reformed. What is wrong with you?"

Betty moved some files to the coffee table and plopped down next to Jewel. "Don't be too hard on him. I swear it's every man's fantasy."

"I think that fantasy has created more than a few lesbians." Jewel winked at Darrell. "Besides, he's harmless."

Sally put her hands on her hips. "Did he tell you about his third leg?"

"He did. And I told him you said it was a Chihuahua's."

"That was a really low blow, baby."

He actually has the balls to look insulted. "Well, if the leg fits, Darrell."

He rolled the chair back and stood. "Is there someplace we could talk in private?"

Sally suddenly looked around frantically. "Where's Bruce?"

Jewel nodded toward the door. "Carole has him in her office with the door closed. He wouldn't stop barking at Mr. Sensitivity here. I just texted her you were back."

At that moment Carole peeked around Peggy from the doorway at the same instant Bruce jumped from her arms growling and headed for Darrell.

"Oh, hell no!" She threw her hands in the air. "He's still here?"

Sally snagged the leash from its hook, clipped it to Bruce's collar while he almost convulsed snapping and barking at Darrell, and absently handed the lead to Carole, who grudgingly pulled him from the room.

Once they were out in the hall, Peg stepped around Sally and held out her hand. "I never actually met you before. I mean, I've heard an awful lot about you. I'm Peggy Russo."

He touched her fingertips to his lips. "Such a pleasure meeting you. Darrell Normand at your service." He flourished a bow. "It's nice to know there's someone in this establishment with manners."

"Since you just let yourself in, I'd say it's pretty good manners that none of us have called the police." Betty didn't try to keep the distain from her voice.

"There wasn't anyone at the front desk."

"Oh, of course, so that's an invitation to just waltz in and take over my office." Sally crossed her arms and glared at him, knowing it was useless to argue, but she couldn't help herself.

Peggy held a hand up. "Stop. All of you." When they were quiet and staring at her, she turned her attention to Darrell. "Mr. Normand, I'm afraid my introduction wasn't about manners. I just wanted to be able to say I'd actually met the biggest asshole on the face of the earth."

For a few moments, stunned silence hung over the room until Jewel clapped and said, "Bravo," as the other women chortled.

Darrell put his hands on his hips. "Really, Sally? I don't know what you've told everyone."

"The truth."

"Well, there's two sides to every story."

"No, Darrell, there's actually three. But how would you know any of them since you were drunk the whole time?" Betty asked with a smirk.

"You know, I came here to try to make peace."

"Oh, come on, I can see right through your narcissistic bullshit. It's been an awfully long day, and I have no patience. Now, please leave before I lose my temper and start screaming." Sally's back was hurting. She wanted to cry over remembering high school, her rape, and everything that had happened with Tom. She couldn't take anymore and sat on the arm of the couch next to Betty who reached for her hand and held it in friendly reassurance.

"Darrell, please, you don't want her to start screaming. It can get really loud when she's mad."

"You're telling me? Jeez, every time we had sex, she practically burst my eardrums. I'm pretty sure that's why

I'm losing my hearing."

There was a community gasp, and all eyes were now on Sally. Betty cackled. "Oh, gosh, that's true. I remember that time we were staying with friends in New Orleans, and you decided to show up. They ended up giving the two of you the studio across the courtyard, so you'd have some privacy, and none of us got any sleep that night with Sally's periodic screaming. The next morning, I apologized and told them her back had gone out."

"I remember that. I'd gone to the courtyard with my coffee and had to reassure everyone that she was fine."

"Oh, and there was the time we were in Mexico and one of her old beaus had followed us there and—"

"Thelma! You can stop now." Sally felt like her face was on fire.

"Hey, you told me you only did that with me. When was this Mexico thing?"

"It's none of your business. Just leave."

Darrell was now sporting a cocky grin. "You know, I bet there're a lot of stories your friends would love hearing, like about that time you wanted to tie me up and then the—"

"Darrell!" Sally stood abruptly. "Okay, everyone, out!" She waited until her friends reluctantly filed out then slammed the door. "This is blackmail. You know that, don't you?"

"What's a little blackmail between friends. We've known each other a long, long time. And we know things about each other no one else knows."

"Until today, you mean." She ambled to the couch and slid down into it.

He took a chair across from her. "I've missed you."

"I haven't missed you. But I have thought of you a lot. Every time my back hurts so much I can't function, or when my hips lock up and I can barely walk, or when I catch a reflection of myself limping around like an old cripple. So, yeah, asshole, I've thought of you *a lot*."

"You still look as beautiful. I've always thought you were one of the prettiest women I've ever seen."

For a brief second, she felt a slight warmth somewhere around her heart, but it was quickly gone. "Cut the crap and get to what you're doing here."

He sat forward in the chair and leaned in toward her. "I'm looking for a place. I thought I could rent for a while then hopefully buy."

"You're moving back?" The idea made her stomach knot.

He nodded.

"Why?"

"Moving to Los Angeles and going to work for *that woman* made me realize how fucked up I was."

"*That woman* has a name. Madeleine, I believe. Or Maddy as you liked to call her when you were throwing her in my face."

"Look, there was never anything real between us. All she wanted was an escort and a *boy* to boss around and do her bidding."

"And all you wanted was a nurse and a purse. Sounds like a match made in heaven to me."

"I deserve that. And I'm so fucking sorry for all of it. I felt really guilty for what I let happen to you, and I couldn't stand the way you looked at me after that. I saw the repulsion and pain in your eyes, and I couldn't take it. I screwed up everything and can't take any of it back. But I want you to know that I have regretted every single miserable day not sticking around and being here for you."

Sally felt like there must be something wrong with her. She was listening to him and almost believed what she was hearing. Watching him, she couldn't remember him ever looking sincere before. But she was sure of one thing. She didn't have any fight left in her right now, and she was so damned tired.

"Darrell, I'll make a deal with you. I'm too exhausted to talk about all this right now. And I've still got things to go over with the girls before I can go home and get some sleep. If you just back off for twenty-four hours and let me take care of business and get some rest, I can meet you tomorrow evening for drinks or…oh, sorry, I forgot. Okay not drinks, maybe dinner or something, and we can discuss whatever you want. But right now isn't the time or place."

His eyes brightened in victory, a look Sally remembered all too well when he managed to get his way.

"You can still have drinks. It won't bother me. How about drinks *and* dinner? My treat."

"Oh, damned right, Darrell. It's definitely going to be your treat."

She stood, held the door open, and waited for him to step out of her office. Just before she closed it behind him, she heard, "I'll be in touch." *Of course, you will*, she thought and leaned against the door wondering how men could be so obtuse…but mostly, how Tom could have crushed her like he did and how she would ever get over it.

Chapter 31

Thomas

Thomas stood, gave Betty a peck on the cheek, and pulled a chair out for her. "Thank you for agreeing to meet me for dinner."

When they were seated, she looked him in the eyes and put a hand on his arm. "I'm glad you called me about Sally's watch, but you could have dropped it by the office or put it in her mailbox."

He sighed and laid fingers gently on top of hers. "Indeed, I could have, but we both know why I contacted you."

She withdrew her hand. "To talk about her…about what happened. Tommy, I agreed because I've got some questions of my own. I'm not taking everything Sally thinks she remembers at face value. But I expect some damn honest answers from you, because right now I could kick myself for pushing her to take you on as a client. I had no idea things would move so fast between the two of you. She holds most men off for years."

He leaned back in his seat and crossed his arms. "You're no more surprised than I am. We had a connection. Everything just clicked like we'd known each other our whole lives."

"Well, you almost have except she just didn't remember it."

Put like that, the thought made him sad, and he glanced away with a slight shake of his head before looking back at her. "Your questions? Ask away, then it's my turn."

The waitress came and took their drink order. When she left, Betty put her reading glasses on and stared at the menu thoughtfully. "I want to know what happened in high school." She looked up and put the glasses on top of her head. "Everything, Tommy, I mean *everything*."

"I had a crush on her. We liked the same things, were in several of the same classes. We partnered in lab, sometimes met after school to work on assignments. The chemistry teacher had let us come in after classes to work on a project in one of the annexes. It was just the two of us, and a thunderstorm had blown in out of nowhere. She grabbed my hand, led me outside, and talked about how much she loved storms. It started raining, and she did this little pagan dance then said—"

"Glorious, isn't it?"

He smiled and nodded.

"She's been saying that ever since I've known her."

"And still does. Anyway, she looked so damned enticing I said, 'Yes, very glorious,' and kissed her. I didn't know I was going to do it. It was spontaneous, in the moment. But more than that, she kissed me back."

"Sally? Wasn't she seeing that college guy then?"

Thomas shrugged. "Yeah, she was, and that's why she pulled away. She told me she had a boyfriend, and I think she felt a little guilty. But the way she'd kissed me was like she meant it. I was confused. It was almost as if she'd slapped me. Instead of saying I understood, I got defensive. I told her the guys had dared me to do it and I really hadn't wanted to. I was young, an idiot with a crush on a girl that thought I was her friend, and I blew it."

Betty's eyes narrowed, and she leaned forward, lowering her voice. "That in itself was a jackass thing to tell her, but did you know about Billy raping her?"

He leaned in and looked her in the eyes with as much sincerity as he felt. "For the love of God, hell no. Does anyone get it? I had the biggest crush on her. I would have wanted to kill anyone who harmed her. Billy wouldn't have told me. And if he had, he would have said it was consensual, in which case I kind of doubt I would have kissed her."

"Maybe you thought you could score, too."

He leaned back again. "I get how it could look that way. Believe me, I understand how she could have thought that. But that wasn't what happened. I had no idea about any of it, much less how it happened. So, do you know? Can you enlighten me?"

Their drinks came, and they placed their dinner orders. When the waitress left, Betty rested her arms on the table. "Evidently, something to do with her helping him with homework. I remember her always helping other kids, especially those that couldn't afford a tutor. He'd asked her to come over one evening, and when she got there, he told her his parents were out of town. He'd been drinking and smoking pot…who knows what else. She tried to leave, but he convinced her he really needed her to stay and help him with an essay or something. And when she was settled and going over things with him, I guess he just pounced."

Thomas felt sick, pushed his drink to the side, and put his hand to his mouth. After a moment, he brought it down and clenched his other hand. "And she would have fought, and he would have hurt her. The little bastard, he was always a piece of shit, but I put up with him because we were in sports together. I haven't seen him in years, but I'd love nothing more than to knock the living hell out of him."

"Well, you might get your chance. Our class is having that big fiftieth reunion in a few months and is honoring E.T. Duncan, the author who wrote *The Reunion*. Surely, you've been contacted about it."

For a brief moment he thought about telling her the truth, that he and Elaine had written it, based off what happened with Sally all those years ago…that he and his deceased wife were E.T. Duncan. But he wasn't ready to share that yet. "Is Billy going to be there?" He hated the idea of Sally having to see him so soon after remembering what he'd done to her.

Betty shrugged. "I don't know. I've been so busy with Widower Whisperers and at the hospital with Adi I haven't kept up. Truthfully, with all that's happened, I don't know if Sally still plans on going." Suddenly, Betty's eyes got huge. "Look, quick." She pointed toward the hostess station.

At first, he didn't see what she was talking about then leaned to his left to look between two columns blocking his view. And there she was in all her glory, Sally Estes, with a man he didn't recognize. His heart went up to his throat, and he felt sucker punched. Sitting up straight, he stared at Betty suspiciously. "Did she see us? Did you tell her we were meeting? And who in the hell is that man she's with?"

"Whoa, down boy…just stay calm. No, I'm pretty sure she didn't see us. They went to the other side, away from the bar area. No, I did not tell her I was meeting you or what I was doing after work. She probably assumed I was going to the hospital. And that man, my friend, is Sally's ex...kind of ex, since they were off again more than they were on. And now, he's supposed to be an ex-alcoholic, here to prove to her that he's changed. God only knows what he really wants."

Thomas put his hand out. "Okay, let me get this straight. This is the guy that she has PTSD from...the narcissist that gives her flashbacks and makes her shudder and shake?"

"That would be him. Darrell Normand in the flesh."

"And just like that, she's gone back with him?" He wanted to hurl.

Betty shook her head. "I hope not. He just showed up."

"What do you mean just showed up?"

"She didn't tell you anything, did she?"

He took a deep breath. "No, I guess our girl likes to keep a lot to herself."

"Darrell moved off to Los Angeles with some woman, and they were going to do this big business deal together. She had tons of money, and I guess he thought it was his chance to get his share. Things had gone sour between him and Sally after the accident."

"The one that left her with the limp and all that pain?"

She nodded. "The one Darrell caused."

Thomas felt the color drain from his face.

"Oh dear, she didn't tell you about that either. Well, Darrell's a drunk...or was, if he's to be believed. They'd been broken up, but he'd talked her into having drinks with him. He's a charmer that one, and of course he wanted to go early...never one to miss a happy hour. He insisted on ordering the signature martini, and after they each had a couple, they were pretty well lit. Sally just wanted to go home, but on the way, he claimed to be starving and coerced her into having dinner. It turned out to be an excuse for him to drink more. He had another martini there, but she refused and opted for water. Then he ordered a bottle of wine with dinner. Sally just took a couple of sips to be polite, but he finished off the bottle and chugged the rest of her glass when they were leaving."

Thomas shook his head. "He sure wasn't fit to drive. Was it a car accident?"

Betty leaned back with a smug look on her face. "Let's just say it was more like a train wreck. Sally was furious at him and at herself for agreeing to go out with him in the first place. She tried talking him into letting her drive, but like a great con and typical drunk, he convinced her he was okay. When they got to her house, he parked in the driveway in back and tried to talk her into letting him come in. She told him no and offered to call an Uber for him. Of course, he refused. She got tired of arguing and was getting out of the car. He jumped from his side and went around to hers while she was getting her purse. He grabbed her and was trying to kiss her, put his hands where she didn't want them. She jerked away from him, her foot twisted, and she went sideways off her high heel wedges."

"So, you're saying he was trying to force himself on her?"

Betty nodded. "It's a disease…alcoholism. In his mind, I guess he didn't think there was anything wrong with it, since they were off and on for a few years."

Thomas shook his head and took a swig of his drink.

"There is never a good excuse for a man to push himself on a woman who doesn't want it."

"Of course, there isn't. You and I know that but try telling it to a majority of the men out there. Anyway, she'd dropped her phone in the process of trying to get away from him, and he picked it up, put it in his pocket, and because her foot hurt like hell, Darrell ended up helping her into the house. They made it as far as the couch in her living room then he excused himself to use the restroom and never came back."

"What do you mean he never came back?"

She shrugged again. "It was a Sunday morning, and we had plans…breakfast at Mozart's then walking it off at one of the trails around the lake. She was really big into marathons and was always looking for an excuse to jog. I was supposed to pick Sally up at her house. I texted and called to let her know I was on the way but never got a response. When I honked, she didn't come out. It was clear Darrell was there because of his car in the drive, so I let myself in prepared to catch them in bed. I was pissed. But what I found was Sally on the living room floor and that son-of-bitch passed out on top of her bed."

"What happened to Sally?"

"When Darrell never came back to the living room, Sally tried to stand to go look for him and get her phone. Her foot had started swelling and bruising, the pain was excruciating, and she wanted to go to the ER. She stood, the pain causing her leg to go out from under her, and her back hit the corner of the coffee table then she went down and hit the floor sideways on her hip. She told me she'd screamed for Darrell, but he'd never come. She'd tried crawling but was too weak to get very far. She was like that all night…finally passing out from the pain and sheer exhaustion."

"Jesus, I can't even imagine…it makes me sick to think about the suffering she must have gone through."

"You have no idea. When I got there, she couldn't get up or move. I called an ambulance then woke Darrell up. He didn't remember anything about the night before. Her phone was on the bed next to him. I guess in his stupor, the ringing and text alerts bothered him, and he'd shut it off. Sally ended up having back *and* hip surgery. Three disks were smashed from hitting the table. The foot wasn't broken but had soft tissue damage, and over the years, she's had to have two surgeries on it and has never been the same. Never been without pain, never been able to wear the same clothes or heels, though sometimes she's tried when she wants to impress someone."

Thomas smiled. "I felt so awful for her that day. She was making a valiant effort, but I could tell she was having trouble walking in those heels. It must have hurt like hell. So, she was really trying to impress me?"

Betty leaned back and smirked. "Tommy, even at our ripe old ages, we've still got some vanity left in us. Though she didn't admit it till later, she was flattered and a little intrigued by the whole thing…she's a woman. She wanted to look good. Funny thing about her is she's the last person you'd think of as a hopeless romantic, but deep down she believes in it. She always says, 'Love is all there is or ever will be.' "

Funny, Ellie used to say almost the exact same thing. "But she's been hurt so much…"

"So many, many times."

Chapter 32

Sally

Sally and Darrell were finishing their meals, and in an odd way she was glad she'd agreed to join him. They'd been friends for over fifteen years, a great deal of that time with benefits. There was a part of her that had genuinely missed him. And being with him when he was sober was somewhat enjoyable.

"But, Darrell, where do you want to rent?"

"I was hoping somewhere close to you or maybe you'd like to lease out your spare bedroom."

She was taking a sip of tea and almost choked. "Oh no, you don't. Forget it, it's not happening."

"Because of you being out all night and coming in the next morning with *the look*?" He gave her the little boy grin and tilted his head. "Don't lie to me, baby. I'm well aware of what you look like when you've been having sex all night. Surely, you haven't forgotten."

She could feel her cheeks burning and took another sip. "None of it's any of your business. You gave those rights up three years ago when you laid in my bed talking to another woman like I wasn't even there."

"I fucked up. I was angry at you because I felt so guilty for the accident. I wanted to punish you for making me feel that way, if that makes any sense to you." He shrugged. "I learned a lot about myself in therapy.

But you've always been *my girl*, my friend, my constant, and you will always be my business. Something's eating at you. I can see it in your eyes. I've made you sad often enough that I know *that* look, too."

He'd always had a way of making her want to share her most intimate thoughts with him, and over the years, she had…as he'd done with her. "I don't know, Darrell. I'm really confused. I didn't think I had it left in me after everything with you."

"What? Tell me, baby." He put a hand over hers and squeezed. "You always deserved a hell of a lot better than me…we both know that."

"To love again…fall hopelessly *in* love."

She took her hand back, pushed her half-eaten plate to the side, rested her elbows on the table, and put her head in her hands, trying to get her thoughts together. When she looked back at him, her eyes were misty, but she was determined to tell him everything, starting with Billy Markham raping her. When she finished her story about Tom, ending with him getting a girl pregnant in high school, proving he was just another lech, Darrell moved over to the chair next to her, pushed it close to hers, and wrapped his arms around her.

"Pardon me, I don't mean to intrude on anything *personal*."

That voice! The sarcasm. Sally pulled away from the embrace to find Tom standing in front of them with Betty closing in. "Sorry, I tried to stop him," she said apologetically.

Tom completely ignored her. "You won't answer or return my texts or phone calls, so I met with Betty to return your watch. You left it the other morning. But since you're here…such a small world…I decided to do it in person." He calmly took her watch from his jean's pocket and laid it on the table. "And you must be?"

Darrell stood and held out his hand. "Darrell Normand, an old friend of Sally's."

"Ah, yes, Betty's been filling me in about you. I guess it's like they say, with friends like you, who needs enemies?" He ignored the other man's hand and kept his eyes on Sally.

"Tom!"

"Tommy!"

Darrell withdrew his offer to shake. "No, ladies, it's okay. I deserved that, baby." He looked earnestly down at Sally.

Betty was behind Thomas tugging on his shirt. "We need to go *now*."

He glanced in the other man's direction. "Darrell…" He gave a slight tilt of his head, hesitated, then looked at Sally again. "*Baby*, enjoy the rest of your evening." Turning, he took Betty's elbow and led her out the front door without a backward glance.

Sally wasn't aware she'd been holding her breath until they'd left and suddenly exhaled loudly, causing Darrell to turn and stare down at her again.

"Thomas Fitzsimmons, I presume?"

She nodded.

"Nice-looking man. I won't ask if he's better in bed than I am."

"Darrell! *Really*?"

He sat, scooting the chair close. "I know you. I know the way you shut down and don't return calls…the way you ghost people."

"Well, I learned from the best. You were a great teacher."

"I'm sorry for everything, and I want to prove it to you. I want to win you back but not unless you give this guy a chance. Hear him out at least. Maybe he really didn't know about the Billy guy."

Her stomach was knotted as she shook her head. "I can't…I remember how I felt back then, like the wind being knocked out of me. It's the kind of shame and embarrassment you never get over. And it doesn't help that I remember I cared a great deal about Tom…I guess I had my own crush going on but thought he saw me as just a friend…I don't want to relive anymore pain. I cried every day for weeks and felt like my heart had been torn out of me. Poor Patrick, the nerdy college guy I was dating, was oblivious, and I let him stay that way. I've had enough heartache to last me the rest of what I have left of my life."

"And I caused a lot of it."

"Oh, stop, damn it, you're making us both seem pathetic. Believe it or not, Darrell, you're not all that…I got over you, and you taught me so many lessons."

He looked down and shook his head. "If you're trying to be cruel, you're doing a good job of it. But this isn't like you."

"Why? Because I'm being truthful and not trying to spare your feelings?"

"Is that what you did all those years, spare my feelings?"

She looked him in the eyes. "Yes, I did…because I cared about you."

"Do you still care about me?"

She bit her lip, glanced away, then met his eyes again, determined to be nothing but truthful. "Yes, but not the way I feel about Tom. You and I were friends for such a long time. It was easy, and we were comfortable with each other. When we were both finally single at the same time and were sleeping together, for a while I thought I was in love with you. But your drinking, your forgetting entire conversations, much less that you lost complete chunks of time…drunken binges where you'd call me and tell me how much you loved me and wanted to be with me, only to turn around later and forget it all and accuse me of imagining or making it up. The narcissistic things you'd say and do."

"That was the booze, baby. The counselor explained to me that alcoholics mimic narcissists. Do you know what it's like not to remember all those things, to lose those chunks of your life, to blackout entire days or weeks?"

She gave him an incredulous look. "You think I might have some small idea, Darrell, after everything I told you earlier? See, this is what always happened. Whatever was going on with me, you made it about you." She was starting to get angry. "Have you ever genuinely cared about how anyone else was feeling? Tom, I can't imagine what he felt walking up while you were giving me a hug. No matter what I think of him or what he did back then, I don't want to see him hurt. And there you were, calling me baby, acting like we were *together*."

"You used to like it when I called you baby."

"No, no, I didn't. You call every female baby. I hated it and I tried to tell you how much, but you couldn't hear me, because all you could think about was yourself and when you could get your hands on the next drink."

"You know I couldn't help it. I'm like a little boy in an old-man costume."

"That's just it. I don't want a little boy, a bad boy,

any *boy*…I want a grown-ass man, and he just walked out of here with my best friend."

She stood, tossed her napkin on the table, and pushed her chair back, wanting desperately to get home and just be alone. "Here's the truth without sparing your feelings. You'll never change, Darrell. You're too old now. Even if you never take another drink, which I pray you don't, that personality is ingrained in you, and there's nothing you can do about it. I used to believe you could, but I was wrong. My mother always told me a leopard doesn't change its spots, but I didn't believe her. I thought I was so special I could help anyone, and they'd change for me or because of me. But I sure as hell proved myself wrong enough times. But not anymore…I'm done. Thanks for dinner, *baby*."

She felt him watching her as she headed for the exit, but she didn't care. Suddenly, for the first time she could remember with Darrell, she felt empowered. Finally, she'd broken the hold he'd had on her. The come hither, go away, the feeling sorry for him, the little fibs to spare his feelings, the covering up for him, making excuses for him, the tug he'd always managed to keep on her heartstrings…they were broken now, and she sighed with relief. At almost seventy years old, she had learned to take her life back. And it felt damn good.

Chapter 33

Thomas

It had been a few days since the incident at the restaurant. Betty had been furious with him for going up to Sally's table with his badass routine, and now she wasn't talking to him either. Thomas was heading into The Widower Whisperers' headquarters to try to catch Frank before he left for lunch, just as Darrell was walking out the front door. They both stopped and stared at each other.

"It won't do you any good," Darrell said, backtracking into the doorway.

"What?" Thomas asked suspiciously.

"Lily's the only one in there. All the girls are at an early lunch."

Thomas shrugged. "I came to see Frank."

"He's with the girls. Doesn't really matter as far as I'm concerned. Sally's refusing to speak to me. Betty hates me. I'm the biggest asshole Peg's ever met." He grinned. "I think Jewel kind of liked me, but she's gone back to Dallas and her girlfriend."

Thomas wasn't about to feel sorry for him, but he was curious. "What did you do to Sally this time?"

"I know you've made up your mind about me, and I don't blame you for it." Darrell methodically took his sunglasses from his shirt pocket, put them on, and started walking. "How about lunch? Maybe I can clear some things up for you."

At first, Thomas was shocked at the invitation and just watched him walk away then the next moment he was hot on his heels. "What do you mean clear up some things?"

Darrell slowed down and glanced over his shoulder. "I figure if you really do care about Sally, you're bound to have questions…just like I do."

"Just like you do?"

"You answer questions with questions. Do you realize that?"

"No, I don't. Where are you going, and would you slow the hell down?"

Darrell stopped short and turned to face him. "I'm hungry. I'm going to walk until I find food or get to my car, whichever comes first."

"There's a cafeteria around the corner."

"You mean like for old people? Perfect. You in?"

Thomas nodded. *What the hell. Maybe I can learn something that will help me with Sally.*

They walked side by side the rest of the way in silence and didn't speak again until they'd gotten their trays of food and were seated. After each man meticulously arranged their dishes and set their trays on an empty table next to them, Darrell started chuckling.

"Well, if this isn't the perfect picture of a couple of old farts. I would have put my green beans next to the liver and onions, but…"

Thomas stuck a fork in his chess pie and took a bite. "You eat your way, and I'll eat mine."

"Like dessert first?"

His mouth was full, and he nodded.

"I'm jealous." Darrell took his hat off and placed it in an empty chair.

Thomas's stomach did a flip-flop, unsure of what he was referring to, and he looked up from his food.

Darrell picked up his fork and pointed at the other man's head. "All that thick white hair." He sighed. "Life isn't fair sometimes."

For the first time, Thomas focused on the other man's bald head with the scruffy gray around the bottom with a feeling of superiority that made him smile childishly. "You know what they say about bald men. Aren't you all supposed to have big…appendages?"

Darrell looked stunned then thoughtful. "Well, maybe not so much after a certain age."

"That's odd."

"What?"

"I didn't expect you to actually be humble."

Darrell swallowed his food then took a sip of water. "Oh, trust me, there was nothing humble about me when I was on the booze. I built myself up by putting other people down…hurting people I loved."

"So, you have it all under control now?"

"I will never have it under control. There will always be the urge to have just that one drink to calm my nerves or to give me that little boost of courage or to numb my reality."

For a moment, Thomas believed he could see the pain behind Mr. Normand's eyes and felt sorry for him. "It's got to be tough."

"Hardest thing I've ever done…getting sober. But it was worth it just to see how badly I'd screwed up my entire life. My wife…I still love her. She's the mother of my children. But she kicked me out when she found out

I was having an affair. I'd had good jobs, made damn good money…but I blew it on booze, a few drugs here and there. Eventually, I'd get fired. It was more than the affair; it was always having to pick up the pieces and try to keep things together while I was always the good-time boy, the quintessential life of the party.

"I lived with a couple of women over the years after, but it always ended up the same. Sally and I had worked together briefly when she was going through her last divorce. We became friends, told each other everything…at least as much of everything as you tell the opposite sex. We flirted, but nothing came of it. She always held me off. I never really thought anything *would* come of it. She stuck around while I went through different women, was always there for support when I was down. Then one day we were both single at the same time. And I pushed it, the sex thing. She'd warned me it would ruin our friendship, and it did. Along with me getting drunk and thinking I was madly in love with her, then the next day, resenting her because I'd acted like that. I was never fair to her."

Thomas had stopped eating and was staring at him. "But she cared about you. You were her friend, and she stuck around to be there for you." It was a statement, not a question.

He nodded. "You know the old saying about hurting the ones you love. But there are different kinds of love, you know that."

Thomas thought about his first wife, Gayle, and how they'd been more friends than anything…then about Elaine and how she'd been like his soulmate, sharing likes, dislikes, values, morals, everything…then how he felt about Sally, almost like she'd been his first love and he'd never gotten over her… "To a degree I know. But I haven't had your vast experience." It came out sharper than he'd intended.

"Whoa! So, let me ask you something. Did you know back then about her getting raped by your friend?"

The question caught him off guard, and Thomas leaned back in the chair. "I did not. If I had, I'd have probably done something I would have regretted."

"Yeah, I'd love to get my hands on that asswipe. I might be a drunk, but I've never raped anyone."

"But you did push yourself on her when the whole *accident* happened."

Darrell looked down at his plate and ran a hand over the top of his shiny head. "For the longest time, I thought Sally had made it up. I didn't remember any of it. After I got sober, bits and pieces starting coming through. But I wouldn't have raped her. I was just trying to get her to let me go in with her…I didn't know she'd twist away like that and hurt her foot."

For some reason, Thomas wanted to believe him. "Listen, I think I've loved Sally in my own way from the time we were teenagers, if a crush can be called love. I didn't know about her being raped, and I regret with all my heart what I said to her."

"You said you don't have my experience. What about the girl you got pregnant who had to leave school?"

Chapter 34

Darrell

"So, that was the rumor?" He shook his head. "Gayle was my best friend's sister. Victor died in Vietnam along with our friend, Dale, the father of Gayle's baby. I married her to give the baby a father out of respect for the sacrifice my friends made."

Darrell was nonplussed, pushed his plate away, and stared steadily at Thomas. *Unbelievable. This guy's a fucking saint.* "So, you're saying that you didn't get anyone pregnant in high school, but that you honored them by giving her a husband, a name, and a father for the baby."

"Correct. Gayle did drop out. But gossip went around because I'd been seen with her...sharing our grief."

Darrell let out a long slow whistle. "So, you really are one of the good guys."

Thomas shrugged. "Either one of them would have done the same for me and my child if it had been reversed. Plus, I cared about Gayle. She was like a kid sister. Our families were best friends. It hardly makes me a saint."

Darrell's own shortcomings were tugging on his conscience. "Does the child know?"

"Indeed, Victoria Dale is a beautiful woman now

209

who has given us amazing grandchildren. And yes, we explained it to her when she was old enough to understand. She still thinks of me as her father. Gayle and I had a daughter together, Annabelle, and they're as close as any sisters could be."

Darrell's head bent, and he stared at his hands resting on the table. "I have two daughters, too. But I messed everything up with them. I cheated on my wife, lied, twisted everything trying to blame it on her." He glanced up and almost flinched at the condescending look on Thomas's face. "I know what you're thinking. But I was a damn good father all those years they were growing up."

"I'm not judging you. Things happen. People change. We all have to live with the consequences of our actions."

Darrell was starting to feel genuine respect for the man sitting across from him and wanted to open up. "I'd started having a few health issues. I'd never taken that good of care of myself. The sedentary life of an accountant. They put me on medications, you know blood pressure, etc., and I started feeling weird like in my mind…paranoid, I guess.

"About that time, Mary, my wife, got her license and started working for a real estate company. The girls were away at college, and she was bored. There was always something going on and afterhours events. It seemed like she was never home, and I…I was fucking jealous. I'd convinced myself she was sleeping with her broker. I started drinking more which was a lousy mix with the meds. It was like I'd gone middle-aged crazy. Then a client complained that I was intoxicated at a meeting I had with him, and I got laid off."

Darrell rubbed a vibrating hand over the top of his skull before holding it out in front of him. "See this. This is what all the damn medications have done to me. I've got tremors now."

Thomas nodded. "I understand all the side effects of meds. It's something Elaine and I researched in depth. There are things you can do to help get off them."

Darrell put the hand in his lap and held it steady with the other one. "Anyway, long story short, I ended up having an affair with Mary's best friend. I don't know why. I was just craving some attention and…I was being vengeful. You know, what's good for the goose is also good for the gander and vice versa. Turns out she wasn't having an affair at all but was getting paid to work extra hours for some of the hot-shot agents so she could surprise me with a trip to Europe for our thirtieth anniversary." He paused, a look of agony marring his otherwise pleasant face.

"Jesus," Thomas whispered.

"Of course, Mary found out and confronted her friend first. I was trapped. There was no way out except for her *kicking* me out. I made things worse and moved in with her friend who was widowed. That's when I really became a drunk. My daughters wouldn't have anything to do with me…had blocked my number even. Eventually, I left Houston and moved here to Austin, made up a whole new background of lies for myself, and went to work in the insurance business. I missed my daughters' graduations from college, their weddings, the birth of my first two grandchildren." He shrugged. "The rest is a long story. We're okay now, and they tolerate me, but I spent all those years hiding in a bottle, going from one woman to another…still in love with my ex-wife."

There was something accusing in Thomas's eyes. "Sally…you're thinking about her and what she meant to me…if anything."

Again, Thomas silently nodded.

"I care about her. And I love her in my own way. I was never fair to her, since I was still in love with the mother of my children. We were good friends. A hell of a lot better friends than we were lovers. I was a liar and a cheat with her. Sometimes I hated that she could see through me and for being one of the only people who knew the truth about me and would call me out. I love you; I hate you; I hate that I love you, like that song. Then the accident and I ruined her life. I couldn't accept what I'd done, so I hurt her even more. And then she was finally finished. If it makes you feel any better, she was never really in love with me. Not the way I think she is with you."

"Huh, you think so?"

"She as much as told me, right before she walked out on me the other night at the restaurant." He leaned in, lowering his voice. "So, tell me something, Saint Thomas, what happened to your first marriage?"

Thomas ignored the barb and leaned forward, his eyes staring earnestly into Darrell's. "I told you, she was like a little sister. I was like a big brother. We loved each other but were never *in love*. We pretended, tried to make a go of it until we finally agreed it was time to let each other go. And that's what we did. No drama, no fighting. Just mutual respect for each other and our children."

Darrell had a lump in his throat for how badly he'd screwed his own life up. "And Sally?"

The shrug again. "I fell for her the second I saw her

sitting at my desk when I walked into class. She was pretty and funny and smart and whimsical. She was my first and last crush." Thomas told him the story about kissing her, feeling rejected, and lying to save face. "Elaine was my soulmate, but she understood that there really are different kinds of love just like you said, and that given the chance, Sally just might end up being the love of my life. I was skeptical. Couldn't imagine life without Ellie. But the first time Sally came traipsing into the business warehouse in high heels and unabashedly admitted she couldn't walk in the damn things, I felt a pull on my heartstrings."

"You know it's the damnedest thing about that woman. She is vain as hell, and one minute your thinking what a fucking diva she is then the next, she's laughing at herself and making jokes. And she has a way of putting people at ease, like her home is your home and that you can confide in her, tell her anything."

Thomas raised an eyebrow. "Sounds like you still care about her."

"Losing her and getting sober made me realize how much she really meant to me. I was so used to her always being there, having her shoulder to cry on... When she wasn't there anymore, it hurt like hell. Hurt enough for me to start thinking about what I'd done to everyone I ever cared about. I'm moving back here with the intention of getting her back. But I told her she has to give you a chance."

Thomas chuckled, stood, and held out his hand. "Well, let the best man win."

Darrell pushed his chair back, got up, and they shook. "Just one thing though."

"What?"

"I kind of like you. You think we can still hang out and be bros?"

Thomas threw an arm around his shoulder and squeezed. "Absolutely, my friend." He then turned Darrell to face him. "But you do one thing to hurt Sally Estes again and I will run you out of this town and destroy what life you have left." He smiled, gave him a pat on the back, and they started walking out.

As they passed the teenage hostess, she hollered at them. "Hey, goodbye, you crazy kids. Come back real soon."

Darrell stopped, glanced over his shoulder, then stared at Thomas. "Tell me she did not just call us *crazy kids*. I can't stand being talked to like I'm a feeble dimwit."

Thomas's face was flushed, and he gave Darrell a little nudge. "Just keep walking, bro, just keep walking."

Chapter 35

The BABs (Bad Ass Bitches)

Frank slapped his hands flat on the conference table then stood. "Ladies, I don't know what the hell is going on between you all, but you seriously need to stop and get your respective shit together. We were supposed to use this time to talk about the problem clients and make some decisions on the best way to handle them. Carole, you're about the only one who's acting like she's not one of the mean girls in high school."

Carole looked at Frank and shook her head. "Well, lunch sure wasn't any more fun than this meeting. I've never seen them like this. Oh sure, there's constant bickering, especially between Thelma and Louise, but it's not like Peg to be so quiet. She's usually rattling off everything she's thinking." She stared at her friend accusingly, followed by Frank.

"Hey, I'm just trying to stay out of this one. I wasn't there. I don't know what happened. Doors slamming scare me."

"I didn't mean to slam it." Betty turned sideways on the couch to look at her.

"Oh whatever! And, Sally, you weren't nice to Bruce earlier when he wanted your attention. I've never seen you like that."

Frank glanced at his watch. "Well, it's four-thirty,

and as delightful as this has been, I think I'm going to leave and find a happy hour somewhere. You want to join me, Peggy?"

She didn't have to be asked twice, jumped from her seat, then started to head out the door with him.

"Halt!"

Peggy turned and stared wide-eyed at Carole.

"You sit your butt right back down on that couch. No one but Frank is leaving here until we get this thing straightened out."

Frank gave a weak grin. "Call me when you're through." He made sure his whisper was loud enough for all of them to hear then scurried out of the conference room.

Peg stuck her hands on her hips. "Look at you all. If I didn't know any better, I'd say that man is afraid of the way you're acting."

"Well, no one likes stepping on a hornet's nest. He'll get over it. Sit!" Carole went to the small fridge hidden in the credenza, pulled out a bottle of champagne, and started opening it.

Sally scowled from where she sat at the head of the table as far away as she could get from Betty. "And exactly what are we celebrating?"

Opening another door, Carole grabbed four flutes by their stems and set them on the table. "Oh, you and Betty of course. Congratulations on whatever this nonsense is about because you've just succeeded in making me want to go back and listen to more crap from that batshit crazy ass who's really *still* married but stalking me. He claims he's trying to figure out how to *win the girl*, which would be me. He has no sense of reality and doesn't care that I'm engaged to Calam or that he has a wife. But after dealing with this all afternoon, I'll take him any day."

"What do you mean still married? I thought we vetted him." Sally looked concerned.

"Ah, he's a clever one. He *was* divorced. But they recently went to Vegas and remarried…so, during the time he was being vetted, he was technically single. And quit trying to change the subject." She filled the glasses and passed them around then sat at the opposite end of the table. "Peggy, do you have any clue what happened?"

She shook her head then took a sip. "All I know is that it's been going on since last week. It was easy to ignore at first…well, make that until today. I heard some of the screaming going on one morning between the doors opening and slamming. I think Betty went out with Tommy and Sally went out with Darrell, but after that I'm not sure what happened."

"Betty, why were you out with Thomas?"

She'd already drained her glass, was licking the bubbly residue off her lips, and held it out for more. "Okay, this is not my fault. I was trying to be a good friend."

"Hmph," Sally snorted.

"Oh, get off your high horse. I wasn't doing anything wrong. He contacted me because you were too childish to return his calls or texts. You know…doing your runaway ghosting thing you always do."

Sally started to speak, but Carole stopped her. "You'll have your turn. Proceed, Betty."

"So, Sally left her watch that night she slept with him. I guess she was in such a hurry to get home to Darrell—"

"Oh, you bitch! You know damn good and well I didn't know he was there."

Betty looked at her askance with a little shrug. "Maybe."

Carole glared at Sally. "Would you stop? Please? Seriously, I want to get to the bottom of all this and have it over with. We're Widower Whisperers for goodness sakes." She refilled Betty's glass. "And *you*, quit pushing her buttons. We all know she didn't know Darrell was at her house."

"It's fun antagonizing her." Betty gave a smug catlike grin.

"Yeah, and you've been doing it since you all were teenagers, and that's how you still act. Jeez, just go on."

"Okay, Tommy contacted me because he wanted to return the watch, so I agreed to meet him for dinner. I figured he really just wanted to talk, and I was anxious to get some info out of him. *And* I was making headway, thank you very much, when Sally came waltzing into the same restaurant with old reprobate Darrell."

"I didn't even see you all."

Carole gave Sally the evil eye, and Betty went on.

"Well, we saw *them*, and then it was pretty useless trying to get Tommy to talk after that. All he could think about was her there with another man which happened to be her old beau. He's crazy about her. It's obvious. He was trying to act all cool and all about Darrell, but his jaw was so tight I thought he was going to break some teeth."

Sally perked right up. "Really?"

"Really. I wasn't there flirting with him or trying to steal your man. The real reason I met him was I wanted to hear from him what had happened back then. I wanted to know in my heart that he hadn't known about the rape. You might not believe this, but I was feeling guilty about pushing you into taking him on as a client and ending up this hurt and miserable. And then seeing you with Darrell. It pissed me off."

"When you all walked up, he was trying to console me. I'd just told him about Tom and the part where he got that poor girl pregnant."

Betty let out a snort of disgust. "Sally, Sally, Sally, will you never learn? Darrell was simply trying to slip back into your good graces. What better situation for him than to decide to move back here right after you've had a heartbreaking experience. I bet he's already planning on helping you put the pieces back together."

"I walked out on him that night."

Peggy gasped, and Carole turned to look at her.

"Don't act so surprised. I told him he'd never change even if he never took another drink, and I walked out. I was upset when he called me baby in front of Tom and—"

"Oh, wait, wait. You don't get to do that." Betty held a red-nailed finger in the air as if testing to see which way the wind was blowing.

"What?"

"Play both ends against the middle. You think Tommy's this awful person that tried to set you up as a laughingstock back in high school, knowing about Billy, by kissing you. From what I hear, you kissed him back…enough for him to have felt that you liked him, which you admit you did. But it doesn't make sense. I believe him when he says he had a crush on you and would have kicked Billy's ass if he'd known. I mean he isn't doubting your story. Why are you doubting his?

"Then you've got Darrell. None of this is any of his business, yet you were out with him, spilling your guts…letting him *comfort* you. Oh, but wait, you walk out on him having known he was never going to change for almost twenty years. I think you just took your frustrations out on him because he was there. You'll feel bad at some point and open that door back up again."

Sally had her thumbnail in her mouth worrying it between her teeth then released a big sigh. "Okay, I'm sorry. You're right. When Tom was standing there and surprised us, my stomach did a flip, and then when I saw you behind him, it did a big old jealous flop. I really think I was falling in love with him. I remember now how crazy I was about him way back then. That's why what he did hurt so much.

"I know you wouldn't try to steal him away. It's just sometimes I'm envious of you. I see you in your cute outfits, wearing heels, making you look all sexy and young, and then I see myself hobbling along in ugly old flats, limping my way through life. And you've always got so much energy, while I don't feel like I have any from the constant pain. I guess what I'm saying is, I wouldn't blame Tom if he did want to date you."

Carole was now pouring the last of the champagne and reached for another bottle. "Hallelujah."

Betty got up, went to Sally, and gave her a hug. "You are still beautiful, you know that. Tommy so does *not* want to date me. I tried my damnedest, but there was no way I could convince him not to go up to your all's table. I might have left claw marks on his shoulder when I tried to hold him back. That man was crushing on you fifty years ago, and he is again. But I was so mad at him for doing that. Confession…it scared me. I'd told him about what Darrell did, about how the accident happened. I could see the anger in his eyes. I didn't know if he was going to coldcock him or what. Then when I saw you all embracing, I couldn't reach Tommy fast enough. I totally lost it when we got outside."

"You all still sound like you're in high school to me." Peggy offered her opinion with a giant smile. Everyone turned to look at her then they all broke into giggles of relief.

"You know, I feel exactly the way I did when I was seventeen. Take away the aging, ailing body, and I'm that same person. Flirting with Tom, getting to laugh and feel joy again, I didn't think about age. Sometimes, when I look in the mirror, I see myself the way I used to be. Now that I remember Tom, that's how I saw him when I left his house that morning…the same handsome boy from all those years ago." Sally held out her glass for a refill while Betty took the chair next to her.

Peggy brought her and Betty's glasses to the table and joined them. "Gosh, I kind of feel the same way, especially when I'm with Frank. I mean we both know we're old physically, but inside we're still the same."

"Okay, speaking of age, there is something that I really, really don't like." Sally paused to make sure all eyes were on her. "When those disgustingly young little pricks call me honey, sweetheart, or some other saccharine name like sugar or sweety." She shuddered. "I cannot stand *love*."

Betty chuckled. "Tell me about it. Don't you all remember that time we were doing our Saturday night thing and this cocky little waiter kept using that term over and over? Sally finally explained to him in great detail how older people do not appreciate punks using endearments that should only be used by loved ones and treating them like they're doddering old fools or little kids."

Everyone nodded and smiled.

Peggy raised her hand. "Oh, oh, *kids*...like that teenage cashier at the cafeteria around the corner. Remember how she's always calling us *you crazy kids*? That makes me an insane old lady."

Sally nodded. "I'd love to have a food fight and get her right in the face with a cream pie."

"Let's do it." Peg chugged her champagne, set the flute on the table, and stood, defiance shining in her soft gray eyes.

Chapter 36

"Down, girl!" Carole stood and retrieved a bottle of wine from the fridge. "Oops, out of the bubbly."

Peg looked around expectantly, but no one moved to back her quest for vengeance. "Really? You all aren't going to go with me?"

Betty put a consoling hand on her arm. "Sit! First of all, we're all exhausted and tipsy. I do not plan on getting arrested for disorderly conduct."

"It would be so worth it."

"Peg, you do not want the Austin police to arrest you for disorderly conduct *and* public intoxication. With the four of us, it would definitely make the papers, and we have the business to consider. I worked for the force, and things were a lot more lenient back then. It's a whole new ball game now." Carole finished opening the wine.

Peggy slumped to her chair and held her glass out. "Well, it would have been fun."

Sally chuckled. "I agree, but the girls are right. Darrell got arrested once for being drunk in public. It was no picnic and very expensive."

"Speaking of, what *are* you all going to do?"

"I don't know, Carole. I can't stand Mr. Normand…never could. And I feel bad for Tommy, but this is not my circus, not my monkeys. I don't want to try to stay friends with him and hurt Sally. Plus, I'm still really mad about the way he acted that night. But I do

223

believe him about not knowing she'd been raped. He was too angry and possessive when he saw her with Darrell." Betty shrugged. "I've been avoiding him since then."

"Look, I'm sorry, Betty. I'm really just mad at myself and taking it out on you. I'm such a damn stickler for the rules, and then I go and break my own. First when I agreed to take Tom on as a client then when I slept with him."

Betty rolled her eyes. "Uh, no. I don't think what you were doing with him was sleeping."

Sally held her glass out in a mock toast. "Touché. And you're not totally correct, there was a little bit of sleeping, but the sex part was awesome." Now they were all staring at her. "Oh, come on, you know you've been dying to ask."

"We didn't have to. As brokenhearted as you've been, it was kind of obvious." Carole put the bottle on the table and sat. "Are you at least going to talk to him?"

She tucked a ginger strand of hair behind her ear and shook her head as tears welled in her eyes and started trickling from the corners. "I don't want to do this anymore. I don't want to hurt like this ever again. I was just starting to get over the damage Darrell had done, and then Tom comes into my life and turns it upside down. If he wasn't guilty on some level, he would have told me. He would have made me remember instead of blindsiding me like that."

Betty shook her head at the other women. "So what do you plan on doing?"

She wiped at her wet cheeks. "Nothing. I don't want to talk to either one of them. I am officially done with men. I've got Bruce, and that's all the testosterone I can handle."

"Oh, I forgot to tell you. When we got back from lunch and everyone hightailed it in here for the meeting, I stopped by and got messages from Lily. Seems like Mr. Normand came by looking for Sally, and Mr. Fitzsimmons was getting ready to come in the building just as Darrell was leaving. Evidently, they walked off together."

This got everyone's attention. "Together?" they asked in unison.

Peg nodded. "According to Lily she could see them through the glass door. She'd already explained to Darrell that everyone was at lunch. As he was going out, she saw him stop and talk to Thomas then walk off, and Thomas follow him."

"Well that's not really, together-together." Betty waved a dismissive hand.

"Oh, no, they were together-together. Lily got up to look out the front window, and she saw Thomas catch up to him."

Sally put her hands out in front of her. "That's it. I'm done."

"What are you going to do about the fiftieth reunion? It's a few months away. You're going, aren't you? You can be my date. Adi will probably still be in rehab."

"I don't give a damn about the reunion. Besides, I don't think I could handle it. What if Billy Markham's there? I don't think I could be in the same room with him. And Tom, he'll more than likely show up just to taunt me." She stood. "Hell, I can't think about any of that right now. I'm still trying to process remembering things from fifty-plus years ago. And now I get to live with the image of Tom and Darrell hanging out together. That's just what I needed."

Sally grabbed her purse hanging on the back of the chair and headed for the door.

"Oh, no, you don't." Betty jumped up and grabbed her arm. "Where do you think you're going?"

"Home. I'm tired."

"And drunk. I'll get us an Uber. I'm going home with you."

Sally turned angrily toward her friend then meeting her eyes she couldn't hold it in any longer and burst out crying, allowing herself to be held in the nurturing arms of her best friend.

Chapter 37

Six Weeks Later
Sally

Sally glanced over at Peggy as she tossed her suitcase in the back of the SUV and climbed in the passenger side. "Thanks for agreeing to go with me."

"Oh, girl, it's fine. I'm excited about it. I know Betty wanted to do the Big Easy with you, but with Adi getting out of rehab and having outpatient physical therapy, she really felt like she needed to be here for him."

"I know and she should. But I'm excited to show you my hometown since you've never been there. And I'm glad to have the company. I've had mixed feelings about what to do with grand-mère's house when Charles passes. Evidently, he's not doing very well."

Peggy squinched her face up. "I'm sorry. I know how much you care about him."

"Yeah, I do. He's a good man and was good for Mom. You know, they'd known each other before she married my father. I'm pretty sure he was one of my mother's paramours. I always knew she was unhappy leaving New Orleans and moving here, but she did it because of Dad's job."

"Frank said his family was originally from Louisiana. It's a small world."

"He's okay about you going with me, isn't he?"

"Oh, sure. Things have been moving so quickly between us I think we both need a little break to try and figure out where it's going."

"You love him, don't you? Like you're *in* love with him, huh?"

They were pulling into a grocery store parking lot, and Peg got unusually quiet, staring straight ahead like she'd seen a ghost. "Hey, are you okay?"

She shook her head. "Just keep driving."

"No…why? We need to get a few things for the road trip." Sally had been looking for a parking spot when she followed Peggy's gaze. There, by a spot near the shopping cart return, was Tom, loading groceries into the back of a vehicle she didn't recognize. Next to him was a strikingly beautiful woman with long, almost black hair and creamy light brown skin. She was smiling up at him as he closed the hatch and turned toward her.

Without thinking, Sally hit the brakes, throwing them both forward, and witnessed the woman hug Tom then give him a peck on the cheek.

"Oh shit," Peg said under her breath as Sally threw the car in reverse and backed out to the exit.

"I'm going to hurl."

"Pull over and I'll drive."

Sally's grip on the steering wheel was so tight her knuckles were white. "Did he see us?"

"His attention was too focused on her."

She looked at Peg askance. "Oh, thanks, that isn't exactly what I wanted to hear."

"Well then you shouldn't have asked. Pull the damn car over before you kill us. I think I've already got whiplash from that stop you made."

Sally swung into a shopping center and threw the car

into park. Feeling her eyes well up in tears, she turned sideways and stared into Peg's empathetic ones. "Maybe it wasn't him...maybe..."

"It was Thomas Fitzsimmons, Sally. But maybe there's an explanation...like she's an old friend of his or his late wife."

"Old friend? Did you see her? She was young enough to be his daughter."

"So maybe she *was* his daughter."

"No, she didn't look anything like him, and clearly she was at least part Native American."

"Have you ever seen pictures of his family...his children?"

"Oh, I could kick myself. There was an office/den type room I just glanced at when he was showing me around, but I didn't go in. I noticed family pictures, but I was so absorbed with Tom and the dogs. I've tried finding him on social media, but there isn't anything, not on him, his wife..." She finally released her death grip on the wheel and ran a hand over her damp face.

Peggy opened her door, got out, went around to the driver's side, and opened that door. "Are you still wanting to do this? If so, get out and let me drive until you've got yourself under control."

Sally nodded and obediently got out, grateful to have someone else take over.

****

After a stop in Natchitoches for a late lunch at Lasyone's and to stock up on meat pies, they made it safely into New Orleans as lights came on all over the city, bathing the darkness with a soft golden glow.

Sally drove slowly down St. Charles pointing out places of interest and enjoying Peggy's endless questions

229

as she watched the nightlife filled with tourists and locals alike, standing in line for the streetcars or to get into restaurants. "Over there, that's the Columns, a lovely old hotel with a beautiful bar, and there's always music of some sort. Mom used to meet her friends there for drinks."

"Was the family home close?"

"Oh, yeah, not far at all. I'm glad Charles wanted us to be there in time for a light aperitif and some hors d'oeuvres. Translation...he'll probably be serving us Sazeracs and a four-course meal."

"I'm glad he asked us to stay there. I'm already exhausted."

"Oh, I promise, he'll charm the pants right off of you. He is a character even at his age."

They'd done a U-turn on St. Charles onto Washington and made a right onto Prytania Street, past Lafayette Cemetery. Sally nodded toward it, explaining, "If we'd gone straight, we'd have ended up in front of Commander's Palace." Next she pointed out the Opera House and different homes, giving an account of their history and who lived in them or previously owned them. Slowly, she pulled over to the low curb and stopped in front of a pale pink home with white columns and decorative ironwork surrounding the porch and balcony. A massive natural gas lantern hung over the front door. "This is it."

"Oh, wow. *This* is your family home?"

Sally smiled with the pride she always felt looking at its beautiful Italianate exterior.

Peg turned to her wistfully. "I do not know how sick your stepdad is or how much longer he's got. But do *not* lease this to anyone."

"Actually, I had an idea while we were driving. I was thinking about possibly living here part time. New Orleans would be a fabulous place to open The Widow Whisperers. I could start out renting a spot at the Rink. I noticed there was a for-lease sign when we drove by. Charles has usufruct until he dies. I could live here with him. Help him out. He's made the offer several times. There's an elevator, so I wouldn't have to worry about stairs, except for the ones going to the third floor. Eventually, I could throw parties here for the clients…there're all sorts of possibilities."

Peggy's eyes narrowed as she studied her friend. "This has to do with Thomas, doesn't it?"

"He's moved on. I need to do the same." She opened her door and got out, not wanting to give Peg the chance to argue with her.

She stood at the wrought iron gate punching a number into the digital lock when her friend sidled up next to her and whispered, "Be careful, Sally Estes. Don't make decisions because of assumptions and the fact you're hurt."

At that moment, the front door was thrown open, and a tall, debonair man stepped under the gaslight, his silver hair pulled into a ponytail and a smile that took twenty years off his weathered face. "Bienvenue, Mon Cheri," he called out, his arms opened wide.

Sally flew through the open gate and hobbled as fast as she could up the steps to his waiting arms, forgetting Peg standing on the sidewalk watching the reunion in silence.

Chapter 38

Thomas

Thomas helped Jean put the last of her belongings into the back of her car. "So this is it, huh?"

She hugged him tightly then pulled away and stared into his eyes. "It's not like we'll never see each other again. Dallas isn't that far away. It'll be good for me to be closer to the children and grandchildren. We're getting old, Thomas, and I for one want to spend as much time with my loved ones as I can."

"Why do I feel like I was admonished in the kindest way possible?"

"Because you were. I'm glad you're moving back out here. The girls tell me you've been spending more one-on-one time with them. That's good."

"But?"

"But, damn it, Elaine was right about you and Sally. And I haven't wanted to say this, but you should have told her everything right from the get-go. What were you thinking?"

They were experiencing the last dry, dog days of summer just before autumn brought cooling breezes and unexpected thunderstorms. He felt the hot Austin sun beating down on his head and neck, his chambray shirt damp from the exertion of helping Jean load the last of her personal items. He squinted at her. "That's just it! I *wasn't* thinking. Could we please go inside to have this discussion?"

Jean ran a hand across the beads of sweat on her forehead, pushing her damp bangs out of her eyes. Nodding, she headed for the house and its cool interior. Silently, she went into the kitchen and poured them both glasses of tea then sat at the farm table and stared absently out the window. "Days like this, I bet you miss Colorado."

Thomas sat across from her. "I was up there a couple of weeks ago. I miss it, but so much of it's not the same without Ellie. I'm actually thinking about selling the house."

Jean reached for two napkins, folded them, and set one under each of their sweating glasses. "Is that something you really want to do?"

He shrugged. "I always thought I'd go back there. But you've got a valid point. We are getting old, and it's important for me to be here with the kids. They've got their own lives, but the grandkids won't always be this young, and eventually they'll have their friends and activities and won't have time for an old fart like me. I need to enjoy them while I can."

"Humph. I think you're leaving out the Sally Estes part."

He gave a bittersweet smile. "Hope springs eternal. However, she won't have anything to do with me. I'm completely blocked…a persona non grata."

Jean set her glass down with a thud. "Where in the hell is your backbone? You could have gone to her house, shown up at her work. You could have waited for her on the sidewalk if you had to."

He ran his hands through his hair and gave her a

tortured look. "I did all that except for making a public spectacle of myself and waiting on the sidewalk. No one ever answered at her house, and once, I ignored Lily and went up anyway. She'd locked her office door. I made such a nuisance of myself Frank came and got me and asked me to leave before the ladies called the police. Now, he's not telling me anything because Peg asked him not to. I guess our friendship's upsetting Sally. I don't know what else to do."

"You were never a quitter, Thomas. When you and Elaine were working on a project and doing research and experiments, you would keep trying until you made headway. So try again."

"I can't, damn it!"

"Why on earth not?"

"She's gone. Darrell said he heard from Jewel that she took off for New Orleans and no one knows when she'll be back."

"Why there?"

"Her home. That's where she was originally from. Her mother moved back after her father died to help take care of Sally's ailing grandmother until she passed. Somewhere in there, her mom remarried, and they lived in the family home."

"I was under the impression her mother had died years ago. But I do remember Elaine reading up on her and there being something about the stepdad, a physician if my memory's correct. Still being alive and under the Napoleonic Code, he has the right to live in the house until his death. Very interesting state." Jean looked thoughtfully at her tea then back at Thomas. "Go to New Orleans then."

He felt his face burning. "I did. I flew there instead

of staying in Colorado. I rented a car and found the house. I stood like a blithering idiot at the locked gate and was told, by a particularly odd woman, that no one by that name was there before she slammed the rather formidable door in my…well, not exactly my face. So, I walked around…make that I stalked, sweating like I was in a sauna then finally went back to my rental and continued to wait. She pulled up an hour or so later in her car. I started to approach, but a man in a suit got out of the passenger side, opened her door, helped her out, and put an arm around her as they walked up to the porch."

They stared at each other for a few tense moments then Jean waved a dismissive hand in front of her. "Oh, that doesn't mean anything. It could have been anyone…a family member…an old friend."

"Well, what it meant was that I felt like a complete creep spying on her, besides the fact it made me sick to my stomach. I went straight back to the Monteleone, had a few drinks at the Carousel Bar, went to bed, and left first thing the next morning."

"It's not likely she'd have taken up with someone so quickly. It's not her style."

He shrugged. "I thought the same thing. But who really knows? Maybe it's another one she's known for years like Mr. Normand."

"So, this Darrell, you're still in touch with him?"

"Not a very likely friendship, I know. But he's kind of hard not to like."

"And he's a wellspring of information on Ms. Estes."

"There is that."

"Is he still in touch with her?"

Thomas leaned back and twirled the ice in his tea.

"From what I know, he's tried with about as much luck as I've had. What bothers me is he says Sally has always talked about wanting to live there again."

"In New Orleans? What about her children? She's got a daughter and son."

"Evidently, her son's a pilot and rarely home, and her daughter and husband live part time in other states where they have homes. Her granddaughter's grown now and living in New Mexico."

"Oh my, sounds like it might be lonely for her. I take it she still has family in Louisiana."

"According to Mr. Normand, yes. That's something else that irks me, and I know it shouldn't. He still wants her back, and he knows her so much better than I do."

She reached out and touched her fingers to his hand. "Don't. He might know her, but I doubt he understands her. Wait for her. Give her time to process everything and to heal. You *are* going to go to the reunion, aren't you?" He hesitated before responding. She removed her hand and leaned back, crossing her arms over her chest.

"Don't give me that look."

"This isn't just about you, Thomas. This is honoring my sister as well. We'd discussed me being there to help represent her."

"You don't have to explain that to me, Jean. I'm very well aware. And I plan on going because of that and…" He stopped without finishing.

"And? What…retribution? Are you hoping Billy Markham will be there?"

"Let's just say, if he is there and Sally shows up, I don't want her facing him alone."

"And what do you intend on doing?"

"Exactly what I should have done fifty-three years

ago."

"But you didn't know about the rape then."

"No, but I do now." He stood, ending the conversation, and looked at his watch. "I'll walk you out to your car. I'd feel better if you make it to Dallas before dark."

Chapter 39

Sally

"I wish you weren't staying. I don't like leaving you alone."

Sally glanced at Peg with an *are you serious* look. "I'm hardly alone. There's Charles and Naomi. I have old friends and family I haven't even visited with yet."

"Oh, Naomi, she is a saint. I mean it. A little weird and kind of scary, but as ornery as Charles is, I don't know how she puts up with him twenty-four seven."

Sally chuckled. "He's lucky to have her working for him. There's no way he could take care of that house by himself. She started out as his nurse, just coming to check on him a couple of times a week. He must have made her an offer to move in that she couldn't refuse. Besides, you just aren't used to his ol' southern charm. It's that Cajun background of his that makes him a pistol."

"Don't get me wrong, I really do like him, but he'd be a lot to handle. Anyway, back to the subject of *you*. I'm not sure why you decided to stay, but I really do need to get back. And what about Bruce?"

"Oh, he's fine. Betty's having a good time with him, and Carole said she could take him for a few days. Calum told her Michael would love playing with him." Sally stopped at a light and touched Peg's shoulder. "Hey, everything's going to be fine...*I'm* going to be fine."

"I'm worried you're running away. I'm worried about you driving back to Austin by yourself. I'm worried you're going to stay here and never come back." There was a honk behind them. "The light's green."

Sally put her hand back on the steering wheel and took off into the slowly creeping traffic going to Louis Armstrong New Orleans International Airport. "I'm not running away. This is good for me. After the accident and the surgeries then starting the business, I haven't had a chance to come home in years. I need some time and space to think...to heal. I've always loved it here. Mom used to say I had swamp water in my veins. That's why my books are always set here. I'd actually thought about moving back when I got out of college, but I ended up getting married instead.

"I would have come back after my first divorce, but the kids were settled and happy with their schools in Austin, and I didn't want to take them away like my parents did me."

"I know...I get it...but..."

"But I'll be okay. Charles is thrilled to have me staying at the house. Usually, I stay with different friends. You know, he won't be around a whole lot longer, so this means a lot to him. And I've got more research to do about opening up an office here. I promise I'll be back. I have a house and Bruce to take care of, and don't forget my children and granddaughter. And I'm relying on you, my friend, to keep me posted on what's going on at Widower Whisperers. There's not much I can't take care of from here. Besides, you have Frank to get back to. The way he's been calling and texting the last few days, I take it he misses you."

Sally caught Peggy's surreptitious smile before she turned her head and looked out the window. "Okay, girlfriend, I saw that grin. What are you trying not too successfully to hide?"

"I can't. I'm no good with secrets. I never have been."

"Clearly. So what's up? Obviously, something's going on with you and Frank." A car pulled in front of them to go around the truck in front of it, and Sally hit the brakes throwing them both forward. "Asshole. You okay?"

"Yeah, I'm fine. Good reflexes. Is it always like this going to the airport?"

"I don't know. It's probably because of people heading for Baton Rouge for the weekend. There's a big LSU game tomorrow." She glanced in the rearview mirror then back at her friend. "Hey, you, don't avoid my question. Fess up, what's going on with you two?"

"Oh, damn it! You promise not to say anything to anyone? And I mean anyone."

Sally held the steering wheel with her left hand, crossed her heart with her right, and then pressed her index finger and thumb together and made the motion of zipping her mouth.

"Would you put both freaking hands on the steering wheel? Besides, that's not good enough. You have to swear."

"Fine, I swear."

Peggy gave her a dubious look then sighed. "Okay, you're right. Frank really, really misses me. He went to Dallas to help with the new office for a few days, and he said it wasn't the same without me being there. He's back in Austin now. I guess he and Thomas and Darrell got together and…"

Sally shot her a look, stopping her. "I do not want to hear about Tom or Darrell. And I especially don't want to hear about them hanging out together. I just can't believe that's even a thing. How does that happen? I don't know. Is it like a douchebag thing? What do they do, compare stories? And you wonder why I don't want to go back and have to—"

Peg cleared her throat putting an end to her friend's tirade, and when Sally stole a glance at her, she could see the disparaging look on her face. "Okay! You're right. I need to get over it. This was about you, and I made it about me. I'm sorry."

"You really, *really* do need to get over it." She gave a heavy sigh and turning in her seat to look at Sally, crossed her arms. "Honestly, I'm sick of this shit, so I'm going to put it right out there. Maybe, just maybe, Sally fucking Estes, you need to quit being so self-absorbed. First off, Thomas lost his wife. He was there through her long-suffering battle with MS. I'm sure he got lonely. You know friends back away when people are dealing with things like that. I'm sure it's good for him to be friends with Frank and vice versa.

"And then Darrell…good ol' Darrell. You know, at some point, for your own sake, you need to try to forgive him for what happened. He has to live everyday with the knowledge of what he did to you…what he did to his ex-wife, his family. It can't be easy for him, especially now that he's sober and has gotten help with his addiction. I'm sorry he caused your accident. I'm sorry he treated you so terribly. But he was a drunk. He was an addict. He had a disease. I can't even imagine the demons that man lives with every day of his life. Did it ever occur to you that besides having you in common…by that I mean they both care deeply about you… did you ever stop to think that someone like Thomas is probably really good for Darrell?"

"Damn it, I shouldn't have taken I-10." Sally turned off to get on the Transcontinental access to the road leading to Airline Drive and glanced at Peggy. "I get it. You think I'm a self-centered bitch."

"That isn't what I said, and you know it. But since all this with Thomas, you've pretty much thought of no one but yourself. I know you're hurt, and you have to be traumatized to have remembered the rape. I feel for you, I really do. But, Sally, for the love of everything holy, you've just run away without giving either one of them a chance. Not that Darrell really deserves one or is what you need. But what about Thomas? Couldn't you have given him a chance? Couldn't you have at least sat down with him and asked your questions and heard him out? You're basing everything on speculation, not facts. None of this is like you."

Sally was silent the rest of the way. Pulling up in front of Southwest, she stopped, stared at her friend, and shook her head. "I don't know what I'm like anymore. But here we are." They both got out and went to the back. Sally opened the hatch, and Peggy pulled her suitcase out and shouldered her carry-on. "Thanks for being truthful with me. I'm going to miss you."

The two women hugged, and the car waiting behind them to take their spot honked. They pulled apart. "What is it you were going to tell me about Frank?"

Peggy rolled her luggage to the curb and smiled. "Oh, just that he's talking about us living together and I'm going to say yes."

A stab of pain went through Sally's heart, and she wanted to burst into tears. She was losing everyone. They'd all found someone to be happy with. All of them but her. She forced a smile as the car behind honked again. "Congratulations. I think it's wonderful."

Peg nodded with a worried look on her face. "Go on before that guy blows a gasket. I love you."

Sally started to get in her car but stopped and looked over the top. "I love you, too, and I'm happy for you."

She slipped behind the wheel and headed back toward the Garden District, her mind flush with the realization she might be alone the rest of her life, and the sadness crept through her, releasing itself in a stream of tears she hadn't been aware she'd been holding back.

Chapter 40

Three Weeks Later

Fall had settled in, and the air was balmy. Charles had taken to sitting in the courtyard in the evenings, enjoying his cocktails and cigarettes among the gardenias, fruiting satsumas, and Meyer lemons. Sally had met friends at Commander's for their martini lunch and was still a little tipsy when she joined him at the umbrellaed bistro table, a bottled water in hand.

"You have a good time today?"

She nodded, took a deep breath, and let her nostrils fill with the old familiar heady scents. "Hmmm, I remember being a kid here at my grandparents' house. Everyone sitting out here with drinks, smoking." She reached behind her and pulled a bloom from a ginger lily and brought it to her nose. "Oh, I so love all the smells mingling together...even your cigarette smoke."

"Do you want one?"

She shook her head. "Gave them up a few years ago. But thanks."

"Too bad."

Sally tilted her head to the side. "One of the hardest things I ever did." She stood, went to a tree, and looked over the ripening lemons.

"Pick some to take home with you."

She turned and stared at him then lifted a shoulder.

"I'm not going anywhere…for a while."

"I remember helping my father plant that tree and the satsuma." He nodded to the opposite end of the small, enclosed yard filled with blooming beds.

Her brows drew together in confusion as she sauntered back to the little table. "What are you talking about?"

"Aw, Cher, she never told you?"

"Who…Elizabeth?"

He nodded. "Oui, ta mère…your mamma."

"About?"

"Me."

"What about you? What is it I don't know?"

Charles ground the cigarette in the ashtray then emptied it into the silver silent butler, tarnish almost obscuring the delicate initials etched across the top. He caught her following his movements. "A wedding gift from your grand-mere." He shrugged.

"And?" she encouraged.

He took a sip of bourbon, set the crystal Baccara tumbler on the wrought iron tabletop, and lit another smoke. He inhaled and exhaled deeply, watching the smoke curl lazily in the growing dusk. His eyes narrowed as if thinking. "I loved her from the moment I saw her. I was just a child. We were a poor Cajun family who'd moved from Lafayette to the Big Easy. The family was large, but there was more opportunity here to find jobs. Mon père…my papa, he was good with plants, had the green thumb, you know?" As if having second thoughts, he put the cigarette out.

Sally settled back into the chair opposite him. "Hmmm, I do now. Go on."

Pulling a cigar from the pocket of his cardigan, he

lazily lit it then set it in the crystal ashtray. "He eventually opened a small nursery in the Irish Channel where we lived and did yardwork and landscaping for the wealthy people Uptown and here in the Garden District. It was a good business then and provided work for me and a couple of my older brothers who were still at home."

He took a long drag. "I remember it being late afternoon…what your folks called cocktail time. We were just finishing up and getting our tools from the back here as the adults…your grandparents and some of their friends started coming out with their drinks and smokes. We were gathering our tools, trying to get out of the courtyard when I heard Elizabeth's young voice looking for her maman. She stood in the opening of the gallery there." He pointed with the glowing end of the cheroot, and she glanced at the now screened-in gallery with floor-to-ceiling windows opening onto it from inside.

"She was there at the top of those steps in a frilly little dress with her espresso-colored hair plaited in a long braid hanging over her shoulder, a bow clipped to its end. Wisps of escaping curls framed her perfect heart-shaped face. She had her tiny hands on her hips and was tapping her foot impatiently."

Sally leaned back and stared up at the darkening sky. "Oh, Mamma, she never changed. She did that her whole life when she was irritated about something or someone. Which was quite often."

Charles chuckled. "That she did. Your mamma was quite the character. But I was fascinated by her. Just stood there with my mouth gaping open. My father practically pried the spade I was holding out of my hand and tapped me under the chin to get my lips closed."

"So, how old were you all?"

"Oh, I was nine or ten, and she was probably eleven or twelve then. An older woman, you see."

She smiled and tried to picture the courtyard as it had been eighty-something years ago.

"It hasn't changed that much…all these years. I helped plant the gardenias over there. They were your mamma's favorite up until the day she died. When they were blooming, after we were married, I'd pick a fresh one every day and put it in your grandmother's Waterford bowl she liked to float them in." He pointed again with the cigar. "And the big camellia over there, I helped plant that."

Sally stared at him in wonderment. "I had no idea you had so much history here or with her."

"Oh, mon Cheri, she didn't know I was alive back then. That perfect little nose of hers was stuck so high in the air there's no way she could have seen a small Cajun boy like me. We were the *help* and invisible." Her brows scrunched together. "You look like Liz when you do that."

"Me? Look like my mom?"

He nodded. "You have some of her traits. The coloring you got from your papa, but those ice blue eyes are from your French roots. I see some of her in you."

"So, if you were invisible, how did you all ever get to know each other?" Sally had always had her suspicions about their relationship.

He sighed deeply, took another draw of the stogie, and exhaled. "It was college. I'd graduated high school a year early and was taking some courses at Tulane, still working part time for my father. I was determined to make something of myself."

"And you did. You became one of the most respected doctors at Ochsner's if I remember correctly."

He gave a little smirk. "Now, I don't know if I'd go so far as to say that exactly."

"Oh, please, spare me, Charles! Humble does *not* look good on you."

He chortled and shook his head. "Never did." His brown eyes twinkled, and he raised his glass. "*À votre santé.*" Taking a sip, he looked thoughtful.

"Go on. Tell me how you finally got together."

He glanced at her then at his glass and grinned. "Elizabeth had turned into such a beautiful young woman. By then, she'd been going to Tulane for a couple of years and was entrenched in sorority life, and as Shakespeare said so eloquently, the world was her oyster." He shrugged. "I saw her on campus, flitting from one social event to another. Then one night I was doing research in the library. I was having trouble deciding if I wanted to be an attorney like your grand-père or a doctor like old man Evansworth.

"I was between shelves searching for a particular book. I don't even remember what it was now. But I heard whispers and a book being slammed down on one of the tables. I pulled a couple of books from a shelf and took a peak. Your mamma was arguing with a young man. I recognized him as one of the football players. He grabbed her by the shoulders, and she jerked away from him and started to sit. He reached for her and turned her to face him. I could hear her words, 'just leave me alone.' He stepped closer, and she was practically bent backwards over the chair he had her pressed up against. I don't know what got into me, but I stepped from my hiding place and walked to the table. 'Miss Elizabeth,' I said, 'is everything okay?' He backed away from her and told me to fuck off, they were having a private conversation."

Charles chuckled at the memory. "By then, I was about six foot three and at least one-hundred-eighty pounds. I'd worked landscaping my entire life and had been picked on by and fought with four older brothers. A punk like him didn't intimidate me. I pulled myself up to my full height and just smiled, my eyes never leaving his."

Sally shifted in her chair and stared at him. "Did he back off?"

"Oh, oui. He scurried away with his tail between his legs. That type usually does…the ones who think they're big men on campus and it's their right to browbeat and bully women."

"So, was Mother grateful? Did you all hit it off after that?"

He stared at her with an amused look. "Elizabeth Toussaint? Surely you jest. No, she gave me a scathing look and in no uncertain terms told me she'd had the situation under control."

Sally smiled. "That sounds like Mamma. Did she remember you? Know who you were?"

"Aw, that's the thing. She acted like she didn't, but I found out much later that she'd known *exactly* who I was." His eyes glowed with the memory. "And just like that, we miraculously ended up running into each other on campus, and oddly, Liz was in one of my classes the next semester."

"She ended up stalking you and you got together." It wasn't a question and didn't surprise Sally in the least. Eliza, Liz, Elizabeth, Lizzy…whatever you called her...always went after, and usually got, whatever she wanted.

He nodded. "We started studying together, and one thing led to another. We had a brief affair. I wasn't all that available though. I was working as many hours as I could to help pay for school. Even with the scholarships it was expensive. And I spent most of my free time studying, not going to games and partying."

"And being my mother, she drifted away to someone more *fun*...someone like my father whose family had money and connections."

"Precisely."

Chapter 41

Sally knew she must have had a disbelieving look on her face. "So, she basically dumped you, and you took her back all those years later?"

He gave her an endearing yet condescending smile. "Ah, that's just it. Life is never that simple. Mon Cher, there was also a war…you've heard of it, World War II. Life was exciting and crazy. Young people grew up quickly. Some grew old in a matter of years; some didn't have the chance to grow old at all. You had a war too, Vietnam. So sad for your generation. Jacques was idealistic and enlisted. It broke his mother's heart."

She nodded. "I can only imagine. Your only child. But he came home unscathed, didn't he?"

"Aw, physically, oui. But emotionally…I believe there are things he never got over. He lost so many friends…watched them be blown to bits, die before his eyes. But now he has found himself and is extremely happy." Charles looked sorrowful for a moment then shrugged. "Anyway, I was sent overseas as a medic and your father—"

"Had a clerical job in the states at Alexandria Air Force Base, right here in Louisiana."

He nodded. "By then, Lizzy had talked your grandparents into letting her go to LSU in Baton Rouge. Oh, she told me she'd dated around, but your father would come to see her, or he would have her come visit him at the base. He had money, his own car, would buy her gifts from the commissary. I saw her a couple of times when I was on leave…but she got pregnant."

Sally couldn't imagine the horrified look on her face. "Oh damn, this isn't where you tell me you're my real father, is it?"

He'd been taking a swig of bourbon and almost choked. "Oh mon seigneur, heavens no! Look at you. You have your mother's sapphire eyes, but the rest of you is your father, from your copper hair to that ornery grin with those alluring dimples and freckles. Besides, after she'd started dating him, the affair part of our relationship ended."

For some reason, Sally was both relieved and disappointed. "Confession. When I found out about you after my father died, I had these quixotic thoughts that you might have been my father. It didn't take a genius to figure out the timing and that they had to get married. I was born three weeks short of nine months after what they claimed was their wedding date, though I never saw a license." She shrugged. "That in itself was odd. Then after she'd passed, through some of my mother's friends, I'd learned she wasn't exactly loyal to my father…evidently ever. It hurt, but it also explained a lot about my childhood and her constant absences."

"Your mother was beautiful and spoiled, and today we would call her a narcissist. Sadly, she never got over being moved to Texas from Louisiana…from here, her parents, her friends…New Orleans, her favorite place in the world. It jaded her…her resentment was a torturous cross for her to bear. Unfortunately, it trickled down to you. But know this, Cher, she loved you deeply…with her whole heart…as much as she had to give, she did try to give to you. Then when your father died and you were grown and married for the second time, I believe, she eventually came back here to help take care of your grandmother. By that time Elizabeth had mellowed…changed. I was one of the attending physicians when Mrs. Toussaint was hospitalized after her stroke. Your mother and I became reacquainted."

"And you ended up marrying her after everything in the past?"

He relit the cigar and released a curl of blue smoke against the night sky. "Young people…they look at us and think we're old fools. They know what it's like to fall in lust and have the all-consuming desire for another to dictate their lives, and they believe their relationships to be the *end all* of their short existence on this earth. But *they* are the fools. We have been through all of that…and know that it's but a fleeting thing. With the years comes emotional maturity."

He arched a knowing brow, knocked an ash off, and took another long draw. "What? You look concerned."

"Should you be doing that?"

"Smoking?" He glanced at the glowing end of his cheroot. "Probably not. But I'm ninety-six, and the cancer is slowly killing me. I choose to be happy these last days of my life." He snuffed it out in the ashtray. "Don't look so sad. I've had an amazing, long life, and I've been blessed beyond belief."

Sally sniffed away the tears that threatened to fall at the thought of losing him, too.

"Cher, stop that. Your maman has been waiting for me. Aw, where was I?"

"You were talking about getting older and emotional maturity."

He reached out and wiped a little trickle from the corner of her eye. "Yes, I was." He rested his arms on the table, leaned forward, and held her eyes. "You know, there are reasons God doesn't give us everything we want when we're young. He is wise and knows that some things must wait until we're older…he gives us something to *look forward* to. After my wife died, I thought that was all there was to my existence, and it had ended.

"There is a song by Peggy Lee, 'Is That All There Is?' But I digress. Anyway, your mother ended up coming home, and we reconnected. This time around it was *special*. We'd lived our youth, made our mistakes, raised our children, knew who we were and what we wanted and *didn't* want. We wanted each other. Only then, it was a sweeter, kinder, less-selfish love. And we had that *history*. Do you understand what I'm saying?"

Sally felt a needling in her brain…and flickering images of Tom streaked across her mind. She swallowed hard and slowly met his probing eyes. "I think so."

"Though we hadn't been together all those years, I'd known her as a little girl, as a teenager and a college fem fatal. All the years in between didn't matter. Being with her was like coming home…comfortable, warm…familiar and safe. I know what that's like and how wonderful it is. The young, they are the fools to think they know more than we old people." He put a frail hand over hers and nodded, holding her eyes, then looked out over the courtyard and sighed. "Grow old along with me! The best is yet to be, the last of life, for which the first was made. Our times are in His hand who saith, 'A whole I planned, youth shows but half; Trust God: See all, nor be afraid!' "

Sally rewarded him with a whimsical smile. "Robert Browning…those lines were part of your wedding vows. I think of them often and wish I had what you and my mother had. This isn't just about you and mother, is it?"

He removed his hand and sat back. "No, it's not. You need to start packing your belongings, Sally. Jacques is prepared to drive you home at the end of the week. I've spoken to Betty, and she's told me about Thomas Fitzsimmons and what you believe happened all those years ago. It's time to put on your big-girl panties, as they say, and get the hell back home and face things. You've got enough of your mother in you to go to that damned reunion with your head held high…no matter who shows up. Jacques has offered to be your escort."

Charles' son was one of the best-looking men Sally had ever laid eyes on. "But he's married."

"Oh, Lord, Richard doesn't mind. He'll be relieved to have some time to himself. And what better escort than your handsome stepbrother who also happens to be gay?"

Sally leaned back thoughtfully and took a sip of her water. Everything Charles had said resonated with her. These last few years of her life, she'd wanted nothing else but to eventually find someone, the love of her life…her last love…someone to grow older with…to hold their hand when they took their last breath, or they hold hers. That was one of the real reasons she'd put up with Darrell for so long. But they hadn't had the history or similar backgrounds. Then Tom came along, and ironically she'd thought briefly he had been the one. They'd had the history… "I must still be tipsy."

"Why must you?" he asked grinning.

"Because I'm almost agreeing with you."

"Oh, well then, surely you must be drunk." Again the sparkle in the handsome brown eyes.

She smiled back. "Surely, I must be." And for the first time in weeks, she felt an excited anticipation about going home and whatever awaited her there.

Chapter 42

Thomas

Looking around the apartment, Darrell smiled. "Bro, what a bachelor pad. Are you sure you don't mind?"

Thomas leaned against the kitchen countertop and folded his arms. "I renewed my lease right before finding out Jean was moving to Dallas, and I decided to move back to the lake house. I'm pretty sure they'd let me out of it, but it's kind of nice having a place to come to that's close to the office. It's been vacant for weeks now. You might as well take advantage of it while you're waiting on the renovations of you condo to get finished. There's no sense in you continuing to pay rent on that *suite* you've been staying in."

Frank was staring out at the rush hour traffic downtown and let out a snort of contempt. "More like a shithole if you ask me."

The other two men joined him in the living room, and they all sat. "I don't think either of us will argue that point with you. But when you're on a limited budget and out of work, a guy's gotta do what a guy's gotta do. It's virtually impossible to live on social security alone. Don't get me wrong. I'm glad to have it, but…" Suddenly, Darrell got a serious look on his face. "So, how much do you want, Thomas?"

"To stay here for a few months?"

"Yeah. I'm not a complete charity case…yet."

Thomas shrugged and got a shit-eating grin on his face. "Back off of Sally?"

"Oh, very funny! Tempting, but no! All's fair in love and war, right?"

"Sure. I was kidding with you, okay?" Thomas leaned forward and put his elbows on his knees. "I want nothing but for you to enjoy the place. It's not exactly like she's having anything to do with either one of us anyway."

"She's coming home tomorrow." Their heads turned to Frank who had a sheepish look on his face. "Oh Lord, I wasn't supposed to tell either one of you. It just slipped out. Pretend like I didn't say anything."

Thomas stood and went to the art deco bar cabinet, splashed scotch into a Glencairn whiskey glass, took a sip then turned to face them, holding the glass up. "Anyone care for some?"

"You have no idea," Darrell said under his breath.

Frank stood, slapped him on the back, then joined Thomas at the cabinet. Picking up the bottle, he read the label aloud. "Glenfiddich eighteen-year-old single malt. You won't believe this, but I visited the distillery when I was in Scotland." He set the bottle down and picked up a glass. "Don't mind if I do."

Thomas filled both their glasses and gave Darrell a sideways glance. "Sorry, old chap, I'll move the alcohol out before you move in."

Darrell ran a hand over his slick head and licked his lips. "I'd appreciate it. It's hard sometimes…like now…when Freud here lets it slip that Sally's coming home." He glared at the man. "So, don't stop. Give us the details."

Frank sighed, took a big gulp, then went back to his place on the sofa. "Okay, this is just between us." He looked from one to the other, and they both nodded. "You know, since Peggy and I started living together, I hear things I'm probably not supposed to. She was in the bedroom on the phone with Betty when I got home the other night. She had laundry going and didn't hear me come in. They were talking about some man driving back with her. Sorry, guys, I don't know who. I just heard Peg say something about being glad Sally had *him* to drive her."

"You didn't ask Peggy what was going on?" Darrell's penetrating eyes never left Frank's face.

"Look, to make this all work, Peg and I have an agreement. I don't talk about you all, and she doesn't share info about Sally. I felt like a creeper and made some noise, so she'd know I was there. She got off the phone real quick and joined me in the kitchen. I asked her what she'd been up to and did I interrupt her talking to someone. She told me she'd just hung up from Betty and that they'd been discussing what they needed to go over with Sally when she got back. I acted like I hadn't heard anything. Peg asked me not to tell anyone then volunteered that she'd be back tomorrow night."

Thomas had been silently staring down at his glass. He drained it, refilled it, and slowly went to sit down next to Frank. Placing his drink on the coffee table, he put a hand on Frank's knee and turned to look at him. "It's okay. I don't want you breaking Peg's trust. Thanks for giving us a heads-up but…" He sighed, removed his hand, and ran it through his hair. "Look, my friends, I have a confession to make."

They both stared at him expectantly. After a long silence, Darrell stood and faced both of them. "Okay, you guys are killing me. I get all this honor stuff and all, but would you just get real? Out with it, Thomas. Say whatever it is you have to tell us. Get it off your damn chest."

Frank looked up at him and tilted his head to the side. "Are you always so fucking impatient?"

Darrell nodded then shook his head. "Hell, I don't know. I've never been this sober before, and all this talk about honor and confessions is giving me the heebie-jeebies. And then Sally coming back with some man…" He put his hands in his pockets, jiggled some loose change, paced in a little circle, then sat on the ottoman across from them. "Look, I'm sorry. This really isn't me. I've always been the happy-go-lucky dude that never let anything get to him. But I guess it's just my guilt. Being around the two of you makes me realize what an absolute shit I've been, and how I've fucked up my life and hurt everyone I ever loved." They were both staring at him. "Stop with the looks of pity…please. Thomas, I'm ready to hear your confession if you're still willing to tell us."

Thomas rested his arms on his legs, staring at his hands fisted together. "I stalked Sally in New Orleans."

There was dead silence in the room then Frank shifted on the couch, took the same pose as Thomas, and looked thoughtful.

Darrell was the first to speak. "So, how did you stalk her? I'm not getting it."

Thomas splayed his hands. "When I went to Colorado…it…well, it just didn't feel right anymore without Elaine there. It seemed all wrong. Then I realized I was doing nothing but thinking about losing her, losing Sally. I called a realtor about selling the place, got on a plane to New Orleans, rented a car, and figured out where her stepfather lived."

"Oh, I could have told you. It's a beautiful place, just a block off St. Charles. Sally and I…" Both men sat up straight and stared at Darrell. "Sorry, man, I guess I was the last person you would have wanted to ask."

"You think?" Frank turned to look at Thomas. "So, what happened?"

"Like an idiot, I went up to the gate, and it was locked. I pressed a buzzer next to it, and a strange woman opened the door and glared out at me as if I was the devil incarnate. I asked to see Ms. Estes and was told no one by that name was there then she slammed the door. I rang the buzzer a few more times, but no one came back. I walked around the neighborhood, taking it all in. Finally, I went back to my car parked down the street and waited."

"Okay, so that's where the stalking came in. But you know, that's not *really* stalking. You should see the things I did trying to find out if my ex-wife was seeing someone else after she kicked me—"

"Darrell! Thomas is trying to tell us what happened."

He held up a hand and gave a slight nod. "My apologies. Continue."

"As I said, I waited. About forty-five minutes had gone by when I saw Sally's car pull into the drive. I stepped from the rental about the same time a nice-looking man emerged from the passenger side, opened her door, and walked up the sidewalk with his arm around her shoulder."

"Oh fuck!" Darrell whispered.

"What? Do you know who he is?" Thomas was on high alert now.

He shook his head. "Sorry, not a clue. The one time I was there, we'd stayed at her friends' studio. It was a spur of the moment thing on my part. I was convinced she was seeing someone there and just showed up. She drove me past the family home but never introduced me to anyone but the people she was staying with, a nice married couple…artists."

"So, you really believed she had someone there she was involved with?"

Darrell glanced at Thomas, shrugged, then looked away. "We had just gone over to the friends-with-benefits thing, and I was drinking all the time and paranoid. She and Betty took off on this trip to New Orleans. I remembered her telling me about some guy she'd dated briefly after her second divorce…" He met the other man's eyes again. "I was in the love-bombing phase. I didn't question her. I guess I didn't want to give her a chance to lie to me. I don't know. I really don't. So, what did you do?"

"I put my tail between my legs and bailed. Went back to the Carousel Bar at the Monteleone where I was staying, sat there drowning my sorrows until I couldn't sit up straight anymore, went to my room and to bed, then caught the first flight I could get back to Austin."

Darrell took a deep breath then expelled it. "Would you be able to recognize him on social media?"

Thomas shrugged. "I doubt it. I didn't get a good look at his face. All I really noticed was dark hair and something on the back of his hand like a tattoo. Maybe in person. I was too upset like I'd been sucker punched."

"It doesn't bode well for either one of us then, does

it?" Darrell asked.

Silently, the other two men shook their heads then downed their glasses of scotch. Thomas stood. "Let's get out of here and get dinner." After his friends had slipped into the hall, he turned off the lights and held the door open thinking about the time Sally was there and how terribly wrong it had all turned out. His appetite gone, he slowly closed the door wondering how he could possibly eat with the lump that had formed in his throat.

Chapter 43

Sally

Sally played with Bruce and baby talked as he ran around in circles squeaking like one of his toys, stopping to give her high-fives and paw at the air. When he settled down, she picked him up and closed the back door. "Thanks for taking such good care of him and bringing him home. I would have been glad to come get him."

"I figured you'd just spent eight hours in the car and didn't need to get back out. Besides, Adi's been staying with me, and I needed a break." Betty tilted her head at the wineglasses on the island. "Is it wine time yet?"

Sally glanced at the kitchen clock. "Oh, it's been time for hours. I was hoping you'd stay and have some with me. Pizza's on the way."

"Twist my arm."

Sally looked at her friend askance as she poured. "So, what's going on at home?" They grabbed their glasses and headed for the porch.

"Oh, nothing, really. Adi truly is wonderful, and I love him dearly. I really, really do." Betty made herself at home on the couch as Sally lit the coffee table's firepit before settling in.

"But?"

"But sometimes it's a lot. He's doing really well. But I have to help him with everything, and he's still not getting around all that great without using the wheelchair." She stared thoughtfully at her glass for a minute and tapped the rim. "I think he should have stayed in rehab longer."

Sally took a sip of chardonnay. "Hmmm, I was wondering about that. Back surgery then knee surgery. I didn't expect him to be out this soon."

"What can I say? He's Greek and stubborn as they come."

"I thought he was going to be living with Max and Angelina."

"Humph, that didn't last a New York minute."

"What happened? She was so adamant about taking care of her father."

Betty swirled her wine then took a swig. "Oh, yeah, she was. She left Max in Houston, as you know, and he took care of selling the home there, etc. They were staying at Adi's house, but he insisted on leaving rehab much earlier than he should have and came home. It turned into a nightmare for all three of them."

"Was Max jealous of Angel's time taking care of him?"

Betty smirked. "Just the opposite. Max was great and a huge help. It takes someone strong to maneuver someone Adi's size around."

"Ah, let me guess. Your Adonis was the one to get jealous."

"Bingo! He wasn't getting undivided attention from his daughter. Then to top it off, Max had moved things to make it easier for everyone to get around with Adi having to use the wheelchair. You would have thought he'd blown the house up."

"Oh, dear. So, you…being you, ended up offering

for him to stay at your house." It wasn't a question.

Betty nodded and set her glass on the table and faced Sally. "He's a damn pain in the ass. But, Sally…"

"What?"

"He's my pain in the ass, and I'm in love with him. I missed him so much when he was in the hospital and rehab I thought I was going crazy. All of a sudden…after all these years, I was lonely in my own house by myself…even with my dogs and Bruce there."

Sally felt her heart jump to her throat. Again, that awareness that everyone had someone but her. That sick feeling that she would spend the rest of her life alone…die alone. And tears welled behind her eyes. She swallowed hard, fighting to keep them at bay. "I'm happy for you, my friend. You deserve to love and be loved back."

Betty rewarded her with a winsome smile. "Yeah, I know. But you deserve that too. Enough about me. What's going on?"

Sally feigned shock. "Me? Absolutely nothing. Oh, but I did a lot of research, and I want us to open an office in New Orleans. Remember having coffee at Still Perkin' at the Rink? They've got a great space for rent. It would be perfect right there in the heart of the Garden District with Lafayette Cemetery and Commander's Palace just down the street."

Betty looked at her suspiciously. "You're planning on moving there, aren't you? Don't lie to me. You always wanted to move back."

Sally finished her wine and put her glass next to Betty's, wishing she'd brought the bottle out with them. "I'm thinking about living there part time. Charles would love to have the company. He's not going to be with us much longer. I talked to several of my old friends and some cousins, and they all thought The Widower Whisperers being there is a wonderful idea." She saw the skeptical look on the other woman's face and rushed on to reassure her. "It wouldn't be all the time. I'd be back here a lot. There's the headquarters here. My kids and my granddaughter will be visiting. And there's you and Peg and Carole."

She put her fingertips lightly on Betty's arm just before her friend stood. "I need more wine. Do you want some?"

"Just bring the bottle, please."

When Betty returned, Jacques was with her carrying a glass, the open bottle of wine, an unopened one, and a corkscrew. "You didn't tell me this handsome devil was upstairs."

"My stepsister has convinced me to stay in her granddaughter's room. Quite nice, actually, though I could help her with a little decorating advice."

The two women looked at each other and grinned. "So, Jacques, what do you think of Sally's plan to stay with your father and open one of our offices there in your hometown?"

He poured wine all around, took a seat next to Betty, and held his glass up in a toast. "Here's to beautiful women and equally beautiful men. *À votre santé*!" They clinked glasses, and he looked thoughtful. "For all intents and purposes, it is Sally's house. True, my father has use of it until his eminent death, but it's been in her family for generations and should remain so. Charles would enjoy the company." He turned to Sally and smiled. "I have to admit that when your mother and my father got married, I was more than a little resentful. I didn't like you very much." He shrugged. "Being an only child and you the daughter my papa never had…"

"Oh, say no more. I really kind of *hated* you back then. You were such a snob, and we were forced to do those family dinners together when I'd come to town. I was sure you were a male chauvinist pig the way you acted around your wife and positive you were having an affair."

"Ha, not hardly. I couldn't stand her though. As the years went by, she became more entrenched in *Carnival* and the krewes, the parties, the luncheons. Oh let's not forget the King and Queen of Mardi Gras. It became tedious. I was bored and irritated. And that ex-husband of yours was quite the pontificating asshole, wasn't he?"

"*Quite*," Betty interjected before her friend could respond. "So, what happened to make you leave all that?"

"Richard happened. As you know, I went into the medical field like Charles. But I was struggling with PTSD the entire time. It lingered long after Vietnam, long after I quit the service. I started going to counseling and group sessions with other veterans…with other people who *got it*…got what I'd been going through all those years. That's where I met him. He understood me. We started going for coffee after the meetings. Soon it was drinks. I realized he was gay but told myself I wasn't…that we were just friends. Before I knew what was happening, I felt something I'd never felt before. Pure, joyous romantic love for another human being. Unadulterated, unconditional. When that happens to you, you don't walk away and let it go."

Betty stared pointedly at Sally.

"Go ahead and say it. After the ride here, I doubt

Jacques and I have any secrets. And you certainly didn't have any trouble calling Charles and apprising him of everything."

Betty grinned. "You're absolutely right. I didn't. Not in the least. What I want to know is what you're going to do about all this. Peggy told me about you all seeing Tommy with that other woman." She held a hand up. "No, don't you dare get upset with her. I cajoled it out of her. And to be honest, I wouldn't blame Tommy if he *was* dating someone else. The idea was for him to be able to start living again, not wait for the almighty Sally Estes to come off her high horse and give him a chance to exonerate himself for something he probably didn't do or even know about fifty years ago."

"Bravo! My sentiments exactly." Jacques gave her a golf clap and propped an ankle on the opposite knee. "Please, go on."

"Thank you. Anyway, you don't have any idea who that woman was. I think you should pull your act together and talk to Tommy. You're not a good liar, and you were never good at hiding your feelings. Peg said she could tell how sad you were, and she hated coming home without you."

Sally held a finger up. "First of all, I'm surprised you haven't talked to him for me."

Betty shook her head vigorously. "I'm not ever doing that again. I remember what happened the last time. We ended up not talking for days."

Sally smirked. "Good. Secondly, I'm still reeling from remembering him all those years ago, as well as Billy and the rape. That's a lot to process. I'm not good for anyone right now, whether Tom's innocent or not." She held up three fingers. "This has all hurt like hell…first the memories then seeing him with that woman. I'm not like you two. Maybe I wasn't cut out to be in love. I've cried more the last few months than I can remember since high school. I can't handle the pain."

"So, what are you going to do?"

"Do you know if Tom is going to be at the reunion?"

Betty shook her head. "I had Marla email me a list of the people attending, but his name wasn't on it."

"And Billy Markham?"

"No, but a lot of people show up and pay at the door. You know that."

Sally looked down at her hands thoughtfully then smiled and stared at her best friend and Jacques. "In answer to your question, I'm going to go to that damned reunion with my head held high and this handsome devil on my arm, and I'll dare anyone to rain on my parade."

She saw the surreptitious looks pass between the other two and couldn't help but wonder if they were keeping something from her.

Chapter 44

Sally

She was leaving The Widower Whisperers early to go home and get ready for the reunion, just as Thomas Fitzsimmons opened the front door. Startled, she stopped short and gasped. They stood awkwardly staring at each other for a brief moment before he broke the silence. "Sally…it's nice to see you."

Did she imagine it, or had his voice actually cracked? Feeling a flutter in her stomach and the weakness in her legs, she only nodded, not trusting herself to speak.

"Um, well…I was just on my way to see Frank." He glanced awkwardly at his watch. "So, I best be getting to it then."

Still unable to force herself to speak, she made a move to walk past him, and he gently touched her arm. She came to an abrupt halt, her heart thudding so loud in her ears she was positive he heard it too. Turning her head, she met his hazel eyes with her own tormented ones.

"Sally," he whispered.

She couldn't breathe, the pounding wouldn't stop, and the breathlessness was making her light-headed. She tore her gaze away and looked down at his fingers resting lightly on her forearm and shook her head. Slowly, he removed them, stepped back, and opened the door for her. Forcing her leaden feet to move forward, she made it to the sidewalk and took several deep breaths, pain gripping her heart like a vice.

Jacques, who had parked in front of the building to pick her up, stepped from the car and went to her. "Are you all right?"

She lifted her head and stared at him. "No, I'm not…I don't know if I'll ever be okay again."

Holding onto her arm, he helped her to the car. Once inside, he turned and met her eyes. "The man who walked in just now, that was Tom?" Tears had pooled, and she blinked a couple of times then nodded. "Nice-looking man."

She couldn't hold back any longer, and the tears burst forth. Leaning over, he let her cry her heart out as he held her in his arms.

****

Thomas

His office door slammed, and Frank jerked his head up from the documents he'd been going over. "What the—"

"Sorry, didn't mean to do that." Thomas glowered at him then sat sullenly in the guest chair.

Frank gave a deep sigh, laid his pen on the desk, and leaned back. "Apology accepted. So what happened?"

Thomas put his elbows on his knees, head in his hands, and rubbed his temples. After a few seconds, he looked up. "I ran smack dab into Sally Estes. That's what happened."

"Did you all talk?"

"I did. I said something about it being nice to see her. I was on my way to see you."

"And?"

"And she didn't fucking respond…just nodded. She started to walk past me. I touched her arm and said her name…nothing…she just stared at me like I was insane."

"Come on…maybe she didn't know what to say…maybe the cat had her tongue, or…or she was embarrassed."

He shook his head. "She looked down at my hand on her arm, and I felt like the biggest fool…like she thought I was some kind of abuser. I stepped back and opened the door for her, and she waltzed right out into some other man's arms. No…no, that's not quite true. It wasn't just *some other* man…it was the guy I saw her with in New Orleans."

Frank let out a low whistle, picked up the pen, and started tapping the desk with it. "So, that was the *him* that was driving her home. But the reunion's tonight. What are you going to do?"

Thomas shrugged. "I've got no choice. I'm going to go with my heart on my sleeve, act like nothing's wrong, and pray this whole charade doesn't blow up in front of everyone. I just don't know if I'm a good enough actor."

****

Betty leaned over to Sally sitting next to her at the banquet table. "Holy bejesus, everyone is so old."

Sally's forehead wrinkled, and her eyebrows drew together. She put a hand up to cup her mouth and moved closer in an attempt to be heard over the pounding music from the '60s and '70s. "Well, we are at our fiftieth reunion. How's Adi holding up?"

Betty reached over and lovingly ran fingertips over her fiancé's hand resting on the arm of his wheelchair then tilted her head back to her friend's. "He's fine. He told me earlier he wished he was able to get out and dance with me."

"Aw, that's so sweet. It's really nice he's here. You know, you could always go shake a leg with Jacques. He'd probably appreciate being rescued from that pack of gray-haired single women that have him cornered."

"Why doesn't he just tell those wolves he's gay?"

Sally shrugged and smiled. "He's trying to be honorable and give the impression he's *my man.* Besides, he might be gay, but he still loves women…and attention…he is a man after all." She looked around uncomfortably. "I don't recognize most of these people, so don't go off and leave me. I've had a few come up and tell me I still have the most beautiful red hair…I told one woman she too could have my color and gave her the name of my stylist."

Betty chortled. "Hey, you might have high school amnesia, but these people are so ancient even I don't know who half of them are. Come to think of it, they might not even know who they are."

"Any sign of Billy Markham?"

She took a sip from her plastic Solo cup and shook her head. "Seriously, I doubt I'd know him if I saw him. I keep having to stare at those badge things with our graduation pictures on them to try to figure out who people are. Thank goodness *we* haven't changed."

Sally suppressed a giggle. "Yes, and humble as ever. What about Tom? Have you seen him?"

Betty looked uncomfortable, shook her head, then stared out at the dance floor.

A warning signal surged through her, and Sally tapped her friend's shoulder. When Betty looked at her, she stared knowingly into her eyes. "What's up? What are you not telling me?"

Just then the music stopped, and Gladys Mason waddled up to the podium and took the screeching microphone. Tapping it a few times and saying, "Testing, testing, one, two, three," she seemed convinced it was ready for her auspicious announcement.

"Hello, everyone! I am so excited to see this wonderful turnout for our fiftieth reunion! Look at all you fabulous people!" She paused, waiting for the applause of the three people clapping to die down. "Oh, what an enthusiastic group!" She smiled like her career as an emcee was dependent on it. "Now to the part we've all been waiting for. As promised, we are honored to have with us tonight none other than E.T. Duncan, the author…or I should say, one of the coauthors of one of my favorite bestsellers, *The Reunion*. Not only that, but the movie version is to be released in a couple of months, and we'll all be given free passes to it's opening. It's my pleasure to welcome Thomas Duncan Fitzsimmons, or as most of you know him, our own Tommy."

There was applause mingled with whispers and gasps, not the least of which was Sally's, as Thomas entered the vast room overlooking downtown Austin with an entourage that included two younger women, Frank, Peggy, Jean, and of all people, Darrell Normand.

Chapter 45

"What the hell?" Sally hissed, glared at Betty, then stood.

The applause had stopped, and just as Gladys was handing the mic to Thomas, a drunken voice from the back called out. "Awesome ol' Tommy Zitsimmons. Always the goody two-shoes…the little mister do-gooder…or is that goober?" The man laughed at his own joke then snorted.

Thomas ignored him and took the microphone. "Gladys, a big thank you for the warm welcome and to the heckler in the back." There was a brief awkward chuckle among the crowd. "First off, I can't take credit for writing *The Reunion*. It was a vision of my late wife, Elaine, inspired by my high school days and something that happened at our fortieth reunion." He paused and looked at Sally who was staring at him in disbelief while Betty was calmly trying to get her to sit back down. Their eyes met, and he smiled.

"Oh, for the love of Christ, would you just get on with it and quit making goo-goo eyes at fucking Sally Estes? Some of us need another drink." The man stood, knocking his folding chair over as a couple of the women at his table were attempting to get him to sit and be quiet.

Darrell, who had been standing at the end of the stage, inconspicuously slipped off and headed toward the back of the room as Jacques made his way to Sally's side.

The belligerent man irritably shrugged the women off and staggered a few steps forward.

Thomas stared at him as he approached, realizing it was Billy Markham…of course it was. Turning, he handed the microphone to Frank and was stepping from the stage, but Darrell got there first, glanced at the man's badge with his name on it, and blocked him from going any farther, seconds before Thomas pulled up behind him.

"I've got this, Darrell."

Glancing over his shoulder, he murmured, "No, you don't, Thomas. Go back up there and finish your presentation. I understand this. I used to be him." Then he looked back at Billy and grinned. "What did you just say about Sally?"

"Oh, come on, man, the bar's back there behind the stage. I don't know who the hell you are, baldy, but you know…everyone here knows about Sally fucking Estes, or maybe I should say fucking Sally Estes. And that shmuck behind you had the biggest crush on her…" He swayed, chuckled, then wiped at his nose with the back of his hand and sniffed. "If he only knew that I…"

He never finished the sentence as Darrell's fist made contact with his jaw. Billy had a stunned look on his face but managed to get his foot up and catch Darrell squarely in the groin. The crowd gasped as one, and Darrell doubled over, just as Thomas stepped around him and grabbed Billy by the throat. The room went deadly silent, watching him swing desperately at their honored guest, his arms too short to make contact.

Thomas glared at Billy's reddening face and bulging eyes as he sputtered, spit dribbling from the corners of his mouth, and he wanted to squeeze harder. Suddenly realizing what he was doing, he released him, watching as he dropped to the floor trying to get his breath. "You're not worth it," he hissed and turned, looking for Sally, but she was gone, and so was her date. He looked back to see Darrell helping a couple of women get Billy to his feet and hopefully on his way home.

Up on stage, Frank sat the mic in its stand and gave a sigh. "Okay, folks, you don't know me, but I'm a friend of Thomas and Sally. My name is Frank, and that's my girlfriend, Peggy. Those two beautiful women behind me to my right are Thomas's daughters, Victoria and Annabelle. The lovely lady here on my left is Elaine Fitzsimmons' sister, Jean. Now that the excitement's over, how about getting on with things? Let's give a big welcome to Jean Reynolds who's here to speak to us about—"

****

Sally didn't hear the rest of Frank's speech as she closed the door to the ladies' room. Leaning against the wall, she took several deep breaths then stood and checked under the stalls to make sure she was alone. Resting her hands on the sink's cabinet, she stared at the tears streaming down her face. She was so damned angry...angry at herself. Angry at Billy Markham...mortified about what had just transpired. She grabbed a couple of paper towels, wet them, and was dabbing at her cheeks when Betty came blasting through the door.

"Are you okay?"

"Do I look like I'm okay?"

"No, you look like shit!"

Sally turned on her. "How much of this did you know?" The door flew open again, and they both turned to stare at a flustered Peggy. "And you! You were up on stage with them!" Sally shook her head. "What in the hell were you and Frank thinking?"

"Oh, no, you don't! You stop right there. First of all that *woman* we saw Thomas with…the one you convinced yourself must have been a girlfriend. She really is his daughter. They all showed up to the house so we could Uber here together…the guys wanted to support him. I was shocked, told Frank and Darrell about us seeing them together, and the whole story came out."

Sally closed her eyes and took a deep breath. "What story?"

Peggy took a step forward. "Look, I didn't betray you, okay? I didn't know any of this until right before we got here. Oh dear, are you going to faint?"

Betty grabbed a stool from under the vanity and put her hands on Sally's shoulders. "Sit! You're going to need to when you hear what she has to say."

Sally did as she was told then glanced accusingly over her shoulder. "*Et tu*, Brute? I knew there was something you weren't telling me."

"Do *not* blame Betty. She saw us all getting out of our rides together and wanted to know what the hell was going on. I briefed her…but I didn't even find out everything until we were waiting to go on stage."

Sally stared at her expectantly. "I'm growing older, Peggy. I'm having trouble breathing, and I might hyperventilate, so would you please just spit it out?" She noticed her two friends exchange a look, and her heart went up to her throat. "What?"

"Okay, damn it! We were all wrong about everything. Thomas never got anyone pregnant in high school. Two of his best friends were killed in Vietnam.

His ex-wife, Gayle, was Victor's little sister, and she'd gotten pregnant by the other friend, Dale, right before they were deployed. She didn't even know she was pregnant until after he died. You might remember Dale. He was one of the only Native Americans at our school."

As the truth dawned on her, Sally felt ill and put a hand to her mouth. "And Tom…he…"

"Married her to give the child a name and a father." Peggy took off her glasses and stared pointedly at her friend before putting them back on. "And that's not all. The book he wrote with his wife, Elaine…about an unrequited love he had in high school…a girl who didn't remember him at their reunion?"

Betty cleared her throat. "Does that sound like anyone we might know?"

"Oh God," Sally moaned, putting her head in her hands.

"But here's one of the best parts. Tommy went to New Orleans to try to talk to you. And that crazy lady, who works for Charles—"

"Naomi," Peggy filled in for Betty.

"Yes, thank you. Naomi told him there was no one there by that name and closed the door in his face. When he was getting back in his car, he saw you with Jacques, and now he thinks the two of you are an item."

Sally glared up accusingly at Peggy. "And you didn't tell him the truth?"

"Don't give me that look, little missy! I just found that little tidbit out after Frank glanced out into the audience and saw the two of you together."

Chapter 46

Thomas left the rest of the ceremony to Frank and Jean and started searching for Sally. He'd finally given up and was heading toward the men's room when he saw her date sitting in the lobby just outside the short hall leading to the restrooms. He was approaching but stopped short as the man looked up from his cell.

Jacques nodded. "She's in the loo. You might as well go in, everybody else has."

With his heart in his throat but curious, he advanced and held out his hand. "I'm Thomas Fitzsimmons and you?"

They shook, and her date gave him a cocky grin. "Yeah, I kind of got that. Dr. Jacques Schexnayder…Sally's *gay* stepbrother."

Thomas felt like a weight had been lifted, and his expression must have shown it because the other man let out a laugh as his hand was pumped harder up and down. "Well, in that case, Dr. Schexnayder, it is indeed a pleasure meeting you."

"I think you can just call me Jacques. I feel like we've known each other for years," he said, extracting his hand and giving Thomas an unexpected hug. "Now, would you do me a favor and go in there and claim that woman? I don't think I can take another moment of her sulking about, trying to pretend she isn't miserable over you."

Thomas gave him a lighthearted pat on the back, straightened his tie, and headed toward the ladies' room.

****

Peggy and Betty had slipped from the bathroom unnoticed and found Jacques sitting in the lobby grinning from ear to ear. As the three made their way back to the reunion, they caught each other up on what had happened since the confrontation with Billy Markham. Once again, there was laughter and the sound of old friends reminiscing and sharing stories while music filled the room. Betty, the dancing queen, whispered to Adi and pushed his wheelchair out on the dance floor. Peggy found Frank, and he whisked her out to join their friends, and she filled him in on what had occurred in the bathroom and about Thomas's arrival. Darrell was already cutting the rug with Victoria, and Jacques asked the other daughter to dance. Yet all the while an unacknowledged expectation filled the air.

The band was taking a break when Sally and Thomas entered, and there was a perceptible hush in the room. Making their way self-consciously to their seats, Sally noticed several people nodding at them and smiling, and she squeezed Tom's hand for reassurance. Making sure she was seated and comfortable, he caught the eyes of his daughters and motioned for them to come over.

Victoria bent and gave her a hug. "When they were writing the book, Elaine told us all about you. We were hoping Dad wouldn't be too stubborn about The Widower Whisperers thing. Great concept. It's nice finally meeting you in person."

For a moment Sally felt like the old fool she knew she was and blushed. "Thank you…we have a lot to talk about," she answered, thinking how beautiful both girls were as Annabelle stepped up and wrapped her arms around her.

"I'm Anna. It's wonderful to meet you. I look forward to getting to know your family, soon, I hope. I always knew Elaine was right about you two. She *knew* things." She pulled away and gave her a devilish wink that made Sally smile.

Unobserved, Frank had stepped onto the stage and hooked his phone to the microphone, and the first strains of one of Sally's mother's favorite tunes drifted to them. "Oops, girls, sorry. They're playing our song. Sally, would you do me the honor?"

Flustered, she shook her head. "Tom, I can't…my back—"

"Just hold onto me," he interrupted, held out his hands, and helped her to her feet.

Grudgingly, she allowed herself to be led to the dance floor, laced her hands behind his neck, and whispered, "Everyone's watching us."

He put his arms protectively around her waist and glanced around. "Indeed they are."

As they started to dance, she tilted her head back and stared into his eyes. "You know, Tom, we don't have a song."

"We do now," he said and twirled her around the floor to Etta James singing "At Last."

Epilogue

Charles looked his most debonair as he walked her down the stairs of her old family home in New Orleans. And Sally was as happy as she could ever remember being. They were all there. Peggy, Betty, Carole, Jean, and Jewel stood as her bridesmaids with her daughter, Amber, maid of honor. Tom had Darrell, Jacques, Jacob, and his daughters, with Frank serving as his best man.

The evening was overcast and warm, but the house and yard were brightly lit. After the ceremony, Sally stood on the exact spot where Charles described her mother standing all those many years ago, in the doorway of the covered gallery. She looked around the courtyard filled with food, drink, laughter, and most importantly love and wondered what her mother would have thought, hoping she would have been genuinely happy for her.

"What are you thinking about with that beautiful smile, Mrs. Fitzsimmons?"

She accepted the glass of champagne Tom held up to her. "Oh, just about how everything in my life has led to this…here…now…us. That God really did save the best for last."

He nodded and took the couple of steps up to join her, glancing over the group of people that meant the most to them. Pointing with his flute at Darrell talking to an attractive woman who was grinning up at him flirtatiously, he smiled. "Seems like our friend's found someone interesting to talk to."

Sally looked where he was pointing and almost choked on the sip she'd just taken. "Sorry, that's Cousin Gloria. I heard she recently lost her husband."

"Oh, I'm sorry."

"No, no don't be. He was close to a hundred years old. I think he lasted a lot longer than she'd expected." She saw the curious look on Tom's face and giggled. "He was her sixth and loaded. If Darrell plays his cards right, he just might end up being her lucky number seven."

He raised his eyebrows and took her hand, helping her step down. "Well then, I wish him the best of luck."

She stopped walking and glanced around the enclosed yard that she'd always loved then turned toward Tom. "I wish us all love and luck…"

"Toast!" Charles called out from his chair where he and Bruce were holding court.

The couple walked up and stood behind him, Sally resting her free hand on his shoulder. Charles put a frail one on her hers. "Elizabeth would be so proud of you," he said as if in answer to her own musings. He held his glass up. "To the newlyweds!" Everyone raised their glasses in a chorus of well wishes.

Tom and Sally stared at each other a moment then up at the darkened sky. "To Elaine," they said in unison. Their glasses clinked, and the courtyard was filled with the tinkling of flutes and the echoes of their toast. And, as if on cue…the heavens split, and the moon winked brightly through the clouds as a cool welcoming breeze washed over them.

Coming Soon…

Book 2 of The Widower Whispers Series, Forever's Not So Awfully Long…

A word about the author…

Tina Fausett was born and raised in Oklahoma City and attended both the University of Central Oklahoma and Oklahoma University, majoring in History and English. She's a published poet and novelist, as well as an oil painter and historic home specialist. She's owned an antique store and art gallery and currently runs a company called Red Hot Mamma's Pickles in Oklahoma City where she lives in an historic neighborhood. Having lived in the Garden District in New Orleans, her passions for art, antiques, writing, the paranormal and travel were reignited. She now tries to spend her time between the two cities she loves. Tina has a daughter, son and granddaughter that are her main focus.

Find Tina Here:
Facebook   Page:
https://www.facebook.com/tina.fausett
Twitter: @TinaFausett
Blog: http://Lifehappensthenyouwrite.blog